The Interpretation of Magic

The Shifter's Heart Book 4

Philippa Lodge

The Interpretation of Magic © 2022 Phyllis Laatsch

Cover Art © 2022 Get Covers

All rights reserved. No part of this publication may be reproduced in any form, or by any means, electronic or mechanical, including photocopying, recording, or any information browsing, storage, or retrieval system, without permission in writing from the publisher.

This book is a work of fiction. Names, characters, places, and incidents are products of the author's imagination and are used fictitiously. Any resemblance to actual events or persons, living or dead, is entirely coincidental.

Dedication

To my local romance writing group as it goes from strength to strength.

To the Sprint subset of the writing group and the incentive of NaNoWriMo.

Especially to Gloria, who set me on the path of a psychology-based book title.

And to my family. I wish I could heal you and calm you with magic, but until then, there are hugs.

Content Warning

CHILD IN DANGER, MISTREATMENT of Autism, guns, kidnapping, gang violence, magical violence.

Chapter One

THE SILENCE OF HIS car's speakers, broken only by road noise, the slight crackle of tower to tower transmission and of his Bluetooth headset, told FBI Special Agent Andrew Miller he had finally surprised his half-brother.

Alex Three Feathers cleared his throat. "Um, I'm going to put you on speaker and you're going to repeat what you just said so Beth can hear it, because those were words, but I'm not sure what they meant."

Andrew gritted his teeth. "Are you kidding me right now?"

Alex was hardly ever serious in interpersonal transactions anymore. A good FBI agent, Andrew supposed, in his offbeat, loner way, but not known for his straight-forwardness in normal conversation.

Andrew heard footsteps and a tap on a door and his sister-in-law's, "Come in?"

Then Alex must have muted the phone, because Miller didn't hear the beep of a hang-up.

"Right, Andrew. Tell me again what you just said," Alex's voice was tinny and distorted with the distance of speakerphone.

"I said I'm in Florida -"

"You just got back from there," Alex interrupted.

"Right, from the hawk kidnapping, but this is personal business." He'd been in Florida, come home, then had gotten the call that was changing his life.

Silence and static and road noise, until Beth, who hated silence, asked, "What's going on?"

"I'm on my way to pick up my son from his grandmother."

"See?" Alex said. "I told you it was words and I didn't understand the meaning!" He sounded pissed off and like he was trying to cover it with a joke.

"You have a son?" Beth asked.

He kept his voice even through force of will. "I learned of his existence when he was born and my ex-girlfriend discovered he was a shifter and she wanted child support. He is now five and his mother died in a car accident three days ago."

"Oh, I'm so sorry, Andrew." After another pause, Beth said, "And his grandma…Not your mom."

"No, my ex's mom, who thinks shifters are an abomination in the eyes of the Lord. She says she's going to sue for custody because she wants to save his soul, but she's unwilling or incapable of caring for her grandson, because he is also on the autism spectrum. Which she says is because he's a shifter abomination, etcetera."

"So you have a…secret love child," said Alex.

"I don't have a…a…" He swallowed. "Dammit. OK. Yes."

Alex cleared his throat. "Like, you know…"

"You don't need to say it," Andrew growled. "Like our father."

Since Alex was their father's secret love child and Andrew had sworn to never leave children behind, it rankled deep down in the part of his heart that wanted to hate Andrew Miller Senior instead of spending his whole life trying to win the man's approval and, since his death, to be better than him.

"This is wonderful!" Beth exclaimed and she didn't sound sarcastic or mocking, but her usual enthusiastic self. "A nephew, Alex. We have a nephew! When can we meet him, Andrew?"

Something inside Andrew relaxed, if only by a hair. "I have to get him and see how it goes, but I hope to be home in a few days."

"So he was conceived right around the time of the whole Renaissance Faire thing, right?" Alex asked.

Beth scoffed. "Oh, it doesn't matter! I can't wait to meet him."

Andrew answered anyway. "He was born just after then. I broke up with his mother a few months before and transferred out of Florida to work that case, but I didn't know she was pregnant."

He'd been eager to work the case because Alex was part of the supremacist gang beating up shifters and ultimately kidnapping members of the well-known shifter family, the Catellis. Alex had been undercover, but Andrew didn't know it at the time and had thought he was righting the wrongs of his family by investigating his half-brother.

"And he must have been two when all the commune shit was going down," Alex said. He'd been undercover as Beth's assistant in a shifter commune where predators were taking over from the inside, during which the two of them had came to a truce of sorts.

Andrew turned the question over in his mind, hearing Alex's flat tone and realizing his half-brother was angry. They had made their first tentative steps toward friendship during and after the commune shit, so he likely should have told Alex about the boy after. "It wasn't long after that when she asked for more child support because he'd been diagnosed with ASD. Autism Spectrum Disorder. She sent a bailiff with a court order to summon me to a hearing." She could have called him up at any time from the moment she knew she was pregnant or whenever she or the boy needed something, but had instead taken him to court, which had rankled.

"Oh, sweetie," murmured Beth, the only person in this conversation who was not emotionally stunted.

"I thought we were friends," said Alex with a little quaver, proving he, too, might learn to express feelings.

Andrew still didn't know about himself in that regard. He didn't do drama in his life and inside his mind. Besides, an FBI agent had constant drama from the outside. "She didn't want anyone to know I was the father. She was trying to keep her little wolf pup a secret." Her excuses to keep him out of her life still sounded terrible. "She didn't know I was a shifter until he was born, and then the whole abomination thing kicked in from her mother."

"You should have told me!" Alex half-shouted over Beth's murmur of empathy. His voice lowered to a growl. "You have known this vitally important piece of information for five years and never *fucking* got around to telling me."

Andrew didn't have an answer. He didn't know what answer would be acceptable. His life was partitioned into its categories and until now, his son-he'd-met-twice category hadn't intersected with his half-brother-he-grudgingly-liked category, which overlapped into his work category.

Beth, though, saved him, "Now, Alex, wait. He's telling us now. What do you need from us, Andrew?"

Andrew took a deep breath. "I'm going to need backup. A, uh, support network. I was reading a parenting book on the flight and it said I would need that. I mean: help." He'd told his mom as soon as he found out five years before and she'd hung up on him. Ever since, she'd refused to acknowledge his illegitimate child. He knew it was because of the way his father had treated them all as disposable, but his mother's rejection had cut him.

"We're here for you, Andrew," Beth assured him earnestly. "We're always here. I can't wait to babysit."

Since she'd mentioned - overshared - a few days before that they were trying to get pregnant and so far not having any luck, he wasn't surprised. Her offer, however, meant a lot to him.

"I'm not sure how, how...He's autistic. And part of our agreement was to give me updates on his health and school. He can talk, but doesn't do it much. Honestly, I don't know what I'm going to need. She wouldn't let me visit because she said it upset him and I'm going to pick him up and he doesn't know me. I don't know him."

Did he sound like he was panicking? Yes, he sounded like he was panicking. He pulled his emotions in hard.

He heard the rapid-fire clicking of Beth's keyboard and knew she was already researching it. She was a history professor with wide-ranging, eclectic interests, though shifter mythology was the subject of her doctoral dissertation and the book or books she was working on.

"Hmm," she said. Apparently skimming her search results. "There's lots of types and severities of autism, right? It's called a spectrum, after all. We're going to need more information before we can, you know, get more information."

"We don't know what we don't know at this point," Alex's mocking voice repeated one of Miller's favorite investigative phrases.

"That's about it. I'll forward the documents I have to you, but they're sparse. The situation is constantly changing because he's just a kid and..." Andrew couldn't go on because the wave of despair and confusion was crashing over him again. "Look, I'm almost to the grandmother's house and I'll have to play it by ear."

"Andrew?" Beth said, her voice soft. "You're always welcome here, you know."

Andrew felt his eyes sting, like there might be tears in him somewhere.

Alex sighed. "The kid's going to need more than your tiny, urban apartment."

"I know," said Andrew, tears receding and irritation at all he still had to do to prepare his apartment for a child. He had the building's concierge on alert to let in the people delivering a bed and a dresser. But more than that, a shifter child would need trees and grass and wild things.

Delilah Woods loved her mother very much. Her mother loved her. It was all very uplifting.

That she had to repeat this to herself twenty times a day was less uplifting.

She closed the child psychology textbook on her splintery desk in her mom's front office as the phone rang and her mother called out in an aggravated voice, like always, "Could you get that?" when it was barely past the first ring.

"Serena Woods Accounting, this is Delilah speaking," she sing-songed in her best professional voice.

"She there?" a man grunted.

"May I ask who's calling please?" Del knew damn well it was the same finance manager for RFB Inc. who'd been trying for days to cover his ass by explaining the company's missing money was due to accounting errors. He'd fired an accountant to cover his ass, but her mom was sure the ex-employee was not in on the theft. Her mom paid Delilah the big bucks - small to middling bucks, but free room and board - to answer the phone and track appointments and keep assholes like this one from interrupting her, so she was gatekeeping to the best of her abilities.

"Brad James. I've got to talk to her. She's there, isn't she?"

"She's very busy, sir." Del sang out in her most polite voice. "I'll have to check if she's available."

She put the jerk on hold and let her finger hover over the intercom button for about half a second before her mom appeared in the doorway. "Mr. James?"

Del sighed. "You bet. Sounds pissed."

Her mom wrinkled her nose. "Well, I guess he might have some new bullshit he'll try to feed me. I wouldn't have found the office supply budget problems yesterday without him letting that little turd of information loose."

"Ew, Mom. No."

Her mom went back into her office, closing the door behind her this time. The light on line one stopped blinking.

Delilah opened her textbook again. "Kohlberg's Stages of Moral Development, you will not defeat me today," she announced to the empty room.

Ten minutes later, the little phone light went off and a minute later, her mom came out of her office wearing her ugly snow boots and puffy coat, her laptop bag strap over her shoulder. "I'm going over to RFB now."

"Wait, did you have an appointment?" Del clicked her mouse to wake up her laptop. "I don't see an appointment this afternoon."

"I'm going to call Shalonda on the way. They're walking Mr. James out in handcuffs right now and I'm missing it," she announced as she strode toward the door.

Del would have thought her mom was gleeful, and maybe she was deep down inside, but she was mostly mad she wasn't there to present her findings in an orderly manner before Mr. James got perp-walked. A dramatic "J'accuse!" was good for client relations, she always said - and she claimed she didn't learn anything useful at her mother's knee. Her mother, Del's grandmother, was the epitome of drama, having done palm readings in the back of their candle-and-incense store and put on a hell of a show for customers when she got going.

"OK, I'll transfer the phones to my cell and lock up early, I guess."

But her mom was already gone.

Del really needed some decent coffee. Since she'd started making the coffee in her mom's office it was OK, but her mom insisted on a drip pot, no Keurig, no espresso machine, and Del really wanted a big, nasty mocha with three pumps of caramel.

It was a Starbucks kind of day.

Chapter Two

Del sat through her evening class with an increasing sense of unease about her mom.

They didn't text or call unnecessarily, so she wasn't expecting a report from her on Mr. James' arrest, but she had an unspecified bad feeling all the same.

Since her family was one of the few in the world where an unspecified feeling counted as real information to be shared, she ducked out into the icy courtyard during her break and called her mom. She left a voicemail when her mom didn't pick up, and called her Aunt Moira.

"Hello, darling, what's wrong?" her aunt answered, sounding winded.

"I'm not sure. Mom went to a client site this afternoon and I've had a bad feeling about her ever since. She's not answering her phone."

Aunt Moira took a deep breath and let it out slowly. She didn't have a lot of premonition talent, but was skilled in setting charms in things and in keeping people calm and happy. "Well, Mother left me a message a couple minutes ago on the landline, and I still need to call her back."

"Who is it?" asked a man's voice in the background. Uncle Dave, her aunt's husband, a retired doctor Moira had known since high school, but had only met again five years before. She'd flown out the summer Del was visiting Renaissance Faires out west, doing readings as a fortune teller, the summer her cousin Eloisa had met her husband and been kidnapped. It had been eventful, to say the least.

"My niece, Delilah," she answered. "She's worried about her mom."

Delilah said, "I have to get back to class. Could I call you when I get out? Only it'll be at 9:30." Del's mom was routinely in bed by nine and she didn't inquire into her family's sleep schedules as a rule.

"I'll talk to your Grandmother and tell you what she said." Grandmother hated phones, but now she was living alone, she could no longer require her daughters to place calls for her and answer queries from her granddaughters by talking in the background. "And 9:30 is fine. I'm usually up until eleven."

Del slipped back into her seat after her professor had started lecturing and earned a glare. She hoped it was early enough in the semester that he didn't know her name.

As soon as the class was over, Del packed her notebook away and pulled her tarot cards from their wooden box as she set off for the student parking lot. She shuffled them as she went and cut and yep, there was Justice, her mother's card, at the top of the deck. Then a four of Pentacles reversed - embezzlement, yes that's what her mom was working on. Magician reversed: a con man. She shuffled the cards one more time and cut.

And stopped walking.

Eight of Swords, a woman tied up in a cage of swords. Kidnapping or hostage.

She gripped the deck tightly as she jogged to her car and, with shaking hands, shoved the cards back in their wooden box once she was in her car. She dialed Moira and put the phone on speaker as she pulled out of her parking spot.

Aunt Moira opened with, "Mother is pulling Justice over and over right side up and reversed. Isn't Justice what you always pull for Serena?" As often happened, the conversation just started in the middle. Del didn't know if it was because they were psychic or because they were rude.

"Eight of Swords, Aunt Moira." Going on tangents without answering a question was also how they spoke to each other. "Is it always for a current confinement? Could it be when Eloisa was kidnapped? Why would it crop up now?"

"You know full well it can be completely metaphorical," her aunt replied tartly.

"But I feel like it's danger. Either my mom right now, or something to do with the time Eloisa and Mike were kidnapped. Or both."

"I don't know, I'm sorry. I don't have that gift."

Aunt Moira's gifts were more subtle. Grandmother with her foresight and cards and crystal ball had considered them lesser until a teenage Eloisa and preteen Delilah had sat her down and explained the only reason her shop hadn't failed a hundred times already was because Moira ran it. She had a gift for charming objects and people. The shop had also survived because Del's mom had a magical gift for numbers and wouldn't listen to her mother when she tried to outspend the store's income.

In fact, if Aunt Moira hadn't wanted to find something new to do when Grandmother announced her retirement, Del would have happily been the mysterious psychic in the back of the shop with Moira as the store manager. Del wasn't as good at putting on a show or running a business, though, as proved by her lackluster results at the Renaissance Faires.

She was thinking in circles.

"Is it too late for me to stop by Grandmother's house?"

"Well, let me just wave my magic wand and fix him all better."

Andrew blinked at the sarcastic in-home care-worker, his teeth briefly unclenching, which was as close to jaw-dropping as he ever allowed himself. The fifth babysitter in as many weeks, this one was in her twenties and licensed to work with developmentally disabled kids, but had been a bit rude about shapeshifters when he interviewed her. He'd thought it would be all right until he could find a permanent carer, but apparently, it would not be all right.

It might never be all right ever again.

The carer before was recommended as a shifter babysitter, but had no idea what to do about the boy's ASD issues. None of them could do both, apparently.

Andrew had taken an emergency leave of absence to fetch the boy from Florida, only to find him rocking in a corner, refusing to make eye contact, and growling softly.

The kid's grandmother had prayed and shouted at him while he gathered his son's things and her pastor had arrived and condemned them both to hell as Andrew scooped up his son and latched him into his car seat. The grandmother and pastor - what a man of God, to hate a small boy for the way he was born - had followed them to the boy's mother's apartment and shouted at him from the hallway as Andrew gathered the rest of the kid's clothes and books and movies into boxes and searched his ex's personal affairs for important papers and things with monetary value.

By the time he was ready to carry some boxes to the rental car, the police showed up about the noise complaint and he'd had to show his emergency custody documents and badge and wait for them to call his boss at the FBI. At least the grandma had left then, threatening a custody battle as her parting shot.

It wasn't the last time he wondered if his own father would have put up a fight in a similar situation or sent him to his maternal grandparents without a backward glance.

Luckily, the neighbor who was babysitting the night his ex died came by before he left and expressed her sympathy and cried. She was a coyote shifter and the boy cuddled into her as she explained he preferred to be held in his wolf form as he slept. She gave him the written instructions and list of foods he liked. Andrew wasn't sure how much trial and error he would have gone through without those babysitting instructions.

He'd brought all the papers and assessments of the boy's condition and abilities back with him on the ride to Ohio, the child whimpering and whining whenever he wasn't asleep, and sometimes when he was. Andrew had been as gentle as he knew how, which was probably not gentle enough.

Andrew had found him a half-day slot in a preschool for autistic children, but the kid kept shifting and freaking them out. And part-time school still left the other half of the work day and in-home caregivers who kept leaving.

Andrew shook his head. "Look, he's not dangerous. Think of him as a highly intelligent puppy."

"He snapped at me when I went into his room! He tore my jeans. See?"

Miller couldn't see any holes in the jeans where the woman was pointing, but he nodded instead of putting on his reading glasses and crouching to stare at her leg.

"He's just gotten more aggressive over the past week. He doesn't like me and at this point, I don't like him either."

She slapped down the key and keycard, grabbed her backpack from the table by the front door, and stomped out. He wondered if he'd get his extra parking pass back from her.

Maybe he could take unpaid leave until the boy settled in. He'd always been proud to have more vacation time banked than most other agents, but he'd used up most of it already. He usually only used it to visit his mom in Washington State for a week each year. Maybe he could have his mom fly in. Though with her attitude toward illegitimate children, it was probably best if she stayed on the other side of the country.

He suddenly realized he might never be able to travel for the Bureau again and his desk assignment might be permanent. His gut clenched.

He dialed the phone at the county office, desperate to get a new babysitter. The line rang ten times and went to voicemail as Andrew felt his FBI career going up in smoke.

He was on desk duty and would be for the foreseeable future, doing investigative research for the Shifter Task Force, the STF, pulling files and running background checks for field agents and referring deep dives to more experienced researchers and hackers. Buho was the only one who didn't laugh every time he answered the phone. He might have been busting a gut on the inside for all Andrew knew, but he'd been his usual, steady best friend.

His half-brother, Alex Three Feathers, always had a good chuckle. But then, Alex had popularized the use of STFU instead of STF when referring to the task force. He laughed at everything these days, relaxed and giddy in his love for his wife, so Andrew tried not to take it personally.

They were trying to learn to get along, but his father's bastard son still had a chip on his shoulder when it came to Andrew. And vice versa. They'd discovered they could work pretty well as equals since Alex joined the team two years before, but they preferred to not have to work together too often.

When Andrew had arrived from Florida, Alex had gotten in his face, snarling and snapping. Alex had halfway relented after Beth fell thoroughly in love with the child, but it was still Beth who invited them to dinner at their apartment an hour outside the city.

Maybe Beth could take the boy tomorrow afternoon. She'd been good to him when she helped out before. The boy had let Alex cut his food up and help him with his coat, which were good signs. Andrew flipped through the binder for Beth's schedule. She had two classes the next morning and office hours in the afternoon.

"Look Andrew..." Beth was the only person other than his own mother who called him by his first name anymore. "I can dash up and get him from his school at noon if you want, but I really have to be in my office at two. My department head's a stickler about office hours and I've already ducked out twice to help you this semester and we're not even to midterms yet."

"Could you..." he wanted to ask if she could take the boy along to her office, but she shared the space with another assistant professor and was there to meet with students. There was a large population of shifters on the college campus, but surely not everyone would be comfortable with the kid.

"The boy tried to bite his new babysitter," he said instead. "I'm running low on time off. There isn't anyone..." *Oh shit. Am I going to whine and cry about this?*

"Andrew..." Beth sighed. "Look, Alex is out of town, but you know that. I have dinner with some of my high school friends tonight or I'd invite you two over."

He stood in his kitchen, silent and thinking. He could hear Beth breathing, but she wasn't talking. She generally talked through her thoughts, especially when she was enthusiastic about them, so she must not have any ideas.

"I'm sorry, Andrew. Let me know if I can pick him up tomorrow and where to drop him off. He might have to come to my office, which isn't ideal, but everyone knows my spouse is a shifter, so they won't be too shocked."

Andrew let out a breath. "It'll all be fine when he can have an afternoon place, but coming in the middle of the year like he did, there wasn't anything available. It's like the carer said today: if I could wave my magic wand, I would."

Chapter Three

"Hello, this is Ag...Andrew Miller. Your cousin Eloisa Woods-Grey asked me to call you. Unofficially."

Delilah had answered the anonymous number after one ring, because who knew, her mom might be calling from someone else's phone. She was opening the office like usual in the morning after spending half the night wandering through the house, checking if her mom had come home.

She bolted the front door behind herself, because the office was creepy when she was alone. There were only an insurance agency, a chiropractor, and the office for a maid service in the building and once the maids had picked up their cleaning products and gone out for the day, the number of people was the merest trickle.

"Hello, Agent Miller," she answered. She tried to remember what he looked like and had an impression of crew cut, greying blond hair, frown lines, and a don't-give-me-any-bullshit aura. Since she'd seen him in the context of rescuing her cousin and several other people from anti-magic kidnappers, she supposed it was normal that he hadn't been cheerful, though his whole vibe said he was upstanding and honest and, frankly, grumpy.

"I'm calling you unofficially," he repeated, "and am currently on my morning break. Since your mother has only been out of touch with you for a few hours and we have no idea why, the FBI has no involvement."

With a stick up his ass. "I'm aware of that, but all of us in my family have a bad feeling about this and we're highly attuned to those feelings. I can't pinpoint much about her because I can't do it for the people closest to me. And yes, I know it sounds like an excuse, but I've come to the conclusion that my emotions are currently keeping me from going into a trance because I am quite anxious right now."

Silence for a few seconds. "Your cousin Eloisa told me as much about you and your grandmother. If this were an official case, I would have pulled the notes from the kidnapping in Nevada for background."

"OK, so she was on the phone with the main suspect in an embezzlement case, who was trying to give her excuses as to why the books don't add up. My mom has a talent – Talent capital T – for forensic accounting. When she gets a feeling about someone's financials, she will dig and dig until she has proof." Del paused, knowing her argument was going to sound weak. "When I get a feeling because of my capital-T-Talent, all I do is warn them something's going to happen or point out why things aren't working. It's the difference between data and advice."

"Yes," Miller said flatly, clearly losing patience.

Del rushed on in the face of his skepticism. "So the guy called and she spoke to him. While they were on the phone, I guess the cops showed up to arrest him, so she took off out of here with her laptop to hand in her final report. Her client said she got there and downloaded the data – my mom's laptop is not connected to the internet in any way and she keeps it with her and locks it up both here and at home. She has a cell phone, but only activates the GPS when she's lost, plus she turns the phone off most of the time, so it can't be tracked by cell towers. It's off now. Her car has a LoJack feature she enables only at night because we don't live in the best neighborhood. It's not activated, so I can't track her car."

Miller cleared his throat. "I was mainly calling as a favor to your cousin to assure you that adults are allowed to disappear at any time and there has to be evidence of foul play or danger to herself or others to trigger an investigation."

She suppressed a wail of frustration so it came out as a weird squeak. "There's no clear evidence, that's the problem. She lives by her routine, though, and unless she's out of town gathering data for a case, she always, *always* sleeps in her own bed. If she's not going to be in the office, she calls me to find out if there are any messages I haven't sent to her phone."

"Is there any reason to suspect she changed her habits?"

"If you mean did she go on a date and was out all night making the beast with two backs and decided to sleep in her love nest this morning, there has been no evidence she's had sex since I was conceived. Honestly, I don't know how I even happened."

"Uh…"

Too much information, yeah. "The point is I've been sleeping in her guest bedroom – slash – home office for the last seven months and there have been no changes in her patterns or in her aura from what I remember from, well, forever. She gets up, she goes to work, she does accounting, she goes home, she does a little light reading of nonfiction books on accounting. Sometimes in the evenings, she allows herself a true crime show or two, and that's it."

"I need to be back at my desk in two minutes. From what you've said, I would advise you to call the police once 48 hours have passed. There's no law in Ohio saying to wait, but without a credible threat, no one can do anything."

So much for Agent Miller being any help.

"Hi?" the handsome, young Asian man at the door of her mom's house said.

Delilah was not ashamed to say she gawked as she looked up and down his lean body in an open parka over a t-shirt and jeans. "Lac?"

He pressed his lips together. "Do you need to see ID?"

"No, no!" she said as she undid the thick chain on the door and opened it. "It's definitely your voice from the phone and your aura, but the last time I saw you, you were skinny and kind of a mess."

He winced. "I was barely eighteen and had just spent three weeks traveling 500 miles on foot."

"Yeah, I know, but look at you now! Talk about a glow up! How old are you now?" She did the math in her head. Five and a half years ago Eloisa had been kidnapped and this kid who had just met her came to her rescue. And if that was five, no, six years ago...Goddess, she hated math. "Twenty-three?"

"Twenty-four. I just had my birthday."

"Happy birthday!" She beamed at him. She was five years older than him and suddenly felt very old. Of course, Agent Andrew Miller was even older than her.

He shifted from one foot to the other, radiating discomfort. "Um, it was a month ago, but thanks?"

He cleared his throat after she led him to the kitchen and offered him a drink and he wanted only water, but finally accepted that she make a pot of herbal tea because the kettle was already hot and yes, she was right, it was cold out.

"Tell me what's going on. I don't know how much I can help, I mean, I haven't even officially joined the FBI yet, but my background check is done."

"And you have a degree in criminal justice. Summa cum laude," she pointed out. She still didn't have any degree, so he was way ahead of her. When he blushed, she said, "Eloisa and Mike are very proud of you, you know. And thank you for dropping by. I was glad when El told me you were in town."

She launched into her story again and Lac listened carefully, nodding. When she finished he asked, "Have you gone to see the people at the company she was working for?"

She shook her head and poured the herbal tea, offering him sugar or honey, both of which he declined. "I talked to the client contact a couple times."

He blew on his tea and sniffed. "Eloisa's always giving me peppermint, too."

"It's soothing and I've been a mess for the last three days. I reported Mom missing yesterday, but they took my statement and shrugged and said she's allowed to disappear if she wants and they weren't going to open an investigation. I didn't tell the cops I'm psychic, so it's not that they think I'm crazy, either. I mean, Agent Miller already knew and he was zero help."

He nodded, all calm and placid on the outside, but she could feel his aura flare as he thought. She opened the box with her favorite tarot deck and started shuffling, as she had done a hundred times in the last three days. She picked two cards. Justice. Eight of Swords. "I hate that I can't really see for my family and loved ones," she sighed.

"Do mine," he said. "Maybe you can see me figuring this out."

She smiled and handed him the cards to shuffle and cut into five piles. When she laid the cards out, the vision hit her immediately and she found herself humming as images and possible stories flashed out into the future. "I see your magic user. You're still with Aura, right? I met her a couple summers ago when I visited El and Mike, but you were out of town."

He blushed and agreed.

"You and Aura are going to have a lot of trouble. Not soon, but not a long way into the future. In the next year or two. There's going to be trouble and pain and separation. You're going to hurt and weep and... I'm sorry." She rubbed her eyes before she went on. "It's uncertain after that point. You'll both be in danger and there's a dog. Not a wolf, not a shifter as far as I can see, but a pet dog?"

Lac blinked at her, frowning. "You know, pets aren't really a shifter thing."

She shook her head. "I don't know anything about the dog, just the word 'dog' is coming to me. Aura's power is magnificent, but not limitless. You need..." In frustration, she thumped her fist on the table, startling Lac. "I don't know what you need, but it's blue."

"Blue. Dog."

She shook her head. "It's gone. The vision is gone. There's some little stuff about you doing well in your career, but being frustrated by the limits it sets on you, then a big mess with Aura, then it's cloudy and dangerous...maybe several years off."

He glared down at the cards. Finally, he rubbed his face and leaned both elbows on the table to stare into his tea. "Yeah, well."

"Not every college romance works out in the end," she said, patting him on the arm before gathering the cards. "I'm sorry. I shouldn't have told you, but the blob of danger in the future seemed important."

"Eloisa said you weren't having visions."

"I'm not having visions about my mom, who's either hiding or being hidden. I sometimes get warnings and feelings about family, but frustratingly few."

Lac sat back and took a deep breath. "I'm not sure I wanted to be warned. But the future can change, right?"

"Of course," she said soothingly, thinking the trouble and pain and separation had been so strong that she would bet it came true. The blue dog or whatever was so foggy it could easily change.

"Right." He sat for a minute, tapping his fingers on the wooden table top while she poured herself some more peppermint tea and he waved off her silent offer of more. "So it wasn't about your mom at all. OK, what we're going to do is go to where your mom was last seen and ask the people where she went."

She nodded. "Her contact Shalonda said Mom gave the police her statement and a second thumb drive with her report and got in her car and left."

"Did the contact see her leave?"

Del tried to think of what, exactly, the woman at RFB, Inc. had said. "I'm not sure. I'd have to ask Shalonda again. She said mom's car is gone."

Lac set his hands flat on the table and pushed to standing. "It's Friday afternoon, so we'd better get going. Do you have Shalonda's number or should we show up there without forewarning?"

As Delilah drove them the fifteen minutes to RFB, they were both lost in their own thoughts. She was churning over her mom and over Lac's reading and over Agent Miller and the commune in Wyoming and the Renaissance Faires. Her mind was just plain churning.

Finally, as they exited the highway into the office park, she cleared her throat. "I'm sorry about that reading, you know."

Lac took in a deep breath and let it out. "You just report what you see, right?"

She nodded, but still felt bad. "My grandma says she sometimes hid things from her clients. She'd sugarcoat or be, well, nice to them. If it was something major, she would give oblique warnings. But you know the warning they put on psychic chat lines and stuff? For entertainment purposes only. She's an entertainer and only told the whole truth to her most loyal customers and to her friends and family."

He hmmmed.

"Like me, she can't See well for the people she's closest to, so neither of us are getting more than little warnings about what's going on with my mom. And for me, it might be my fears are being expressed in the cards and not anything that's really happening. Just Justice and Eight of Swords over and over with an occasional Magician."

"Do the cards really turn up like that for you? Or are they more of a support for the premonitions, no matter which cards turn up?" Lac asked.

"Some of both. Like I said, I'm pulling Justice, which is what I pull almost every time I think of my mom, and Eight of Swords, which can be kidnapping or jail or some other locked-up type of event."

Another long silence.

Finally, Lac cleared his throat. "So what else can you tell me about Shalonda?"

"She's powerful. She's a vice president at RFB, Inc. or Chief Financial Officer or something, and she takes no shit from anyone. It's surprising Mr. James got away with cooking the books for as long as he did, but she's more big picture than the minutiae that add up to the big picture. She's in charge of profits and losses and loans and all sorts of things."

Lac said, "Yeah, I'm a bit fuzzy about what large corporations do, too."

They both laughed.

She pulled into the parking lot and parked in a guest spot out front. "Ready?"

He smiled at her. God, those cheekbones. "I know absolutely nothing about conducting a questioning or an investigation in real life, you know that, right?"

She nodded solemnly. "We've both watched Law and Order though, right?"

He pushed out his lips in a mock pout. "I've watched a lot of other police procedurals, I'll have you know."

They laughed again and she felt the bond slip into being. "It was good I did your reading earlier, because now you feel like family. El's my cousin who's almost my sister and you're almost her little brother, so does that make us step-siblings? Adoptive cousins?"

He blushed slightly. "Let's tell them I'm your brother and make them wonder."

She squeezed his hand and they got out, ready to ask questions.

Chapter Four

THEY WERE BACK IN Del's car half an hour later.

"I guess we should've called ahead," Delilah said.

Lac sighed gustily. "Awkward."

"But I guess we learned no one saw my mom leave in her car. She said goodbye and shook Shalonda's hand and several people saw her leave the room."

"And her car was gone," Lac added, "from where she parked out of view of the security camera."

"But everyone was busy watching the cops and being interviewed and so on." Del shrugged. "And with Shalonda now on vacation in Argentina…"

Lac shook his head. "Sorry, we didn't learn anything, did we?"

"Shalonda's vacation seems oddly timed."

Lac smiled slightly. "They said she'd been planning it for a long time and going to a wedding."

"But with the investigation and arrest, it seems like she should have rescheduled, don't you think?"

"Yeah, I doubt they would have rescheduled a whole wedding for this. And I mean, she was planning it for a whole year. And maybe this wasn't as big a deal as it felt to your mom. Maybe someone else in the company is handling the day to day concerns of the police investigation."

Del shook her head, but started the car and backed out of the guest spot in front of the glassed-in reception area. It was after five and the sun had set and the clouds were spitting down something that might have been snow if it tried a little harder. "That's not the feeling I got."

Lac said, "Yes. I trust your feelings. Besides, it's the same feeling I got. There's something wrong."

"The cops aren't going to do anything because I had another feeling. Agent Effing Miller isn't going to do anything." She felt the familiar twist in her chest. He hadn't had time for her, but he felt…important. She'd had just enough therapy to know she reacted badly because her dad hadn't had much time for her. Neither had her mom. Thank goddess for Aunt Moira and Grandmother.

Lac leaned back with a heavy breath. "Agent Effing Miller is having a hard time right now, according to my sources. He's got personal stuff going on and he can't do field work. And he keeps leaving the office early."

Del smiled at him in spite of herself as she stopped at the light at the bottom of the on ramp for the highway. "Plugged into the FBI gossip, are you?"

He snorted. "Plugged into Alex, my cousin who's Miller's half-brother. But I heard it from Beth, Alex's wife."

Lac grimaced and pointed toward the light, which had just changed. She accelerated up the ramp.

He grunted softly as she slipped into the flow of traffic between two cars where there wasn't really enough space and the car behind flashed their lights. "Not sure how much of this is common knowledge, but there are rumblings higher up in the FBI that shifters can't be trusted to police other shifters and definitely shouldn't have authority over regular people. I still haven't heard for sure if I'm going to get in. Not absolutely sure I want to if it's true the Bureau is turning against shifters. And they apparently come up with any excuse to nudge a shifter to resign or to find him-slash-her-slash-them at fault for anything bad that goes down."

"I keep seeing dumb shit on social media, but thought it was wing nuts and blowhards."

He chuckled. "Wing nuts and blowhards? Are you fifty years old?"

She smacked his leg with her free hand. "Oh stop. I'm twenty-nine and you know what I mean. How are we kids supposed to talk these days about haters and assholes and conspiracy theorists with loud mouths and a warped idea of what's in their Bible?"

"Yeah, them. I don't know, because I'm not on social media. I hang around with Aura, a few other college friends, mainly other shifters, and with Eloisa and Mike."

"You've got me beat. I hang around with a couple of friends from high school, but most of them moved on with life and finished college and have real jobs and have started families. Mostly I spend time with my mom, my aunt, and my grandmother."

He was silent instead of replying, the wet road whooshing and rumbling under the snow tires of her aging car.

Finally, she said, "I've always identified better with people older than me and younger than me. I mean, Eloisa was big sister and best friend to me. I was too weird to be popular in high school."

"Yeah," he said. After a few seconds he added, "You're an old soul, right?"

She laughed softly, then squinted and reached up to flip the rear view mirror so she wouldn't continue to be blinded by the high beams of the truck or SUV or whatever was behind her. "Compared to Eloisa, I'm brand new."

Lac puffed out a tiny chuckle, more a breath than a laugh. "Eloisa is a thousand years old. You're like, only 200 years old. You've seen a lot and know too much."

She let that sink in. He wasn't wrong. But she'd at least had a fairly normal dating life, which El hadn't managed until Mike Grey. Lots of guys got creeped out because Del would see their futures or she would talk about her family. She'd been dumped harshly a few times and ghosted a few others. She'd managed a while long-distance dating Rob, a sword-fighter she'd met at the Ren Faires that one weird, dangerous summer, but neither had enough money to fly to visit often enough to make a difference. Eventually, they'd broken it off by mutual consent, equally losing interest.

The SUV behind them pulled to the left lane to pass, accelerating like crazy. "Damn kids," she muttered.

"What?" Lac asked.

"The white Escalade tailgated us for the last few miles, blinding me, then it passes like they're on the way to the hospital to have a baby. And—shit!"

She slammed on the brakes as the SUV swerved back into the right lane and stood on their brakes. She was so busy trying to not skid off the road, fishtailing wildly into the left lane to not crash into the back of the SUV that she didn't even honk the horn.

Then the truck accelerated away and she pulled off onto the shoulder and stopped, turning on her flashers, needing to catch her breath. "What the fuck? Seriously, Lac, did you see that?"

He held her hand and squeezed it and she could feel his adrenaline morphing to anger. She sent some calm to him and it calmed her, too. When she let go of his hand, it rushed back, though.

"Want me to drive?" he asked.

"Yes. Please."

She checked there was room to open her door without stepping into traffic and got out, her legs wobbly. They traded seats quickly, getting back in with a shiver as the sleet soaked into their hair.

He drove in silence as she directed him back to her mom's. When they parked out front in her designated spot, he turned to her and looked her over. "Better?"

"I guess. I don't like the coincidence that we came from the place my mom was last sighted and got harassed by Mr. Road Rage."

"Coulda been Ms. Road Rage," he answered.

"Sure. Is there a gender-neutral honorific?"

"Mix," he answered promptly. "Spelled M X."

She nodded, filing it away for future use. "Mx. Road Rage is too much of a coincidence."

"I agree. But I have to fly home tomorrow and can't stay and watch your back."

She thought of Agent Miller, unwilling or maybe unable to help her out. "Who should I call, though?"

He shook his head and handed her the keys. "I know some of the agents on the Shifter Task Force, but half are out of town and the caseload is heavy because the new FBI director is setting them up to fail. Miller on three-quarter time desk duty is messing the task force's work load up pretty bad, too."

They got out and she hit the button to lock the car doors. She unlocked the front door and disarmed the alarm, and they went inside in silence.

"But really, you should call Miller again," Lac said.

"Oh, he won't help unless there's proof she's been kidnapped, but there's no proof because no one is helping." Her voice rose and she was almost wailing at the end.

She stomped to the kitchen and got a cup out for water, drank, then clunked it down on the counter.

Lac was still in the entryway and she heard him speaking softly. Probably Aura, his girlfriend, the one who had her own magic and what seemed to be part of her mother's magic inside her, intense premonitory dreams, and an immense gift for auras, to the point where she could see through walls. Talk about old souls.

He came to the kitchen doorway and pulled the phone away from his face. "I told Miller about the Escalade. I only caught the Ohio plates starting with J and 41 at the end."

"I didn't even see the plates. I was busy trying not to crash." She shuddered again.

"Yeah, assholes rely on the shock to keep you from identifying them. Not sure what they would have done if you hadn't had such good reflexes and your car had been embedded in the back of theirs."

"You're really very sweet, Lac," she said with a smile. "I was watching them because they'd already scared me. Are we eating real food or can I pull out ice cream like every other night?"

"Talk to Miller," he said. "And then I want you to pack and I'll take you to stay with your family."

He held out his phone and she fumbled it slightly. "Hello?" she asked warily.

Miller sighed in her ear. "Meet tomorrow at five?"

She blinked twice, wondering if he always spoke in partial sentences. "OK. I mean, I have to go to my mom's office to check everything's OK, so we could meet there."

"Good. Text me the address." A dog's whine rose in the background of the call, repetitive and insistent. "Five tomorrow."

And he hung up with a beep.

"Is he always so rude?" she asked Lac, handing his phone back.

"I'd say abrupt," Lac said with an eye roll as he pocketed his phone.

"Does he have a dog?"

Lac shook his head. "He just got custody of his son."

The dog's whine. *Wolf's* whine.

"He's having a pretty hard time of it. But that's all I'll say." He clapped his hands. "Text the address to him, call your aunt to say you're coming over, and pack clothes for a couple days."

"Wow, bossy much?" she said with her own eye roll, but she dug into her handbag and pulled out her phone. "I'll call Aunt Moira, but I'm staying here in case Mom comes home."

"I'm still coming down from adrenaline and it's almost supper time in Wyoming, so I'm starving and need protein. What's the best burger place?"

Andrew strode down the hall, following the sound of the little, whining wolf with the drooping tail, the one who had eaten his hamburger and not touched anything else on his plate. The cub had to know how annoying he was, didn't he? No, self-aware wasn't really a symptom of autism. Or of little children. Or was it? The things he'd been reading online, the ones written by people with autism, said they were highly sensitive and attuned to other peoples' moods.

Basically, the more frustrated Andrew got with the whining and scratching, the more the kid would whine and scratch.

Basically, they were both screwed, because Andrew had just about had enough.

His boy was in the corner, slowly scratch, scratch, scratching his way to freedom through the plaster on the wall. Andrew owned his little condo and luckily, the corner his pup was destroying was to the outside of the building, but he was surprised the neighbors hadn't complained yet about the scratching noise and the whining that sometimes escalated to howling (wolf) or wailing (human) and the walking around at all times of the night.

He stood in the doorway in his sweatpants and t-shirt, blinking against the exhaustion and despair which plagued him all the time these days.

As if he had time to help Delilah Woods chase after her mother. OK, so Lac had been halfway convinced there was something weird going on, and the SUV harassing them on the road might not have been a coincidence. Still, there were assholes who cut off people for nothing and Lac had said she entered the highway rather abruptly and maybe this was the car she'd jumped in front of. Andrew clung to the theory that Delilah's mom had decided to take a surprise vacation or had gone off to build a new life for herself.

He rubbed his eyes, then picked the boy up and carried him to the bathroom to brush his teeth for bed, even though it was barely seven. He'd brought the boy's weird wraparound toothbrush from Florida and bought a few more just like it because the kid tended to allow brushing for only a few seconds before chewing on the brush and any nearby fingers, especially when in wolf form.

Andrew set him on the bed and pulled the weighted blanket up. He read the boy a couple books, then said, "Good night, son."

He patted the cub on his head and turned to go, but the whining started up again. He went and got himself ready for bed, too, but came back to find his son in the corner digging to freedom again.

"Come on, we both need to sleep," he said and lifted the cub up to place him back on the bed.

More whining.

Andrew sighed and stripped down to his boxers, climbing into bed before shifting to his wolf form.

He crowded into the child, licking his ears and nuzzling the top of his head, dragging him closer with a paw and claws which looked bigger and more dangerous for their proximity to his tiny cub, fur to fur and holding tight.

Eventually, the little body relaxed and the whining faded away.

And they both slept.

When he woke sometime before dawn, the boy had shifted back to a little, blond boy and was clinging hard to Andrew's paw, rocking and staring at his father's muzzle. Andrew nuzzled him again and licked his ear before shifting back to human, too, reaching down to hitch his boxers back into place over his now-tailless ass.

The boy froze and a little gasp was starting in his throat, the prelude to a whine.

Andrew pulled his stiff body close and held him firmly, humming softly. He didn't know how much time passed, but the child eventually relaxed into him, one hand clutching Miller's wrist the same way he had clutched at a paw.

Miller fell asleep again, feeling like he'd won something.

Chapter Five

Delilah stayed in her car in the mostly deserted office parking lot until she saw the silver sedan roll to a stop two spaces over from her and Agent Miller get out, still in a navy blue FBI suit, tie loose. She wondered if he wasn't cold with no coat, since she was shivering in her puffy jacket.

He looked directly at her over the roof of his car and she instantly remembered, oh yeah, he was really hot for an older guy, and, oh yeah, he did not take any shit at all, ever. From twenty-ish feet away and under a flickering street lamp, she couldn't see his eyes, but her second sight showed his wolf. Focused, intent, protective, dangerous.

She pulled on her fuchsia knit cap and got out, too. "Hi! Thanks for coming."

He nodded brusquely and came around his car, checking in every direction, then returning his gaze to her as he got to the back door on the passenger side. He hesitated and she took two steps forward, noting his eyes were pale, the exact shade unclear, and his short, golden-brown hair silvery at the temples.

"I've brought my son," he said. "My half-brother picked him up from school and kept him for an hour until I could get there."

She nodded, squinting to see through the tinted back window. "Alex Three Feathers is in town?" she asked, not taking her eyes off the faint outline of the child. "Lac told me he wasn't." She wasn't sure if she would have wanted Lac to call Alex. She didn't know Miller, either, really, but Alex Three Feathers had been in on kidnapping her cousin.

"He had essentially a long layover to drop off his laundry and re-pack before flying out again." He still didn't open the car door.

She smiled, flicking her gaze to the man in front of her for a moment. "And kiss his wife."

"Most likely," Miller said tightly.

He finally let out a long, slow breath and opened the door. The child didn't look around, but stared at the seat back in front of him, rocking in his seat, bumping his shoulders against the sides.

Oh, she thought. *Having a pretty hard time* meant something extra when Miller was adapting to a child with whatever issues this one had. She'd had a lot of classes in psychology and knew she had no expertise to diagnose a child, but she had a clue. Miller bent into the car, displaying his fine ass in those dress pants. She upgraded her *Oh yeah, he's hot for an older guy* to *He's hot*.

As he stood with the boy in his arms, she focused on the child again, narrowing her eyes to see the waves of discomfort radiating from his stiff body.

"Shall we go in?" Miller asked with an edge of impatience, shifting the child to one arm to close the door and beep the locks.

She went first up the cement stairs, glad maintenance had done a decent job of clearing the snow and ice, though the sun for an hour or so around noon had probably helped the salt do its work. She unlocked her mom's office and input the alarm code as he glanced around the waiting room and set his child in one of the bright yellow, plastic-covered chairs. The boy pulled his legs up and set his forehead on his knees.

"Are you going to introduce me?" she asked. She liked kids and found it rude to not include them.

Miller stared at her for three seconds before glancing toward his son. "Troy, this is Ms. Woods. We're helping her and her mom with something."

The boy froze at the word "mom," and then rocked harder, one hand toying with his socks.

"Please call me Delilah," she said, crouching a few feet away from Troy. "It's good to meet you, Troy. I have business to talk about with your dad and I'm worried it will distress you." She glanced up at Agent Miller, who frowned. "I'm very worried about my mom."

She didn't touch Troy, but felt his aura flare with pain and anger and so, so much anguish. She held up one hand, pausing a foot away. "Oh sweetie," she whispered, his sorrow radiating until it forced tears from her eyes. "You miss your mom so much. Oh my baby." She wanted to grab onto the child and hug him tight, send in soothing and pull the pain out. This raw, fresh pain.

"His mother passed away a little over a month ago, which is when I brought him to live with me," Agent Miller's voice was even, but confusion and anger radiated from him.

Fear and anger and grief spread outwards from the boy and she sent back calm as best she could.

"You don't understand where she went, do you? You just want your mommy and what you have is your daddy."

She glanced up at Miller, whose frown had deepened, but she realized he wasn't angry at her or at the child, but at the world. "You're very frustrated," she told Miller. "You want to help him but you don't know how. You want to protect him."

Miller looked away.

"You like things to work correctly and want to bring justice to the world. You don't like change and you don't like it when people and events don't fall in line."

She looked back at the boy who was very, very still. She murmured, "And you, Troy, you are perfect the way you are, darling. Your daddy wants to help you. You might never fall into whatever line everyone else thinks is the right line, but you will be yourself and you will heal and your daddy will continue to love you and protect you. You are too young to understand what happened and why your mommy's gone and you don't understand your daddy's rules and everything is different and cold and unknown. You don't know me, either, but I can feel how sad you are."

Troy was watching her out of the corner of his eye and he rocked harder, making the cheap metal frame of the chair squeak. Miller came and sat on the other side of him, not touching him either. Suddenly, the child shrank down in a fuzz of electricity and was a wolf cub swamped by a sweatshirt and loose pants. Miller sighed and started to undress him. Once he was unclothed, the cub shook himself and stepped up onto his dad's lap and hunkered down.

"He lets me…" Miller cleared his throat, the pain in his aura cracking through his neutral expression. "He will let me hold him when he's a wolf. He likes it best when I'm a wolf, too."

"May I pet your head, Troy?" she held out one hand for him to sniff, but he ducked under it and pushed up, so she scratched between his ears. "His sorrow is tempered in this form. Maybe it's comforting to not be human like his mother. She was human, wasn't she?"

"Yes," Miller whispered. "She didn't know I was a shifter until she had the boy. And…" He shook his head and piled Troy's clothes on the chair he'd vacated. "We still need to look around here and you need to show me your mother's computer and things."

She stood from her crouch, her knees wobbling as her thighs burned. She should probably start doing whatever exercise Miller did to tone his legs and ass. But he probably jogged and no, thank you. Maybe wolves liked to run, but psychics were more dignified. At least that's what she told herself.

Andrew looked at the dim, dilapidated waiting room with forty-year-old, yellow-vinyl-covered furniture and truly awful cheap-motel paintings. He cleared his throat. "You don't have a lot of customers come here?"

Delilah Woods shrugged. "Just about never, no. I tried to redecorate when I started working here a few months ago, but Mom said it didn't matter. And since she only hired me because she doesn't like answering the phone or replying to mundane emails and part of my pay is to live with her and eat her food, I figured she didn't want to spend money on it. Still, I rented a carpet cleaner because it was gross even though my mom vacuums often."

He stood up, holding his cub close. So Troy wanted to be a wolf because being human was too much a reminder of his mother? He tucked the boy against his body and tried to focus. "Does she have debts?"

Delilah laughed and rolled her eyes. "No, she's a cheapskate. I mean, we had lean times when I was little, when she was finishing her degree and getting started as an accountant and all, and she probably had debts then. I think Grandmother didn't always have enough food for them when she was little. Everything goes in the bank for a rainy day, only a small portion in stocks and bonds, because they're too risky. It means inflation is eating away at her spending power, but at least the market doesn't crash and wipe out her retirement fund."

Miller shrugged. "It's not ridiculous." His father had left them when he was little and his mom, though she had come from money – or more likely, *because* she had come from money, but her family had lost it all – hadn't known how to survive on the alimony and child support that was half of her previous budget. They'd eaten a lot of beans and rice because she'd blow the budget on steaks when the checks arrived. Every now and then she'd come home with a designer handbag or shoes because she "deserved" it.

He, however, had a steady income, only one dependent, and a big retirement fund, mostly in low-risk investments, with inflation eating away at his spending power.

Delilah went to the desk and sat in the shabby wheeled chair to boot up her desktop computer. "This one is connected to the internet. She has one like it in her office for email and research and the shared calendar, but mostly uses her laptop, which is completely off the net. She'll transfer data with thumb drives, so there's still a risk of viruses and tracking software, but she had them physically remove the chips for WiFi and, uh, what's it called? The cord to plug directly into internet."

"Ethernet," he said distractedly as he watched Delilah log into her computer. She smelled like spice with an undertone of green, growing things. Like running in the forest in spring. He wondered if it was her soaps or lotions or her skin. He forced his mind away from her skin.

"Anyway, there aren't any new email messages, because I also check from my phone and have my own laptop for school."

"School?" he turned his head to look at her. How young was she? He thought back to the fleeting impression he'd had of her during the chaos of kidnappings and Renaissance Faires and the hate group his half-brother had been undercover in. Delilah Woods had been instrumental in locating her cousin, which had meant locating her cousin's werewolf mate and the kidnapped shifters. She'd been an adult back then, but how old?

"Yeah, it's going to be a total of twelve years since I left high school by the time I graduate with my bachelor's, but it is going to happen."

He blinked and did the sums. "Are you thirty?" So young. So very, very young. He shouldn't even be looking at her rounded cheeks, even less at her rounded everything else.

She grinned at him, her pretty face dimpling and dark eyes widening mischievously. "I shouldn't answer that. But no, I'm twenty-nine. I'll graduate spring of next year, if everything goes right."

She knocked on the wood desktop, directing his and the boy's attention to the sound. She continued softly, "My mom being missing still keeps hitting me weird. Like I don't think she could really be gone and here's my life and my plans and they're suddenly up in the air. I had class the day she disappeared and I've only missed one since then, but it's like I'm riding along the tracks and I'm about to run out of fuel or I'll get derailed or something. If we can't find her..." She looked at the cub in his arms, who was watching from the corner of his eye. "My mom is missing from me. Did you know that's how the French say it? It's not just her who's gone, it's a piece of me which is gone."

The cub whined and Andrew rubbed him between the ears. Missing from me. He wondered if he'd ever allowed himself to think about what was missing. His dad when he was little, but he'd acted like it didn't matter when his dad didn't show up for planned visits because he was called to a case. His dad had been his hero and any crumb of attention was worth the wait.

He wondered if Troy had ever noticed he didn't have a dad who visited. Perhaps Andrew's ex had never told him Andrew was coming, so when she cancelled at the last minute, the boy didn't know.

Delilah smiled sadly at Troy before turning back to her screen. "Anyway, I don't see anything different here. I can't log into her computer because I don't know the password, but I can read her emails and see her schedule from this one. She used to have her voice mails in speech-to-text mode and forwarded to email, but decided she didn't like having them available on my computer and phone, in case I got hacked. She's not paranoid, exactly, but she's very security conscious. Maybe because she knows how to wheedle information off the dark corners of the internet, she's extra careful about her info getting out."

Miller nodded. "Hackers can get into anything, but yes, a computer not connected to the internet is your best bet. Of course, not using a computer at all is an even better bet."

"Well, she could work from print-outs or write spreadsheets by hand, but that's impractical. She worries she'll introduce some sort of tracker from the thumb drives and I guess it's possible, right? She buys hers from office supply stores. She just goes in and takes one off the display so no one can mess with it, but I guess when she gets info from the clients, it could have Trojan horses."

Andrew wasn't a research person or a hacker for the Bureau, but he'd put in enough requests for surveillance in his career that yes, he had to agree.

She was still clicking through email folders. "I'm too chaotic for my mom's sense of order, but she's so organized that if she had her way, there'd be a separate folder for each email and they'd all be password protected with a different password and she'd know them all be heart. I've tried to put things into more of a tree so it's coherent. Here it is."

She gestured toward the computer and got up, obviously intending for him to sit and read whatever she'd found. He settled into her chair, finding the bright cushions to be comfortable and warm from her jean-clad butt and the air she'd breathed smelling like mint. Maybe mint gum was the green smell. He wasn't supposed to be noticing her butt or her breath. He eased the kid onto his lap so he could use both hands. The pup pushed his face into Andrew's neck with another whine. Since he was five and not a tiny cub, it meant Andrew got a mouthful of hair every time he lowered his head.

"Troy, could I hold you?" Delilah asked softly.

The cub turned his head slightly, probably watching her from the corner of his eye like he usually did. Finally he turned toward her and she lifted him with an, "Oof, you're a big boy."

And then Andrew did the least logical thing he'd done all day: he didn't take out his reading glasses, instead increasing the size of the font by a couple ticks so he lean back and read from arm's length. He chose to not think of it as vain.

Chapter Six

Andrew was too aware of Delilah Woods carrying his son around the room, cuddling him like a baby, all while carrying on a one-sided conversation about what she was going to have for dinner and how this one painting was her favorite because it was sort of spooky in the way the colors blended around the edges and only hinted at the people in it.

Then the words *possible gang connections* caught his eye. This was the initial email from Shalonda at RFB – no, from her private account – asking for Ms. Woods to put a bid in on a fraud and embezzlement investigation that should look like a simple audit. To keep it quiet because of possible gang connections.

Delilah appeared at his shoulder, still hefting his son. "If you click on this folder, you can see most of the correspondence for the project. The data and final report and things were not sent by email. Let me know if anything needs a password, OK?"

She turned away and he watched stealthily as she moved Troy to one arm and took out her keys to unlock her mom's inner office. "We're going to explore a bit, OK? Let's explore, Troy."

They disappeared and he scanned a few emails, not seeing anything else about gang activity or what sort of gang they were talking about, just about fees and deadlines and meetings. Were they talking about a money-laundering gang or prostitution or guns or drugs? A few guys selling drugs out of the back door of the warehouse? Somewhere in between? Though if there were a hush-hush audit going on, it was certainly bigger than a couple of guys and was somehow wrapped into the company's finances.

He finally clicked the email closed and got up to ask Delilah questions. He found her sitting at her mother's desk with tarot cards arrayed in front of her, his son sitting on the desk, staring at her hands as she pointed out cards. Andrew glanced around the room at the barred window, two tall, beige, dinged-up file cabinets, and a door probably leading to a bathroom.

"Typically, we don't lay out the whole deck at once, just a few cards to help us find the answers we need, but each card has a wide set of meanings depending on what other cards are around it and if it's right side up or upside down. They can also be stubbornly literal. Like before I knew my cousin's boyfriend was a wolf, I kept pulling a Moon card for him." She sorted through her deck and took out a card. "See? There's a little wolf on it and one of the meanings is wildness. Not that Mike is very wild, but we didn't know he was a shifter, see?"

Andrew stopped in the doorway as his kid turned his head and kept Andrew in the corner of his eye. Delilah looked up at him, blinking.

"I remember you pinpointing Mike and Eloisa's location when they were in danger. Can you do that for your mom?"

She leaned back, shuffling the cards she still held. He sat in a vinyl-covered visitor chair which had obviously come from the same 1980s set as the waiting room chairs.

"We've tried a few times, but we're not having any luck. Either she's blocking it, which would be a good thing because it means she's strong, or we're too emotional, though why I could do it for Eloisa and not for her doesn't make sense. Or…"

An idea ignited in the back of his head. *Or* was the key. He had good instincts, he knew, but he downplayed them in return for building a good case based on facts. He was a dog with a bone: an indefatigable bloodhound, according to his bosses. That's what they used to say when he wasn't stuck on desk duty and leaving early all the time. He cleared his throat. "Or?"

Delilah frowned down at the card at the top of her pile. "Eight of Swords again." She set it in front of Troy. "Eight of Swords means trapped or confined. It can also mean we're mentally trapped and if we just opened our eyes, metaphorically and possibly literally, we would see. It can also be the symbol of major weight loss, but I've only come across it in the wild once."

Miller scowled at her. "Go back. She's blocking you, you're blocked because you love her, or?"

Delilah looked up at him, blinking. "Or Eight of Swords." She shook her head and lifted the card to wave at him. "She's blocking, I'm blocked, or someone else is blocking. And we have to figure out how to take the blindfold off. This makes more sense than the literal woman surrounded by swords in the picture."

"Someone else is blocking," he repeated slowly. "Who?"

"Ah. That's the question. Someone with powers. Powerful powers, you know? Capital T Talent." She turned over a card. "Reversed Magician. I'm pulling his card a lot, too. Unmanifested powers or sometimes madness when it's reversed. Right side up means manifested powers, but can also be a con man."

He shook his head. "I'm familiar with powers, but is there a specific type of powers that can block other people from seeing them? On the psychic plane, I mean."

She narrowed her eyes in thought and leaned one elbow on the desk, resting her chin on her hand. "Excellent question. I can dampen the reach of my own aura, but I've never tried to do it to someone else. It seems awfully intrusive. And I can dampen sound and make people not notice me, but they're not my primary strengths. I guess if someone was very strong in those things they might be able to figure out how to block the..." she trailed off, lost in thought, toying with the Magician card.

Troy reached out a paw and tapped her wrist.

"Oh sorry, sweetie. You want more cards?"

He didn't reply, but she took it as a yes and pulled another card. "Justice, which is more about kismet or karma than about mundane laws. Right side up this time. I pull Justice a lot for my mom because she tracks down robbers." She glanced up at Andrew. "You'd probably get the Justice card a lot. You're very big on rules."

He didn't want her to read him.

Or did he?

He looked around the room to find a different subject. "Are the filing cabinets locked?"

Delilah looked at them. "No, I don't think so. She said if someone got this far, they were welcome to what they could find. Which is highly redacted reports, the accounting that gets filed with taxes and is in the public domain, and various research binders which have been sanitized to generalities." She pointed at a shredder next to the cabinets.

Andrew strode to the cabinets and opened the top drawer. "What happens to the thumb drives?" he asked as he pulled out a fat binder, set it on top and opened it to find about ten years of tax returns. He scanned the first pages of the one on top, which was for the year before last. "Where's this year's info?"

She laughed and he turned to look at her. "It's only January. She has the info compiled, of course, but even she doesn't do her taxes this early. It's in her laptop, I bet. Maybe her desk at home."

"Good point." He went back to the binder and turned a few pages. Delilah's mom was making a lot of money. The shittiness of the office didn't reflect it, so either it was all in huge bank accounts or stocks – though Delilah said she didn't play the stock market – or it was missing: lost, stolen, paid out in blackmail, gambled away. He was willing to bet there was no hint of its placement anywhere in these cabinets except as, yes, interest income. He blinked several times. At bank account interest rates, even revised to Certificate of Deposit rates, the amount of interest income on her tax return was a whole lot. "Have there been ransom demands?"

Delilah laughed and paused in telling his son about some other card. "If there had, the cops would have taken this seriously. You would have taken this seriously."

He cringed slightly. He still wasn't sure about taking this seriously. "She has a lot of money, right? Could she have fled to a country with no extradition?"

"What? Just...what? I'm talking Justice card, remember? Rules and laws and sniffing out wrongdoing. If she did flee, it's to escape danger and I assume she would have told the rest of the family about the danger." She stared at the wall, thinking. "Unless she thought she was protecting us by hiding and not telling us?"

"And the thumb drives? The ones her clients give her to work from." He closed the binder and put it back in the drawer, spine up, then lifted the others out one by one with a little shake just to see if there was anything under them or falling out. It wasn't going to be a thorough search, but he could do it later if he thought it necessary.

"She tends to use the same ones they give her to give the report back. I mean, hardly anyone uses thumb drives anymore. Some of her clients say they don't even have them, but she makes them go out and buy a new one."

"She *tends* to use the same ones. Are there times when she doesn't?" He took the last three binders out from where they were jammed to the back of the drawer and opened the thin last one. The lease on the building, copies of the sale documents for her house, including the changes made to one bedroom to make it a tax-deductible office. He flipped back to the house deed and blueprint and saw it was two bedrooms, so figured Delilah was sleeping in her mom's home office.

Delilah snapped a few cards onto the desk as she said, "I've only been working for her for a few months, so only know what she's done during this time. And then she sanitizes them. Like, erases everything then breaks it open and physically removes the data part and destroys it. She's hard core." She paused only slightly before her voice warmed again and she spoke to the boy, "There are four Page cards which often represent children. A Page is an old word to mean a boy who helps out in a king's court. Page of Pentacles, I think fits you best, Troy. Serious and helpful and seeking security."

Helpful, thought Andrew, but didn't scoff out loud because he knew his son was seeking security, true enough.

He put the binders back in and went to the next drawer down, which held hanging file folders with date ranges on them. He pulled one out at random and saw the range referred to the start and end of a case. The basics of it were there: a few names and dates and broad suspicions, followed by pages of research and conclusions, but the reports had words blacked out. *Complete report submitted to client and to police*, he read.

"What happens if she gives the client a report and they don't like it? Or they alter it before giving it to the police?" he asked.

The quiet murmur of Delilah showing every single tarot card to his son stopped. "She always gives a copy directly to the police if the client is going to prosecute."

"And what if the client was the guilty one?" he asked as he put the folder back and took out another.

"She goes over their head, up the structure of the company. Or sometimes straight to the police if the upper levels of the company are crooked."

He wondered why suspected gang activity hadn't merited a trip to the police. Or to the FBI.

Chapter Seven

Del continued to lay out cards for Troy, scrabbling through her deck to find full suits and matches and major arcana. There were cards she didn't think she'd seen in years, ones she maybe didn't understand fully so they didn't speak to her even if she did pull them. She'd have to ask Grandmother and meditate on the cards, if she remembered which ones they were. She wondered if she had some sort of Inner Eye block on them.

The bathroom door opened and closed, the toilet flushing before the muffled sounds of the cupboard under the sink opening and after a minute, closing. Another cabinet drawer scraped and she finished talking about the Two of Cups, one which she saw a whole lot when a couple was getting together or, upside down, when they were breaking up or should not be together.

Agent Miller grunted and swore softly.

"Are you finding anything useful?" she asked tartly.

He let out a long breath. "Just cut my hand on a corner. Do you mind if I take a Band-Aid from the drawer?"

She told him no, she didn't mind.

He came out of the bathroom, smoothing a Band-Aid on the side of his hand. "And no, not finding anything. If we do need to investigate, it'll be a team going through everything page by page, but it's just me and I'm trying to see if there's anything to investigate. It's sanitized, like you said. What she needs to run the business, but nothing secret. Is there a safe? Because surely she doesn't keep all her secrets on one laptop without a backup of some sort. Eventually, the drive would be full. Or the drive would crash and take all her data."

Del considered herself pretty easygoing, but like anyone, she didn't like to be contradicted about something she knew about. "She says she doesn't. She gets a new laptop regularly and has massive amounts of memory installed. She never goes anywhere without her laptop. Even out to eat, she has it in a bag at her feet. She has a safe at home and she locks it in there at night, but I don't think she keeps anything else in there."

Miller turned to look at her, his eyes darting to his son, who was still intent on the cards. She knew he was interested, but wasn't sure how much he would retain.

"How old's Troy?" she asked.

"Five," he answered and didn't offer any other information. "I think I'm about done here. We'll go to your mom's house next."

"I don't know about you two, but I need some dinner," she answered lightly and Troy's attention shifted subtly to her face instead of her hands and cards. "What do you like to eat, Troy?"

A beat of silence, then Miller said, "Burgers and fries. Bacon and eggs in the morning. Carrots and apples sometimes, but bananas are his favorite fruit. Plain macaroni, not even butter on it."

Del smiled at the cub, whose gaze went back to the cards. "What's the best burger place?" she asked the cub.

Another beat of silence and Miller cleared his throat. "He's currently nonverbal, even in human form. The records from his mother and his old doctor said he talked a little, but I haven't heard anything from him since I picked him up."

"Oh," she whispered. Her chest hurt for the poor baby who probably had only ever spoken to his mother, or maybe to a trusted carer of some sort. "Well, which is his favorite?"

"Rally's," Miller answered, his voice tight.

Delilah set her hand palm up next to Troy's paw and asked, "Is Rally's your favorite. Troy?"

He sat back on his haunches, staring at her palm for a moment before touching her hand briefly and yanking it away. She got a strong sense that yes, Rally's was acceptable.

"There's one close to here," she said. "Does your dad know what you like on your burger?"

The cub nodded once, jerkily, and out of the corner of her eye, she saw Miller nod, too.

"What a sweet child." She started to reach out to pet him, but realized maybe he didn't want her to, if he was touch-sensitive. "May I scratch your ears?"

He bent his head forward and allowed her to pet him, not leaning into her or anything, but also not giving off negative vibes. As soon as she stopped, there was a moment of silence, then the cub flashed electricity and power and transformed back into a little boy, kneeling on her mom's desk, buck naked.

Agent Miller picked him up. "Clothing," he said, and went out to the waiting room where he'd left the boy's clothes on a chair.

Del gathered up her tarot and shuffled a few times before slipping them into their box and going out to put on her coat and gather up her things. She watched as Miller gently but firmly put the coat on his son's stiff arms. "Do you remember to ask permission before you touch him?"

Miller paused and looked at her, expression fierce. "What do you mean? I'm not doing anything inappropriate."

"No, no. I'm not saying you're hurting him or anything. Just that we can haul kids around or pick them up without warning and it can be distressing for them. Like I don't expect my nephew to hug me until he decides he wants to."

At Miller's raised eyebrows, she turned to Troy and said, "My nephew's about your age and he's a wolf shifter, too. He's my cousin's son, so strictly speaking, he's my first cousin once removed, but my cousin was always like an older sister to me." She frowned. "They're supposed to come for a visit in a few weeks, but if we can't find my mom in the next few days, I think they're going to come out sooner."

"If it's not safe, they should stay away."

Del held out her hands in an exaggerated shrug. "On the other hand, if my mom is missing and her daughter, sister, and mother need moral support and a dominant wolf shifter protecting the household, it seems like the perfect time."

Miller nodded, expression still unconvinced. "Shall we go?"

"You can follow me in your car, but let me look up the address for the burger place in case you lose me."

After the drive-through, Andrew followed Delilah Woods to her house and parked behind her car in the drive with old, dirty snow icing up around the edges. He carried his kid and their dinner inside.

Delilah invited him into the small, brightly-lit kitchen with pale wooden cupboards and off-white walls, beige-ish, stained, beat-up linoleum floor, and no decorations except a red towel hanging from the handle of an oven. She washed her hands before getting plain white plates and clear plastic cups out. He wrestled the boy out of his coat and carried him to the sink so they could wash their hands. Troy knew the drill and liked playing with the water when they were home. Well, playing in a limited sense. He liked warm water running over his hands and watched intently when Andrew soaped him up. He didn't like baths, but suffered through them, especially if Andrew left the water running to distract him.

Andrew set the boy on a chair, wishing he'd planned ahead and brought the booster seat. He pulled the food out and plated it, then eyeballed the three measly ketchup packets. The kid didn't care if his burger and fries were cold, as long as there was nothing on either except vast quantities of ketchup.

He opened a packet and squeezed it onto his son's burger. "Do you have Heinz ketchup? I mean a bottle? This isn't going to be enough."

"Oh, no. We're not really ketchup eaters." Delilah opened her paper bag and pulled out three more packets which she slid across the table. "Is this enough?"

Andrew assessed the packets, then the small serving of fries, weighing six packs of ketchup against the possibility of there being fries left at the end, which would lead to distress, and nodded. "I hope so."

They ate in silence, his son taking his usual tiny bites and chewing each one endlessly. At least the boy wasn't going to choke. Even in wolf form, he ate like a bird.

It felt domestic. Domesticated. He wondered if Delilah could cook, then grimaced as he realized it might be sexist to expect her to feed him. Instead of going out, he cooked for himself, but simply. Lately, it had been burgers for his son, therefore a lot of burgers for himself. And oven fries, not the crinkly ones, only the shoestring ones, and never, ever tater tots.

That had been a bad night.

His mother was a good cook, though she preferred eating out, which was a problem during the lean times when she'd overspent the alimony and child support. He barely remembered a time when his dad had eaten a meal with them at home, but from what his mom said, he would show up whenever he finished working and insist she cook him something good.

Andrew hoped he would never behave like him.

Chapter Eight

After supper, which was a close call with the ketchup, Andrew washed his kid's hands again.

"If either of you need to use the bathroom, it's the second door on the left," Delilah said as she stacked the plates by the sink where the kid was playing.

Miller felt his son's body tense and dried his hands before carrying him down the narrow, poorly-lit hall with floorboards squeaking under a runner. There was only one more door on each side of the hall, probably the bedrooms. The house couldn't have been more than 800 square feet, plain and not drafty. Delilah's mother had probably replaced or sealed the windows somehow.

Luckily, the boy was completely toilet trained, which Andrew had read wasn't always the case with kids on the autism spectrum. He sure as hell wouldn't have had any idea of how to deal with diapers and toilet training, especially on top of learning everything else about his son as quickly as possible.

When the toilet flushed and the sink turned on, he went in to test the water so it was the right temperature.

Finally, he turned it off and dried Troy's hands on the tiny, fluffy hand towel.

"OK," he said, returning to the kitchen where Delilah had taken care of the dishes and was wiping down the table. "May I look at your mom's home office?"

Delilah sighed. "You know, you're very helpful and I don't think my mom has ever done anything illegal, probably ever, but you are a federal agent."

He nodded. "It's not an official search, but if I found something, I would feel obligated to report it."

She frowned at her hands for a minute and he let her think, his son rocking slightly with his face buried against Andrew's chest.

"OK, so what sort of things are you looking for?" she finally asked.

Andrew nodded. "I can't really say. It's more a case of I'll know it when I see it. We don't know what we don't know."

"How about if I see if there's any info about the RFB case? And maybe anything else she's working on. There are a couple other cases she's done recently with some slightly scary people. Their whole vibe was off when they called."

"And look in the safe."

Delilah spread her hands. "I think I know the code, but she might have changed it. She doesn't write it down and she makes me memorize it."

She went to a drawer, though, and rummaged through it. "Here, Troy," she said with a flourish, "We've got a pack of tarot cards you can use. Be gentle with them, OK? It's my mom's spare deck."

Andrew set his kid down again and sat next to him at the table. He shuffled the cards and cut them, then turned over the top one. Justice.

OK, weird coincidence, since he didn't believe his vibes or whatever made the cards come up in a certain order, more that someone like Delilah used the cards as a conduit for visions. He'd only started believing in visions and powers and so on a few years before during the case where Eloisa

Woods-Grey made people invisible and healed their wounds and so on. He did his job with attention to facts and proof and evidence, so he still doubted a whole lot of things, especially about seeing the future. He was fairly sure his intuition was somewhere on the spectrum of powers, but on the other hand, he had so much expertise in investigating he wasn't sure what was magic and what was experience.

Right then, his intuition was pinging that there was something hidden in Delilah's mom's home office and it was probably not in her safe, which would be the first place anyone tossing the house would look.

He pointed at the word on the card and read it to his son. "Justice. It means bad things are fixed and good people get good things."

And yet here he was, on notice at his job, struggling to take care of his son. What he wanted was his old life back. That would be justice.

But he glanced at his son, who was watching him from the corner of his eye. OK, so justice would be having his son with him and his job back to normal. Maybe not so many trips out of town or late nights. What he wanted was to protect this cub, and for the boy's mother to still be alive, but willing to let Andrew see him. But not have a close relationship to her because she was horrible to him when they were breaking up and nasty about having his baby who was a wolf.

He'd worried about her attitude so much he'd hired a P.I. and had him check on her to make sure she was treating his son fine. The reports were good, but he still wondered if she'd been really a good parent. Whatever that meant.

His son rocked in his seat and let out a little whine, so Andrew turned over another card. Two cups? Upside down, which he knew meant the opposite of whatever two cups meant right side up. He turned it over and read the words out loud while pointing to them, then pointed at the roman numerals and said "I I means two," which was not much of a reading or math lesson, much less the tarot lesson Delilah had been giving in her mother's office.

He turned over another as he heard Delilah's soft footsteps coming up the hall. The Lovers. Well that was embarrassing. He read the words to his kid anyway and pointed out that VI means six.

"Oh the Lovers card means there's a choice coming up in a relationship, not necessarily lovers per se," said Delilah, leaning over the boy's shoulder. She blushed a light pink, though.

Instead of flinching away, the boy took her hand and set it on the stack of cards. She chuckled and said, "I don't think we have time to look at cards again. Your dad and I have to talk about some things and then I'm sure it'll be time for you to go home and go to bed."

Delilah looked at the envelope in her left hand, then the pocket-sized planner in her right.

Andrew Miller looked steadily into her face, holding her gaze when she looked up. So he was hot and intense. And waiting for her to speak.

She held up the envelope. "Right, I found a thumb drive, though Mom always destroys thumb drives. And a key, but I don't know to what. And a set of numbers which might be the password to something or a combination to another safe."

Miller nodded and held out his hand. She'd already put the numbers in her phone, disguised as a phone number for a fictional friend, so she took the key out of the envelope before setting it on his palm, their fingers brushing, his hand warm and hers cold.

She held up the diary, which had a brown cover and was only about 3 by 5 inches. "And a two-year planner. It's more a daily list of activities and clients and such and not a personal diary. I guess it's the little one she usually keeps in her laptop case. I've never looked in it before because we have all the client info on our shared calendar." She flipped it open and paged back to the day she started working for her mom in the late summer. "It contains such fascinating tidbits as 'Hired Del. Billable hours.' Question mark, question mark. 'To answer inquiries, file, etc. Put her on insurance.' She handed me her small business insurance policy and had me figure out how to get added to it, because the part-time retired lady before me had her own health insurance. And here's a good one the next day: 'Report to Barnaby L.' Though I would have to verify if that's the day she turned in the report or if she was telling him about her progress."

"How about the entries for the last few days?" Miller asked.

She grimace-smiled and turned to the day her mom went to RFB. "'Report to Shalonda at RFB' and that's it." She frowned. "Which is kind of weird, because she didn't have an appointment with Shalonda on the calendar and only went there because Mr. James was arrested while she was on the phone with him."

He nodded. "OK, how about the days and weeks of the investigation?"

"How about if I sit down and look through this tonight and let you know what I find?" she snapped, then noticed Troy was rocking on his chair and toned down her aggression. "I mean, I'll read it through and tell you. Until this is a real investigation, I don't feel comfortable turning this over to an FBI agent. As soon as I can convince you or anyone else this is a real missing person case, you can read everything I find."

She held out her hand for the lumpy envelope with the thumb drive and the January 15th and 16th page from the diary with the numbers on it. Obviously reluctant, he handed them back. "Put them back in the safe when you're done. Or someplace safe. Just in case."

"OK." She stepped back.

"All right, son, we're going to go home and go to bed. School in the morning." He picked Troy up and set him on one hip, the boy leaning away from him stiffly. "Then your Aunt Beth is picking you up and taking you to the airport to wave goodbye to Uncle Alex."

Del said, "I'll be in the office for a few hours in the afternoon if they want to come by. We're pretty close to the airport, after all."

Miller narrowed his eyes. "I don't think that's a good idea. If there is a threat, the office would be the first place they look."

"And the house would be the second. Where do you suggest I go?"

He looked at her, mouth set in a stern line. He blinked once. "Not sure. Maybe not hanging around a place with only one egress, though. Here, you can run out the back or climb out a window. There, you're trapped."

She shivered, the idea of being cornered in her mom's office all too vivid in her head. "Well, thanks for that relaxing thought."

He turned toward the front of the house and set Troy on his feet long enough to pull on his coat. "I only relax once the threat is over. Turn on your alarms and make sure everything's locked."

Chapter Nine

AND THEN THEY WERE gone. She watched through the window of the living room as Agent Miller sure-footedly walked across the icy patches on the driveway, put his son into his car seat and buckled him in, then went around, got in, and backed out, seemingly without looking at her.

She checked all the windows and doors and turned on the alarms, like she always did, but with a bit more purposefulness.

Then she turned on her electric blanket to heat her bed while she got ready for sleep and locked the envelope back in the safe in the corner of her mom's home office which was now her room. Once she was under the covers, she opened the diary, figuring she'd flip through it and fall asleep in no time. And yeah, most of it was boring and exactly what she figured her mother would write. Billable hours and deadlines and other stuff that had been added into the project management software afterward. Sometimes she'd been juggling five or six projects at once, all in different stages of completion.

She flipped to the end and started working her way back from the last entry. January 20. January 19. January 18. January 17. January 16. January 15.

Wait, what?

January 15 and 16 should have been missing. It was the page that was torn out, she was pretty sure. She flipped back to the year before and the page wasn't missing from there, either. In fact, they were on facing pages the year before.

She got up and put on her robe and slippers - her mom's thermostat had a timer set to super cold in the house when they were at work and overnight. After pulling the envelope out of the safe, she took out the page. Yep, January 15th and 16th. So whose planner was it from? She compared it to her mom's planner and everything was the same. She turned it over and held it up to the light and: nope, no clue. The numbers looked like her mom's handwriting, but there were only six of them, so it was hard to say. She locked the safe again, keeping the planner page out, and shuffled over to dive back into bed.

She opened the diary to January 15th and squinted at it under her bedside lamp. There was a discolored rough patch in the inside margin, like something had been written in pencil and then erased. Since everything else was in her mom's usual black gel pen and neatly crossed out with a line through it when her mom had been working down a list or had made a change, the erasure was weird. She felt it and could sort of make out the ridges and troughs of writing. She tried to hold it up to the light, but with the words so close to the margin, she was squinting at nothing. She turned on her phone flashlight and set it behind the page.

B.J. = 541 and then something illegible. And while blow jobs were a fun activity, Del didn't think her mom had done one, maybe ever, but probably not in Del's lifetime, and certainly not noted it in her planner. She briefly wondered if Agent Miller liked BJs, but couldn't imagine him handing over that much control to another person. She tried to picture him wrecked with his head back, gasping, and wished she knew what he looked like naked.

And she had to stop that. *Now.* He wasn't interested.

She tilted the little book and looked closely.

And called Agent Miller.

He'd just finished reading his son's favorite book for the fifth time and the kid seemed to be falling asleep when Andrew's cellphone vibrated with an incoming call. Delilah Woods. He had a brief hope that she might be interested in a little pillow talk, maybe leading to phone sex. But he was ridiculous and if she were calling so soon, it was because there was something wrong. He shook his head as he slipped into the hall and answered, his kid going rigid under the blanket.

Andrew stifled his irritation, since the boy wouldn't fall asleep by himself anyway. Even if Andrew wanted phone sex, he'd be cuddling his son to sleep instead.

"Andrew Miller speaking."

"Hi Andrew Miller, I'm sorry to bug you, but I think I figured something out with the planner." Her voice came faster and faster, words tumbling out on top of each other. "There are penciled notes in the margins, like, the margins next to the binding, and they've been erased. I don't know how many there are, but there are numbers and initials and little symbols. Oh, and the page in the safe wasn't even from this planner, but from an identical one. Or, you know, at least with the identical page, so probably by the same company. Which sort of makes sense, because she always had her planner with her laptop, you know?"

Miller blinked, knowing his kid with his sharp wolf ears could hear everything she was saying. His stillness had changed to listening, Andrew was pretty sure. Since the boy liked Delilah and was only five and didn't know eavesdropping wasn't polite, it wasn't surprising.

"Is there a pattern to them? On specific days of the week or dates of significance? Before or after meetings with certain clients.?"

"Hold on, I've only really looked at one and found one more while I was talking." He could hear her breathing as paper rustled just slightly. "There's something every Thursday going back a few months. That's well before she started on the RFB case."

Andrew felt the tingle of intuition again. "Either her disappearance has nothing to do with RFB, or RFB has to do with other cases she's had."

Delilah huffed. "Or she has so many shady characters in her business life it could be anyone or anything."

A little ping of knowing. "Or she went back through the planner and put in information after the fact, hiding it for you to find."

"It does seem pretty systematic. I mean, she obviously was hiding it. The way it's written and erased is the same, so it's like she was inputting the data on each Thursday, then going through and erasing it partially."

He heard the rustling of fabric and forced himself not to think of her in bed. Then he heard the shuffling of cards. She was doing a reading? That was... OK, so if her intuition worked best through cards, then whatever.

He stayed quiet as she murmured softly about wands and queens and a magician.

"I think I've got it," she said. "Pretty sure it's all linked to RFB, but not because of them. I mean, they're part of the pattern. I don't pay a lot of attention to the cases, just to the people who call and email. This guy who got arrested, Brad James, his initials are in here a couple times. I mean other people have the initials BJ, too, but if she's working backwards, I don't imagine she'd use the same initials for more than one person."

Andrew's ears perked up. "Have there been other arrests within RFB? Usually, businesses try to keep financial malfeasance quiet."

"Oh no, he was handcuffed and marched out the same afternoon my mom went missing. The next day, Shalonda, my mom's contact, went on vacation, which had supposedly been planned for a long time."

"I believe you," Andrew blurted out, his intuition adding two and two and getting 500.

"You...OK? About what?"

"About your mom either hiding or being hidden. If she's not already been caught, she's in danger. But it means you're in danger, too."

Silence and Delilah's breathing. "Well, shit."

When his son's ears went up at the bad word, Andrew realized he'd shifted to wolf. He went back into the bedroom and started undressing the cub while Delilah sighed on the phone.

"I was hoping to sleep tonight, but if I'm in danger…"

"I don't think it's an immediate danger, but if you want to come over here…" He swallowed tightly. "That's not a come-on or anything. I usually sleep in my son's bed these days, both as wolves. He's still adjusting to living with me. So you can have my bed." He wished he hadn't said bed, because the attraction to Delilah Woods couldn't go anywhere. He was over forty, she was too young. He didn't have time for a relationship.

"I think you're right. I'll pack a bag."

He forced his wayward lust down and returned to his area of expertise. "Bring everything you can't do without. Everything to do with this case, but also passports, laptops, books you need for class, everything."

"Really? You think someone will break in?"

"Jewelry if you have expensive pieces, weapons," he continued. "I would say your TV and big ticket items, but you need to be subtle, in case anyone's watching. And yes, if they think your mom has evidence hidden at the house, they will come in. Alarms are notoriously easy to get past and if this is as organized an operation as I fear it is, they'll know how to get in.

They'll steal all your things to make it look like a regular burglary and also to fence."

"I…OK?" Her voice was high and thready. "My mom doesn't have much expensive stuff. I mean, you saw the place."

He had only glanced into the front living room and hadn't noticed any tech, just the glimmer of what was probably a TV. "Get a pencil and I'll tell you my address."

"You could text it to me while I pack." She rustled up out of bed and he heard the slide of a closet door.

"True, but I'd rather not have my address on an unsecured phone. I'll give you instructions, too, so you don't use GPS. In fact, turn your GPS off now and your phone off when we hang up. Take the battery out if you can."

"What? But how will I use GPS to get there or call if I get lost, and also how will my family call me? What if my mom tries to call me?"

"She'd understand about being careful, wouldn't she?" Serena Woods sounded like she would go even further to hide herself than staying with a friend and turning her phone off. "Call your other family while you pack."

He gave her the address and basic instructions and said he'd be waiting in the basement parking garage to let her in and to give her his guest parking pass, the one he had on hand for his ever-changing cast of babysitters. He could only credit Blake, the building's concierge, who'd hustled to the elevator to stop the one who'd left in a huff on her way down to the garage when Andrew had called.

"OK, I'm going to call Aunt Moira and tell her where I'll be and that my phone will be off. She'll tell Grandmother and Eloisa for me. I'll get a burner phone tomorrow and use it to check in with them, OK?"

"Sounds good. Can you pull your car into the garage to load it up?" He got up and paced to the hall door, leaning against the jamb with his kid watching him.

"My mom usually parks in there. When there's a lot of snow or ice, instead of digging my car out, we dig out enough to take her car together." She grunted as she lifted something on the other end. "I'm glad I can still think about my mom in the present tense, but what if she doesn't come back?"

"We'll find her. I'll need more evidence there's something going on before I can start an official investigation, but the planner might have enough."

"What if..." Delilah's voice trailed off and he heard a drawer open and then shut a few seconds later. "Sorry, almost dropped the phone. What if there's something hidden I don't know about? In the books or under the floor? I mean, I'm not an expert at searching and just looked in the safe."

"I'll go through it tomorrow after work. We'll stick to the plan to have Beth pick up my son, OK?"

"Troy," she said as he heard more drawers open and shut.

"Yes, Troy." He looked over at the bed where his kid's eyes had been almost shut, but they were open now and he watched out of the corner of one eye.

"I noticed you never call him by his name. Or almost never, anyway."

Andrew froze. She was right. He shook his head. Not something he was going to worry about now. He took a deep breath. "Anyway, put something else of moderate interest or value into the safe when you take out the important things. Make it look like it's the only thing your mother kept in there. If there's dust everywhere but the spot where the thumb drive was, clear a space and put something of value there."

"Ooh, sneaky," she said as if from a distance and he realized she was on speaker.

She rustled around some more and he heard a plastic bag being snapped open. "Bringing my electric blanket and my pillow," she said.

"I'll be waiting for you in the garage. My son won't fall asleep without me, so I'll be carrying him and won't be able to help much."

"OK. I'll see you in about an hour."

They hung up and he wondered if this was going to be a huge mistake. And what if he was wrong and Serena Woods had just gone on a vacation with this Shalonda person?

Chapter Ten

DELILAH ROLLED OVER AT the sound of her alarm, but couldn't find her bedside table. She sat up and opened her eyes and oh, yeah. She was in Andrew Miller's king-size bed in a room easily twice as big as hers, with furniture which probably didn't come from garage sales, new carpets, and an en suite bathroom.

Sadly, though, there was no Andrew Miller in it with her.

She turned her alarm off and wondered why she'd set it so early. But she was glad she'd brought her cheap plug-in clock, since she usually woke up to her phone. Right now, she wanted to check the weather and to see if she had any messages and maybe watch some TikToks, especially a couple of tarot channels which she followed because they seemed legit. She was thinking of doing her own, if she only had the time, but also thought future psychiatric employers might see something like that and hate her. Mystic Marcia – real name Ashley – had offered to have her on an episode through Skype and they'd been trying to find a time. And then this whole thing happened.

But no phone meant she was going to get up and have breakfast with Andrew and Troy Miller. She wondered if Troy's last name was Miller. Probably not, from what Miller had said about his ex.

It had been midnight by the time they'd brought all her things up in the posh elevator, and Troy had been dozing off and then waking up and whining in his room until his dad went and calmed him. Her box and suitcase with her most important worldly possessions were here, plus some evidence of fraud and maybe of what her mother was involved in or investigating or whatever.

Honestly? She was starting to think her mom had gone against her nature and was doing something illegal. Maybe she had gone on "vacation" with Shalonda and they were starting a new life together somewhere with no extradition treaty. Her mom and Shalonda would make a cute couple, though they'd only talk about accounting and finance. Her mom hadn't liked when Delilah probed after meeting Shalonda and feeling the attraction between the two women, but that was mostly because her mom was very private. She'd admitted she'd dated women before she met Delilah's dad. And considering how ineffectual and full of sorry excuses her dad had been when she was growing up, Del couldn't imagine that had been a great inducement for her mom to date other men.

She'd like to think her mom wouldn't leave her holding the bag, pursued by mobsters or whoever was behind this whole…

She stopped to think, then took out her deck for some serious introspection.

Fifteen minutes later, she was dressed and walking into the dining-slash-living room with its row of windows looking out at the roofs of a few houses and the sides of taller buildings.

"Good morning, Troy," she said.

The boy, in cub form, stopped eating his bowl of bacon and eggs and watched her instead.

"Finish your breakfast, sweetie," she said and crouched down to scratch between his ears.

He was tired – she wondered if he'd slept well after being up so late – and confused that she was in the apartment.

"Don't worry, I will do my best to not disrupt your schedule." She stood up and turned to greet Agent Miller where he was standing next to the stove in the open-plan kitchen.

He nodded a greeting. "Would you like bacon and eggs?"

"Just two slices of bacon, please. And some toast and jam? Or peanut butter, maybe. Just point me at the toaster, I can make toast myself."

They were so polite.

She cleared her throat. "I was having some thoughts."

The toast popped up and she put it on her plate and spread peanut butter on both slices.

"Go on," Miller grumbled.

She shivered with pleasure as she thought of other times he might growl at her. She hoped he couldn't tell she was a bit turned on, but he was a shifter with sharp senses and probably used to women reacting to him.

"I took out my cards to help me think, of course. I still don't have a strong sense of where my mom is, but based on things she said and did, I'm pretty sure she knows Shalonda at RFB a lot better than she let on. My mind was rambling when I woke up and I thought maybe they'd run off together. I'm pretty sure they didn't, because though I may have some doubts about what my mom is up to, I don't think it includes leaving the country for any illegal reason."

Miller nodded and waved her to the little table and they sat. A swish of fur and Troy jumped up on the chair next to his father, who gave him another slice of bacon from his own plate. Troy hopped down to nibble at it, dropping it back onto his plate on the floor after each bite, obviously watching and listening.

"If it's OK with you, I'll take the journal and thumb drive to work with me and see if your mother left you evidence of a crime. In that case, I'll be opening a file and will need your signature surrendering the evidence to the

FBI. I don't know if it will show she's been abducted, but if there's proof of a crime, we will look into it, too. At that point, it will probably be taken out of my hands, because I'm with the Shifter team, not Organized Crime, and currently on desk duty. I'm considered unreliable as far as time spent at work, since I will no longer work 24/7. I have other, more important responsibilities at home." He grimaced.

She pointedly did not look at Troy. She just bet Miller resented being "unreliable" in the FBI's eyes, but he was obviously a devoted father who took his "more important responsibilities" very seriously. She had no idea if he loved his son or even understood him, but he was caring for him to the best of his abilities. It was probably the first time he'd commented about it to anyone, too, however obliquely, so she felt honored.

"I'd like it if you stayed here until we can decide how to keep you safe. Beth, Alex's wife, my, uh, sister-in-law I guess, was going to bring my son to me at work when he got out of school, but would you be willing to watch him for about an hour until I get home instead? This apartment is a lot closer to their house and I already rely too much on her, on both of them."

"Did they tell you you rely too much on them?" Delilah asked, feigning innocence.

He shook his head. "Of course not, but they're both busy. Alex is an FBI agent and has been traveling a lot and Beth is a professor with midterms coming up and she's writing a book."

So it wasn't quite bragging, but something about his presence shifted when he talked about his brother and sister-in-law. Maybe he liked them, even loved them. "They're probably happy to help," she answered cheerily. "Give me Beth's number and give her...Arg!" She remembered again that she couldn't turn on her phone. "Could you get me a burner phone when you're out? I'll give you the cash for it. And have Beth call the house phone,

I guess. Definitely write her number down for me before you go, though, so I can use the landline. You have a landline, right?"

He assured her that yes, he had a landline and it had frequent scans against wiretaps, which she wasn't even thinking about until he mentioned it.

Not long after, he asked Troy to shift to boy and when he didn't, Miller gathered up clothes for him and took him to school anyway. She almost said something about the car seat, then remembered the seatbelt dog harness El and Mike had for their son to keep him safe in the car.

Delilah almost asked for a kiss goodbye, but they didn't have that kind of relationship. Yet?

She went to unpack a few things and organize the stuff from her mom's safe. She'd emailed her psych prof before shutting down her phone, so she wasn't expected in class. She pulled out her massive textbook, which other than her car and her aging laptop was the most expensive thing she owned, and started reading and taking notes. After reading the week's assignment, she flipped ahead to the chapter on autism and wished she could Google the most current research. She skimmed the chapter once, then started again more slowly to take notes.

At three o'clock, after she'd painted all her nails and watched a couple of Disney movies and taken a nap, and the time had dragged and dragged without her phone or laptop, the landline rang and she checked the caller ID. It was a blocked number, but she expected no less from an FBI agent's spouse and what Miller had said it would be. The scammers were using spoofed numbers that looked like they were calling from your own area code these days. Legit businesses did, too, but they weren't calling five times a day about her car's warranty. She took a deep breath and answered on the third ring with a simple, "Hello?"

"Hi, this is Beth. Is this Delilah?"

She let out a big breath. "Yes. Shall I meet you out front or in the garage?"

"Garage. I'll talk to you when I get there in about twenty minutes. Should I call you again from down there?"

"That might work best, yes. Or when you're really close. It's kinda dark and creepy down there, or was at night anyway."

Beth laughed. "It's always dark and creepy down there, but they supposedly have a good camera array the concierge guy watches and there's a security guard service going through at random intervals. Do you think Andrew Miller would neglect that?"

Del laughed, too. "Probably not. My mom's the same way with the house and work alarms, but she's not willing to spring for cameras and definitely doesn't want ones linked to the internet and could be hacked."

"Good point," Beth said. "Well, we're driving now. I'm looking forward to meeting you!"

It was more like half an hour later when the landline rang again. Del answered it and with just a few words, was putting on her coat and taking the elevator down to the garage. A small, yellow SUV waited in the loading zone and when Del approached, a tall woman with dark hair got out and smiled like they were long-lost friends. She was probably ten years older than Del, close to Miller's age and, she guessed, to his half-brother's age, too. And a college professor. Did everyone have their life in hand and she was the only one still thrashing around, trying to figure it out?

She shook Del's hand with great enthusiasm. "Beth Ogden. I kept my maiden name, since Three Feathers seemed a bit cultural appropriation-y for me and my degree and publications are all in my original name."

"Delilah Woods from a long chain of matriarchal women who tend to have children out of wedlock and keep naming them Woods," she replied.

"My brother-in-law said you're Eloisa Wood's cousin and you're a magic user, too? I met her in Wyoming when she healed Alex."

"I'm more in premonitions and readings, and the feelings auras give off."

"Oh, fascinating! I've only touched on magic other than shapeshifting in my research, but my mother-in-law is a bobcat shifter – slash – magic user. She has intense premonitions sometimes and can project feelings to calm a crowd or make them afraid." Beth shuddered. "I got hit with the edge of one of those once, and wow. Bad."

They chatted for another minute about magic, Beth asking questions and Del answering them, mostly. And wishing she had professors like Beth instead of like the cranky, glaring psych prof she had this semester.

"So do you want to come in?" Del asked.

"Oh, sorry, I actually have to get going and I don't have a parking permit to stay in the garage. I'm covering a History Club meeting at the college. As if college-age history nerds need faculty supervision! But they meet in the History House, so there has to be someone there and Dr. Stevens had another appointment."

Beth clicked the locks open as Del went around the SUV to the passenger side and opened the door to find Troy in human form, clothes on, but askew.

"He shifted on the way here from wolf, which is why we were a little late. I pulled over to unhook his pet harness and get him into his car seat. He's really good at dressing himself now though, aren't you, Troy?"

Del opened the latches and Troy climbed out on his own. The brush of her hand against him told him he was content with Beth and happy to be home. There was something painful underneath, like maybe today hadn't been the very best day.

"Andrew gave us the car seat, so you don't have to take it out. The harness though, we hand back and forth with Troy's bag. We should probably get a spare or two to keep in the cars he's most likely to ride in. Safety first, right Troy?" She pulled out a small duffel bag and unzipped it to stuff the harness in and hold it out to Del.

Troy was staring off into the middle distance and rocking from foot to foot, but he got a small smile when Beth said his name. Beth held out her hand to tell him goodbye and he touched her palm with one finger, which was a bigger deal than anyone was making of it, though Beth smiled fondly.

Del waved her off, shepherded Troy in front of her, and used the key card Miller had given her to swipe into the elevator, entering the apartment number and access code once inside to make it move. She wondered if it would take her to other floors, too, but didn't want to test it by pressing all the buttons all the way up to the tenth floor. Maybe some other time, if she was still here and got bored again. Maybe Troy would enjoy the adventure, though she was willing to bet the whole building was beige halls with thin, brown carpet like the third floor.

Once back in the apartment - accessed with key card and physical key - and the door locked behind them, she set the duffel on the little table by the front door, wondering if that was the right thing to do. She opened it and found a lunch box, which she took to the kitchen and rinsed the thermos and threw away the trash. She didn't know if Miller reused the sandwich bags, so left them on the counter.

Troy was standing where she'd left him in the short hallway, rocking from foot to foot and staring at the floor.

"Kind of weird to come home without your dad, huh? I'm not one of those babysitters, I'm just babysitting right now, if you see the difference."

He didn't reply, but his shoulders relaxed slightly.

"And I'm sorry I've thrown off your routine. I bet you like your life to be consistent. Honestly, we all do, but I get the feeling you've had so many changes lately that you're still adapting to, so a stranger in your home is a little upsetting."

He nodded once, which was a good start.

"Do you want me to explain the cards some more? I brought the spare deck we looked at last night and if your dad's OK with it, I'm going to give it to you. It's a little different from my usual deck, but mostly the same. I'll go get it out of my stuff, OK? Do you want to wait for me at the kitchen table?"

As she went to get the cards, she berated herself internally for sounding awkward and ridiculous. Her textbook had said verbalizing intentions and the child's possible feelings and reactions might help him be able to verbalize those feelings later. There was a lot about sign language for nonverbal children, but she didn't know any, though she was sure TikTok videos would be a resource, if she only had internet access.

When she arrived in the kitchen, Troy was standing next to his chair, one hand on the table. She sat in the chair she'd used before and started to take the cards out of their box and unwrap them. She paused. "Oh, do you want a snack?"

Troy touched the cards and she smiled. "OK, let's look at some cards. I'm going to show you a reading. You touch the cards again and think about your day and I'll see if the cards tell me anything."

She set the deck in front of him and he stared at them for a few seconds before he patted them. She shuffled them and laid them out in a simple five-card reading, explaining the positions and pointing out the names and attributes of the cards again.

She breathed in and out and boom, the vision came to her. "Your teacher was upset today, but you didn't know why. Probably it's something that doesn't have to do with your school, but it made you uneasy. One of the other children was crying, which also made you uneasy. You spent most of the day as a wolf cub and you were a good boy and very gentle with the others, even if they touched you when you didn't want to be touched, is that right?"

She looked at him in time to see him nod his head once.

"Well done," she said. "It's probably harder in wolf form to tell someone to stop bothering you, but I can see how it would be comforting to have warm fur. Did you do some activities?"

She couldn't See what he'd done, but she bet the folder in his duffel had a list of activities. She got the impression he'd mostly sat and watched.

"And you like Aunt Beth, right? She's very friendly and I can tell she's a good person who loves you. You feel safe with her, which is good." At this point, she was reading his reactions and not his cards. There was one bump left in her reading, though. "And you thought about your mom today, because we talked about moms yesterday and you miss her."

She shouldn't have mentioned it because the pain radiated out of him in a wave much too big for such a small boy and he began to rock side to side.

"I'm sorry, honey," she said softly. "I would bring her back if I could, but no one has that magic."

She saw an image of an older woman, angry and bent over him, pointing in his face and wondered who it was. She'd have to ask about an older woman who prayed and pointed and frightened Troy.

He stood suddenly and struggled to take off his shirt before shifting to wolf with his pants still on. Del crouched next to him and pulled his pants off his tail and back legs, then he trotted out and down the hall. She followed to see him go into his room, where a high, doggy whine started, interspersed with moans.

Shit. She'd leave him alone for a few minutes before going in with a snack. She wondered if she should have made him use the bathroom when they got home, if he was at risk for wetting the floor. OK, so she wasn't used to babysitting anyone, but she was sure she'd broken him and not fed him and forgotten to get him to use the bathroom, all in less than half an hour.

She'd had upset clients before, but never made a five-year-old have a breakdown.

She paced and thought about her mom and wondered if Miller had figured anything out with the planner and thumb drive.

Eventually, she gave up pacing and went and got a banana to take as a peace offering and picked up his clothes to put back on him. She found Troy scratching at the wall in the corner of his room, a little pile of plaster dust growing.

"Oh, sweetie," she said, trying to keep her voice calm. She realized he must have been digging for a lot longer than fifteen minutes, because the damage was fairly extensive and the pile of plaster small. "Hey, I brought you a banana. Your dad said you liked them. Want to get your hands washed and have a snack?"

He stopped scratching, but leaned his forehead against the wall.

"I'm sorry I brought up your mom, but I could tell you were having a hard time about her today. So let's get you shifted, go to the bathroom, clothes on, wash hands, and you can have this banana and we'll talk about happier cards, OK?"

Instead, he sighed deeply. She tentatively scratched between his ears and he let out another sigh. She sat on the floor instead of crouching and kept petting his wiry fur gently until he turned and walked away. Pretty soon, she heard the toilet flush and the sink turn on.

And the water ran and ran and ran. She knocked on the bathroom door and went in, carrying his clothing, to find him in human form, holding his hands under the running water. More self-soothing, she supposed. "I brought you your clothes, Troy. Let's dry your hands and get you dressed so you don't get cold."

Once he'd returned to the table and eaten his banana - she wasn't sure if she was just supposed to give it to him like she had or if she should have cut it up or something - she wiped his hands again and cut the deck before fanning it out. "Take any card, OK? And place it face-up in front of you."

It was a form of quick reading, just to hold one card, of course, but she was more interested in telling him more about the cards again instead of poking into his trauma. She was just glad he still wanted to look at the cards after she had touched his grief. Most children his age didn't understand death and she wondered if anyone had explained it to him.

Chapter Eleven

HALF AN HOUR LATER, the door opened and Miller called out hello and a minute later appeared in the archway to the kitchen, eyes watchful and face neutral as usual. He was giving off waves of intensity and she wasn't sure if it was positive or negative or some of both.

"Talking about cards again," she said breezily.

He nodded. "Good afternoon, Delilah. Good afternoon, Troy."

So formal, but it fit him.

"How was your day?" she asked, then barely kept herself from wincing because she sounded positively domestic. It felt natural to her, which made it even scarier.

He nodded again and came to sit down across from her. "We've linked your mother's journal to an open mob-related case and now the FBI wants to talk to her. They want to talk to you, too, but you say you don't know anything. They'll seize all your work computers and your phone and search your house and office."

Del gaped at him. "Is she going to be arrested?"

Miller's face contracted into deep thought. "I don't believe she's being looked at as a perpetrator, but she's certainly a witness."

Her heart lifted. "So they're going to look for her?"

"Not a serious manhunt, no, but they'd like to trace her movements and get her in for questioning as soon as they can."

Del sat back in her seat. "She's going to need a lawyer. I know she has a few on speed dial, but mostly because they're helping prosecute someone she's found evidence against. She's considered a credible expert witness. There's one who's her lawyer and she pays a retainer and stuff. All the info's in the work computer."

He nodded and apparently thought the conversation was over as he shifted his focus to Troy. "How are you today, son?"

Troy, who'd been rubbing a card on the table with a little scritch, scritch, scritch that reminded her of his wall, pulled his hand into his lap, and then with the rush of power, shifted to wolf cub. He kicked off his sweatpants and his dad helped him out of his shirt, then Troy stepped onto his dad's lap.

"From what I was able to read, his teacher was upset about something and another child was crying. And..." She scrunched up her face. "And I'm afraid I saw in the cards he was upset about his m-o-t-h-e-r, which brought up a lot of pain."

The little cub buried his face in Miller's belly and let out a steady stream of breathy whines.

"I'm sorry, Troy. We will definitely stop talking about it now," Del said.

Miller held the boy closer and soon the whining stopped, though the cub didn't appear to relax. Miller's strong hands were so gentle with his son, handling him carefully and competently. She wondered if he knew how attractive it was to see a good father. Though he'd hinted he didn't know Troy until a few weeks ago. She opened her mouth to ask about it and about the angry older lady who prayed, but didn't want to upset Troy more.

Miller eventually got up and handed the cub to Del, who carried him to the couch and sat, lost in her thoughts, missing her phone worse than ever.

"Did you get me a burner phone while you were out? I really miss being able to Google stuff."

Miller turned from his place at the stove and considered her for a few seconds. "Sorry, I didn't think of it. Tomorrow, I'm taking you to the office with me for questioning and you can ask the Agent In Charge for permission."

Del wrinkled her nose. "Assuming I don't get arrested, right?"

One side of Miller's mouth quirked in amusement. Slightly sardonic amusement, but amusement. "I don't think you'll be arrested. But you might want to really think about everything you know about your mom's business."

Her heart stuttered slightly and she widened her eyes in surprise. "So you think they will arrest me."

"Not arrest. I think they will ask you questions and then we'll go to your office and your house, where you'll point out where information is kept."

She shook her head. "Wait, do they have a search warrant? I don't know if my mom would approve and I know that's pretty important to her."

"You can give us permission." He turned back to whatever he was stirring on the stove top, which was starting to smell really good in a beef sort of way.

"I don't know if I can. I mean, it's her name on everything and I just live and work there. You really don't want stuff to be inadmissible as evidence, right?" Her hand went to her back pocket for her phone, which was still not there. "Dammit! I need the internet. And I need a lawyer, right? And my phone and laptop contain my address book with the lawyers' information."

Miller's shoulders drooped a little. "You can give consent to a search, but you can refuse if you think your mother would. You…should refuse if your mother would. Yes, you should run this by your mom's lawyer. You can search on your own and hand over anything pertaining to the notes in the margins of the diary."

"Which I don't know anything about, except the few notes I found, so that doesn't help. Could I just turn my phone on to get the info I need? And do you have a secured laptop or something so I can search online?" She was realizing she was addicted to the internet or something and wondered if, when everything went back to normal, she would go back to her old patterns.

The negotiation went on for a few more minutes as Miller set Troy on another chair and went into the kitchen, where he made a burger for his son, who sat up, nose twitching when he heard the sizzle.

"Get changed, please, son," Miller said. "We have a rule about eating dinner in human form while wearing clothing."

Troy jumped down from the couch and trotted to the table where his clothes were draped across his chair. He shifted and got dressed yet again.

Del wondered if she should help him and if there were a way to get him easier clothes to take off and on when he struggled with pulling the t-shirt over his head, but he eventually got it on, inside out and backwards, but all by himself. "Good job, Troy," she said, in case this was a relatively new thing and still considered praiseworthy. She hoped she wasn't too condescending.

He stood by the table, watching her from the corner of his eye, then turned his head to watch his father.

"Delilah, would you please set the table?" Miller asked. "Usually I do it for the two of us."

She hopped up. "Sure. And I bet Troy can help me. Troy, could you carry the cups, please?"

Miller opened his mouth to comment, but when she got down plastic cups and turned around with the stack in her hand, Troy had moved to the edge of the kitchen and took them from her while she gathered up the silverware.

He nodded. "Big spoons for stew. I hope you like beef stew. I make a huge pot every couple weeks and freeze it in portions."

She smiled at him, envisioning how he probably followed a recipe to the letter and froze exactly a bowl full at a time. "It's a very predator sort of meal, I guess. And yes, I like beef stew, thank you."

He nodded. So still and solemn he was. So polite. She wanted to mess him up and see the lithe body under his clothes. She blushed and turned toward the table to put the silverware around, narrating her table setting for Troy's benefit. The boy stood there like usual, his attention on her. Maybe she had a head start on understanding him because she could sense his emotions and do a reading for hints about his thoughts, but she wondered if Andrew Miller was sensitive enough. He seemed strict about rules.

After dinner, Andrew turned on his son's favorite movie, a Disney classic with music, and he wondered for the hundredth time if it was the kid's favorite movie or his late mother had played it constantly and Troy had imprinted on it.

"Delilah, could you help me with the dishes, please?" he asked politely. He gaze snagged on her bright pink nail polish, which definitely hadn't been there in the morning. She would say something if she didn't want to do the dishes with it on, right?

She apparently realized he wanted to talk and tore her gaze away from singing princes to follow him into the tiny kitchen. "I'll wash and you dry?" he suggested. They never had enough dishes to run the little dishwasher, so he almost always washed by hand, clearing up as soon as the meal was over.

He filled the sink and used the opportunity to lean and murmur, "In case you have things to ask or tell that my son doesn't need to hear. He has shifter hearing, but probably can't hear over the movie and the water." He reached over her head and flipped on the stove exhaust fan for good measure.

"I need my mom's lawyer's number, which is in our calendar app, so I need to turn on my phone or computer."

He nodded. He knew the warrant was in process, but might be denied, since there was only slim evidence that Delilah's mom, Serena, knew anything useful about the mafia case they were working on. "It would be best to consult with him."

"Her, but yes, thanks."

"Do you know the login info for the app? Could you use a more secure computer and get your information?"

She nodded. "When I set my computer to remember the password, my mom made me memorize it instead, so yes. I'm not sure if I can use another computer, though. I just have it on my desktop at work and my phone and it was complicated to get it set up on my phone. I mean, if anyone was tracking my search history, they could figure it out. I'm no techie."

The music swelled in the other room and he turned on the water. The noise was getting to the edge of hurting his sensitive ears, but he leaned in and asked, "What did you mean about Troy's mother?"

She immediately looked sad and guilty. "I was showing him the cards again and showed the typical layout for a reading. That's how I saw the part about his teacher being upset and a child crying all day. I also saw him being gentle with another child who touched him when he wanted to be left alone. But then I saw the pain about his late mother and mentioned it.

I mean, the pain is the biggest thing in him right now and it's going to be a while. Five-year-olds don't typically understand death, but... has he had it explained to him? Where his mom is and why?"

Andrew nodded and turned off the water, glancing back over his shoulder at his kid, rocking slightly as the villain cackled on the flat screen TV he'd bought when he came home with Troy's DVDs. He'd probably not explained death to the boy in terms he could understand. He felt like slightly less of a failure since Delilah had said little kids didn't understand it anyway, usually.

Delilah reached across him, her body pressed against his for a couple seconds, which blanked his mind right out. She turned the water back on and asked, "Who's the older woman I saw who was yelling and pointing?" Then she turned the water off, again pressing against him.

He braced his hands on the edge of the sink, staring down into the popping bubbles. He turned on the faucet. "His grandmother, I'd guess." He turned it off and picked up a glass, washed it, then rinsed it. "She's extremely anti-shifter. Anti-just about everything except her religion, which is telling her shifters are demons and they should be destroyed or have the devil cast out of them."

"And she had Troy?" Delilah's voice rose sharply just as he turned the water off.

They both winced and looked at the boy, who was seemingly oblivious.

Andrew leaned in, smelling Delilah's floral scent, maybe shampoo. It was very, very enticing. He cleared his throat. "My ex had cut ties with her. She'd needed help when she was pregnant and moved back in, but it was all prayers and accusations for her sin of getting pregnant out of wedlock. At that point, my ex was angry with me for moving away and didn't want to tell me anything. And then she had a baby who shifted to wolf right after he came out and her mother didn't even want to let them back into her house. That's when my ex contacted me and I flew down to take care of them. I got them an apartment and got them set up with social services and child support."

"But when your ex died, he had nowhere else to go." Delilah nodded toward the boy.

He turned the water on again and started washing the pan he'd heated the stew in. "I guess the police called her and she took him in for the two days it took to contact me and for me to get there. He was thoroughly miserable when I got him. She yelled at me about how she wouldn't accept my evil influence and she was sure if he stayed in human form and went to church with her, he'd be healed. Her pastor came when I was packing up the things in their apartment and it was ugly. I got out as fast as I could and had a moving company pack and ship stuff to sort through later. Got Goodwill to come pick up the furniture, and so on."

Delilah let out a shaky breath. "Yeah, we've always had the evil devil nonsense, too. My grandmother had a psychic shop since forever and we had picketers and people coming in, spraying holy water over stuff. We had to call the cops more than once. And cops aren't always super helpful." She shrugged.

He had a twinge of guilt, since he was a cop of sorts and had a healthy dose of skepticism about psychics, especially before he'd learned some of them were real. "The grandmother and preacher kept praying and screaming in the hall about how I was going to hell and she was going to challenge me for custody. It was an upsetting time."

"I can imagine," she said and laid one hand on his arm and squeezed.

"I meant for Troy. It was upsetting for my kid." He was desperate to not show vulnerability, to be big and strong for this woman who smelled like flowers. And he knew what his posturing meant, but she was a witness in a case he was working on and was considering withholding evidence and besides, she was more than ten years younger than him.

She squeezed his arm again. "You're allowed to be upset, you know," she said and picked up the pan he'd just rinsed.

He started on the hamburger pan. "He didn't shift to wolf until we'd been back here a few days and I shifted in front of him. He was relieved and shifted right away. Emotions are…not really simpler in wolf form, but more elemental. My brain is more focused on survival and instinct when I shift and it dulls the emotional side."

"That's funny, because when I do a reading, it's all about the emotion. And this grandmother sounds abusive. She might not have hit him, but she was definitely abusing him. I'm glad you got to him as fast as you could."

He felt a rush of warmth. "I wish I'd been there even faster, but I was on a case and it wasn't like my ex had my number on her fridge or even in her phone in case of emergency." He finished the pan and turned off the water, lowering his voice again. "The thing is, I was in Florida near them on a case. I'd even asked if I could see Troy, but she said no because it would disrupt their routine. She always said no and I didn't push hard enough. She died the day before I came back here."

Delilah made a slight wounded noise. "So maybe if you'd disrupted her routine, she would still be alive."

He took a deep breath. "Maybe. But she could at least have made him more comfortable with me. It had been a couple years since she'd allowed a visit."

He looked over his shoulder and Troy was rocking harder, which he always did at the big fight scenes. At least he hoped it wasn't because of their conversation. "Another thirty minutes or so and the movie will be over, then it's bedtime. Let me get you on my laptop and see if you can access your calendar from there."

She paused, looking at him. "You know I'm not going to let you search anything, right? Not without a lawyer's consent."

"It would be borderline illegal to search the office without a warrant or consent from your mother. We are working on a warrant, but I'm not sure they have enough grounds for one. They'll pressure you tomorrow to either let them in or search yourself, which will have to be up to you, based on what you believe to be your mother's wishes. From here on out, though, you need to not tell me anything about the case and I need to not tell you anything, either."

She frowned.

"I will keep you safe as best I can." He felt this like a deep vow and wondered if she knew it.

Her widened eyes told him she felt his sincerity.

"You can stay here for as long as you need."

"If I don't get arrested."

He smiled. "They don't want to arrest you. They might pressure you to turn over anything you find, but my initial, unofficial glance through your mom's filing cabinets doesn't make me think there's anything there. Until we find a safe or lock box or whatever the key goes to, I doubt you will find anything they want at all."

She nodded, but she was still looking at his mouth. "You have a nice smile," she said, then turned and walked out to the living room, settling on the couch near Troy, but not touching him. She was pointedly not looking back into the kitchen and had her eyes glued to the screen.

He finished wiping down the counters, the little glow in his chest warming him as he went to get his laptop.

Chapter Twelve

AFTER HER FUN, FUN morning of being questioned, Delilah and the lawyer's paralegal, Joy, a fortyish year old woman in an expensive pantsuit, spent several hours after lunch searching her mom's office. The FBI agents had been reluctant to tell them what they were searching for, but gave them a timeframe of the past two years. Del wished she'd kept the planner so she'd know what she was looking for.

Joy was not a joy to work with. Del wasn't sure if she was harsh because she was working so hard to rise up the law firm ladder or she had better things to do than hang out with lowly Delilah, the psychic receptionist student. Del was getting irritation vibes off her as Joy sifted through emails on her mom's ancient desktop computer, printing off a few of them and not explaining why.

There were outright anger vibes when Joy set a stack of file folders on her mom's desk and sat in the desk chair.

Del cleared her throat. "Would you like a cup of coffee? I'm dragging and was going to make some half-caff."

Joy glared at her and turned back to the files, impatiently tucking a stray strand of her sleek, black hair behind her ear.

Del finally snapped. "You know, you don't have to be hostile. We're paying you and your firm well to do this half-assed search. Mom's going to freak out at the invasion of her privacy and the cost. That is, if I ever get her back, if she's not locked up somewhere and if they don't fucking kill her. Which they might already have done, for all you know." She took a deep breath and stood up straighter. "Unless you're hiding her somewhere, I'm not your enemy. The FBI, no matter how heavy-handed, is not the enemy as long as they're trying to find my mother. You are a seriously angry person and I'm going to have to completely sage this office when you're gone."

She stomped out and started some coffee, not glancing at Joy as she went through the inner office to get water from the bathroom sink. She wondered, not for the first time, if OSHA would approve of water from the bathroom, but they didn't have another sink and her mom didn't think it useful to have a water cooler.

She sat down in front of her own stack of files and began to read through them. She'd taken two accounting classes at the community college and had done fine, but not brilliantly, much to her mother's disapproval. It wasn't her fault she was just barely competent on a basic level and numbers didn't speak to her the way cards did. So she read the contracts and other physical documents her mom had seen fit to keep and tried not to think about her mom being locked up or dead. She really hoped her mom was safe, wherever she was. Her hands itched for her cards, but even in the car on the way over, she'd still had the feeling that her mom was OK, just blocked.

She drank her cup of coffee with lots of creamer as she read through a few more documents.

Joy appeared in the doorway, unsmiling. "I'm not finding anything," she announced as she strode to the coffeemaker. "Do you mind if I have some coffee?"

Del looked at the woman's back and narrowed her eyes to see a flare of something conciliatory in her aura. "Go ahead. I mean, it's been half an hour, so it's overcooked, but there's creamer in the mini-fridge if you want."

"Thanks," Joy said stiffly.

Once she'd poured the coffee and looked at, but not used, Del's hazelnut creamer and taken a sip, she turned around.

After she'd stood there for half a minute, ten feet away from Del's desk, Del looked up. "Is there something wrong?"

"I'm sorry about your mother," she said. "And about my attitude. I was supposed to be researching for a trial, but was pulled off of it for this assignment. The young man who is now researching looks good on paper, but is inexperienced and not completely competent, but his star's on the rise."

Del leaned back in her office chair, which squeaked. She stared at Joy for a few seconds as the woman searched the depths of her coffee for enlightenment. "I'm sorry. I didn't know about your workplace stress. I'd be willing to bet it's not the first time you've had a star on the rise get your plum jobs?"

Joy's head came up sharply. "It's the glass ceiling thing, I guess. Or else I'm not as competent as I think. But if fucking Tyler the Whiz Kid fucks this case up, he'll still get a pat on the back and a better office."

"The good news is that this is going to take one day and you'll be back in the office tomorrow."

Joy laughed humorlessly. "To be honest, I'll be spending the weekend analyzing anything we find. I've seen it before, though. Lived through it. Every time you or your mom needs something, I'll be the one sent. Nothing against you, but you're a tiny account. They'll send me on every errand for all the tiny accounts and pretty soon, Tyler the Whiz Kid will be asking me to get him Starbucks while I'm out. I've been there for fifteen years."

Del nodded. "Come sit down and we'll take a break, OK?"

Joy hmphed. "Not a good use of billable hours, not with the FBI sitting outside." But she came and sat in the plastic visitor's chair beside the desk anyway, setting her coffee down with a look of distaste.

"That's just Agent Miller. He's also my friend." He'd also slipped her a burner phone on the ride over, but she hadn't had enough time to set it up.

Joy hmphed again. "Keep telling yourself that."

Del shrugged. "He's doing his best for justice and since my mom's primary driving force is also justice, I feel like it will be fine. I can feel lots of things. Now how about a quick reading?"

Joy stared at her, whole face scrunched up.

"Billable hours, right? My mom can afford it and we need to think of something else for a minute."

"I usually go for a walk, but it's cold." Joy stared at the cards, undecided.

"All right then, a quick one. Set a timer for ten minutes, because surely, you're allowed to take a break."

She hadn't meant it literally, but Joy pulled out a brand new iPhone and told Siri to set a timer.

She shuffled once and handed the cards to Joy. "Shuffle as many times as feels right and then cut the deck into three piles. We'll just do past, present, future, so think about where you've been and where you are now and where you want to go."

Joy shuffled the big deck awkwardly, then cut the cards.

"OK, turn up the top from each pile, left to right for you. Past, present, future."

The past card was one she hated the most: reversed King of Swords, which generally meant an abusive relationship. The present was Ten of Wands, which she knew was great effort without reward. The future, though, made her smile.

She leaned back, visions hitting her. She saw an angry man looming over Joy, an angry woman, a teenage boy, a grown man. "You've had it hard," she said. "Lots of narcissists, lots of verbal abuse. I don't see physical abuse?"

Joy looked surprised, gaze going from Del's face to the cards and back again, then shook her head. "My parents are toxic. I had a few relationships where I kept sleeping with them to placate them without enjoying it. A little physical abuse, but mainly mental, which is as hard or harder, in my opinion. But I've been in therapy for years."

Del nodded. "I see stress and scars in you, but not the great, gaping wound I've seen in others. And the present card means ambition thwarted. Are you sure you've escaped the cycle? Your bosses are demeaning you, either on purpose or by sidelining you and promoting Tyler the Whiz Kid over you. And you're letting them do it, keeping the anger inside instead of asking for new projects and a raise."

Joy's whole face fell. "Dammit, you're right. I...need more therapy, I guess. I thought having two women lawyers join the firm would mean women underlings would be treated better, but they're on the same page as the men. I...no, I won't say more, sorry. I still need this job."

"Well, here's the thing: I'm looking at the future card." Del set one finger on the card and its magic flowed into her. She closed her eyes as the vision rose up. "New opportunities, but you're going to have to make a lot of changes. It might be a new job, or at the least a new position in the company. It might take travel or further education, and I can see a plethora of possible paths, but it's within your reach. How much does law school cost?"

"What?" Joy almost shouted.

Del's eyes popped open. "How much does law school cost and is it worth it to you to pay for it?"

Joy looked minorly freaked out. "Almost a hundred K over three years, not including living expenses. But…"

"How did I know? I don't know. It seems like thwarted ambition for an ambitious paralegal might lead to law school. But is it worth it to you? Can you get a better paralegal job where you'll be appreciated and happy?"

Joy hmphed again. "Not for the kind of pay I'm getting now. I've had offers of half my pay, which would definitely be moving down, not up."

Del nodded. "I'm not very good at taking finances into account, sorry. My mother despairs of me. All I see is you're stuck and unhappy where you are and you don't think they'll ever treat you the way you deserve to be treated. There's a dose of impostor syndrome in there, but I get the feeling you are more than good at your job. Is there something outside law that you want to do? Or something tangential other than paralegal work?"

The seeing faded and Del blinked to come back to reality. Joy was frowning hard, the wrinkles between her eyebrows deep. Del patted her hand and Joy froze in place as a spark of magic flowed between them, telling her of Joy's loneliness and fear and inner strength. She wondered if Joy could read her, too, and if anyone had told her she had good intuition.

"I can't see where you're going to go or what branch of the road you'll take, but I can see the road branching soon. The good thing is whichever branch you choose, you can always branch off again if it doesn't work out. There're lights at the end of a lot of tunnels, wherever you choose to go."

The timer went off and Joy startled. She blinked several times rapidly, then got up, taking her phone, but leaving her substandard coffee behind, and marched into Del's mom's office. Del heard her mom's chair squeak and the slide of file folders.

Del took a deep breath and stacked up her cards again, mixing and shuffling several times, while asking herself what her mom wanted her to find and where it was. She turned over the top card and though it was Justice again, she felt a vision gathering. Another and it was Eight of Swords again, but she pushed aside the literal picture of her mother possibly kidnapped and instead tried to open her mind. Still nothing, but she knew it was here somewhere.

She scooped up the rest of the cards and shuffled again, forcing herself to think of what her mother had hidden and did a layout for lost items, which turned out to be a surprisingly eclectic set of cards. She studied them for a moment, then a vision washed over her. She let it flow through her, her observations and intuition like flashing lights on the edges.

She opened her eyes, turned her head to the left, and smiled to herself.

Chapter Thirteen

Delilah came down the stairs almost at a run, the dour paralegal in her high-heeled boots right behind, less dour than before. Delilah came around Andrew's car as he got out, her face flushed and triumphant. And beautiful.

"We found it!" she announced over his car door.

The paralegal stopped a few feet away and nodded. "I think it's what you're looking for, Special Agent Miller. I'm going to review it and consult with my boss and determine if we should release it to you."

Andrew nodded at her. "Good work."

The paralegal smiled, which seemed like a slightly foreign look on her stern face. "Oh it wasn't me. Delilah figured out where the…items were."

Delilah beamed at her and he was aware he'd missed something in the three hours they'd been inside and time had been creeping by for him on his pointless stakeout. They'd not been even slightly friendly on the way in, but now they were partners.

He looked at the happily blushing young woman and forgot the young part and just appreciated the woman as she bounced on her toes.

"I'm heading back to office, OK?" Joy said.

They didn't quite hug, but there was mutual arm-patting and promises of staying in touch.

Delilah went back up, declaring she needed to tidy up and inviting him to come upstairs to get out of the bitter cold. "Just don't look around, OK? I mean this as a friend and not as a witness in embezzlement, and you as a friend and not an FBI agent."

It was warm enough in his car, which he'd been turning on periodically, but he locked it and came up the stairs, not watching her round ass. Much.

The chairs in the waiting room were dragged out, the end table with ancient magazines had casters and was rolled to the middle of the room, and the rug was folded over, exposing the floorboards. "There was a safe under there, inside the wall. Mom apparently kept her most secret things in there and never told me. But I did a reading, which just sparked my intuition. I mean, my mom refused to get a cleaning service in, but was willing to do half the cleaning, right? It wasn't just me, she's always been like that. Her last assistant said Mom always did the vacuuming and I think it was mainly to hide the drag marks from the chairs. She said it helped her think to vacuum and I was happy to only have to clean the bathroom and do some light dusting, you know?"

All this time, she was carrying file folders into her mother's office and rehanging them in the bottom drawer of the filing cabinet.

"Honestly, we didn't find anything useful in the computers or the files, but the papers and external hard drive we just found..." She grinned at him. "Not going to tell you anything without a subpoena. Anyway, Joy is pretty awesome once you get to know her and now we're both jazzed about this being a big break. They're under-utilizing her at the law office and she knows it, but this case is going to lead to big things for her."

He wanted to help carry, but knew he would be in trouble if he touched anything, since he was there in an official capacity. Or semi-official capacity, he guessed. He probably shouldn't be in here at all and she definitely shouldn't have told him about the safe, even though it was empty now.

Of course, he shouldn't have a witness staying in his home, taking care of his son. He shouldn't have the daughter of a witness-slash-possible suspect staying in his home.

And thinking of his son, he checked his watch. Beth was bringing the boy to them at the office, so he checked his phone to see the text from her had just popped up.

"Beth is about five minutes out with the boy," he said when Delilah came back into the waiting room.

"The boy," she said, raising one eyebrow. "Have I mentioned before how you almost never use his name?"

He nodded. She was right. He was a terrible father. "I'm trying to do better. I don't know why I do it. Beth is almost here with Troy."

She tipped her head, considering him carefully, the said, almost as if she had read his mind, "You're still learning to be a father and trying your very best means you're already a good one, you know?"

He didn't know. He would die for his son, but taking care of him was hard.

"And then it's the weekend." Delilah smiled. "It's been a hell of a week, huh? I really hope there's information on the drive that can help find my mom."

"If she had so much info, she should have been working with the police or the FBI or someone before this," he said bitterly.

Delilah shook her head. "My mom never turns over a report unless it's complete and all her intuitive conclusions have full corroboration with facts."

Andrew sighed. "Yeah, this is a lot bigger than her report. But she probably has some important pieces of the puzzle. We're talking years of work." He could tell her that because she'd been informed of it during her questioning.

She nodded. "Still, she left it all for me to find. I mean, there was a post-it on the folder telling me I'd done a good job and not to worry about her, so now I think she's in hiding. I don't know how to tell her to come out and talk to the FBI, though. She...she doesn't trust the police." Delilah winced.

He nodded and looked at her for a long time while she straightened up her desk, watching her all the way into her mother's office and hearing another cabinet drawer open.

"OK, so if you could help me put the waiting area back together?" she said as she came back out.

She led the way to the corner and crouched down. "See? It's in the wall, but under the floor. I wonder if it was there when she bought this office."

He went to one knee beside her, examining the hole in the floor. "I'm going to guess it wasn't, or whoever showed it to her would know where it was."

"Ooh, yeah, good point," she said, smiling at him. "She would not have liked that. She must have cut the holes herself. My mom is nothing if not dedicated. So anyway, now we know where it is and you can show your FBI friends when they get the warrant. Do you want the key now?"

He shook his head. "You'd better keep it. I'm guessing she will find somewhere else to hide it when she gets back."

She nodded. "On the other hand, she might worry someone had made a copy of the key if I let it out of sight. You're right, I'd better hang on to it."

"Well, once someone finds the safe, it's not very big and they could lift it out and take it somewhere else to drill out the lock."

"Good point. I mean, I don't know anything about cutting open a safe, but yeah, it isn't like Fort Knox in there."

He refrained from telling her Fort Knox wasn't all that exciting, but it was true it was the most secure place on the planet. He wondered if they'd considered renting out space to the truly paranoid. Though the truly paranoid wouldn't want the government in charge of their stuff.

He turned his head and she was still looking at him, crouched down with one hand on an ugly chair to balance herself.

The moment of eye contact stretched out as a low, gruff, semi-feral voice in his head told him to lean in six inches and she would meet him halfway for a kiss. Her cheeks turned pinker and she bit her lower lip, but she didn't move or look away. He could smell she was attracted and, in return, she could probably feel the waves of attraction coming from him.

In the end, she was the one who looked away, breaking the little spell and recalling him to himself. She slid a floorboard back into place, covered it with a big square of linoleum, and flipped the carpet back over it. He rolled the end table back into place and they replaced the chairs where they had been.

Once it was all back together, it was clear the furniture had been moved.

"I should vacuum," Delilah announced just as Andrew's phone vibrated.

"Beth and Troy are downstairs."

"OK, I'll be out in about five minutes. The whole place needs swept with all the dust we pulled out of everywhere, but I'll be quick."

"Troy hates vacuums, so we'll stay outside until you're done."

"Really? I mean it is loud and annoying. This one's not too bad, which isn't saying a lot. I tried to get Mom to get one of those little robot vacs and activate it at night so we didn't have to listen to it, but I guess I know now why she never did. I mean, besides that most of them are WiFi controlled and she hates WiFi."

Andrew got to the doorway and paused, looking back over his shoulder to see Delilah sauntering into the back office again.

He closed the door carefully behind himself and jogged down the stairs.

Beth sprang out of her little SUV, smiling at him as she came around to the passenger side. "The teacher said he had a great day at school today. And by the way, I read today that the safest place in the car is the center of the backseat, but I didn't want to move his car seat there and cause a problem." She opened the door to reveal his son in human form, watching him.

"You know, it probably is the safest. I've had him by the door for his and my convenience, really. Once he's ready to stay in the seat, stay in one form or the other for the whole ride, and learn to be in charge of his own buckles, we'll talk about moving him to the center, unless we need to make space for someone else to ride in the back with him."

Beth nodded. "Yeah, hmm. Might be best to stay where he is for the sake of routine?"

"I don't know," Andrew said. His son was listening avidly. "Troy, I think we can have two slightly different placements if those have consistent rules otherwise?"

Troy nodded sharply once.

"How about we give it a try in my car on the way home?" Andrew said as he bent down to unfasten Troy. His son held still as he lifted him, the bony, warm presence against his chest a balm to his soul.

Yeah. He loved his son. He wondered if his own father had ever had this feeling of devotion and fear and if he'd lost the feeling after he moved out. He'd certainly never shown affection that Andrew could remember. Andrew held Troy closer, adjusting him against his body as the boy shoved his face against Andrew's chest, hot breath on his shirt. He looked down. "Do you want to try moving your seat today?"

Troy shook his head.

"You'd like to think about it a little more?"

A quick nod, more felt than seen.

And Andrew realized he'd had a conversation with Troy, which was a bit of a miracle.

"I'm not going to put you in our car yet, because we're waiting for Delilah to finish upstairs. She's vacuuming, which our wolf ears hate."

The boy paused then tilted his head to the side to glance up at Andrew's face.

Andrew nodded. "We have really sensitive shifter ears, don't we? It means we can hear very quiet things, we can even whisper to each other so no one else can hear us, but when it gets loud, it sometimes hurts."

The boy turned his head back down. Just this position felt like such a sign of trust and love. He'd been doing it since the second day after they arrived in Cleveland and Andrew had figured Troy was hiding his face. But that his son hid his face against Andrew felt important.

Delilah came out the office door and shut it firmly behind herself, twisting the key in the deadbolt. She waved to them and shook the solid, unshakable bars over the window like she had the last time they left and he wondered if it was her mom's routine, too. Her mom probably had more steps to locking up, but it was quite possible some of them were secrets even from Delilah. He just bet there was a hidden camera somewhere or at least a secondary alarm system.

Chapter Fourteen

"Do you think we found everything?" Delilah asked him over dinner.

Dinner was rice and the chicken he'd remembered to remove from the freezer in the morning to defrost in the fridge. He'd marinated the chicken before freezing, because he'd started reading food prep blogs twenty years ago and was actually quite good at feeding himself. And others, if the enthusiastic appreciation from Delilah was any indication. He was good at recognizing lies and she seemed genuine.

"Everything of what?" he asked, realizing he was still thinking about chicken.

"Everything my mom wanted me to find. I think I need to go home and do another reading."

He was not going to look even slightly disbelieving, because he knew instincts and Delilah had a lot of instincts.

She noticed his disbelief anyway and her excitement dimmed.

He shook his head. "I'd be willing to bet there are a lot of things she still has hidden, both in your house and the office and in a safe deposit box or two, plus, I don't know, a gym locker."

She rolled her lips into her mouth, deep in thought as she scooped another bite of rice and chicken onto her fork. She opened her mouth and her lips looked redder and slightly damp and extremely kissable. He glanced over at Troy, who was finishing off his burger and shoestring oven fries, not particularly paying attention.

She said, "Mom didn't go to the gym, just used the treadmill at home to walk for exactly half an hour every day at three miles per hour. Eloisa made her buy it when she realized Mom wasn't getting any exercise."

"She could still have a *locker* in a gym."

Delilah took the bite from her fork and tilted her head in thought as she chewed. "I think she'd hide things somewhere most people would never expect or else someplace Fort Knoxish. But like the stuff today, she would be sure someone she trusted could find it, just in case. I mean, there might be something Grandmother can find and something else Aunt Moira can find. Maybe even some clues sent to Eloisa. I don't think she trusts anyone outside the family."

She stabbed into her salad and tilted her head again. "Leaving something in a locker at the gym would mean an assigned locker and definitely a membership. Otherwise, they would cut the lock off after a while, right?"

He nodded. "Most gyms would, yes. Even with a membership, you usually bring your own lock or rent a lock, just to leave your things while you work out. If they found your papers, they would contact you. If it was a thumb drive, they might plug it in to see whose it was."

She nodded. "Or they'd throw it all away if they couldn't figure it out. But in all these months, she's never gone to a gym as far as I know. Though she occasionally meets with clients, so for all I know, she's actually driving around the Cleveland area, dropping off evidence in an entire network of caches."

"Are there public places with security she goes to regularly to leave important documents? A bank? People she trusts at Starbucks, even?"

She chuckled. "To her, Starbucks is overpriced desserts, not real coffee, so not Starbucks."

He smiled. He could hardly wait to meet her mother, because he wholeheartedly agreed. "They do a decent espresso and the brewed coffee's only slightly expensive."

She rolled her eyes. "True enough. I mean, I get her an Americano all the time because watered-down espresso is fine, just don't go putting any pumps of anything in there or whipped cream on top." Her eyes went a little glassy as she gazed into the middle distance. "A huge mocha cookie crumble frapp in the summer is absolutely the best." She focused on him again and shrugged, apparently embarrassed. "I know it's a shake with coffee in it, but it's a damn, uh darn good shake."

"Troy has heard a lot of grown-up words before, don't worry. He understands they're for grown-ups, right, son?"

Troy was seemingly focused on his banana slices, picking them up daintily between two fingers and nibbling at them, a sure sign he wasn't hungry, but he really loved banana and wasn't going to stop eating it no matter what.

"Do you want to look at cards again this evening Troy? Or watch a movie? Or...What else do you guys do in the evenings?"

"We sometimes read books. Troy has some favorites and I introduce new ones to him from time to time."

She smiled and speared the last bit of lettuce in her salad plate. "I saw the bookshelf in his room."

"Would you two like to pick out a few books while I do the dishes?" he asked.

She frowned slightly. "You cooked, I should do the dishes."

"But you're a guest," he said, because agreeing felt too much like she lived there. It was oddly tempting, but not reality.

She smiled at him, unbothered, so maybe she wasn't interested in moving in. He'd never lived with anyone after leaving his mom's home in

Washington State, though he'd had a few women friends who'd wanted their relationship to be permanent. He'd eventually driven them all off because of his long, irregular work hours where he could be sent across the country on short notice. Or his failure to open up to them about his feelings. Or he'd broken up with them.

It was domestic enough that she was going to read books to his son as a form of evening entertainment.

She helped stack the dishes and carry them to the kitchen, where she asked, "What are we doing tomorrow? It'll be Saturday."

He nodded. "I have to go to the office for a while. Probably about five hours. You're waiting to hear from your lawyers, so you should keep the burner phone handy."

She nodded. "And luckily I'm here to watch Troy. Do they let you bring him to the office as long as he's not disruptive?"

He shook his head. "Absolutely not. There's not a 'Bring Your Kid to Work Day', either, at least not where the kids see anything other than the public areas. I guess the tour goes to the holding cells if there isn't anyone in them. Too many secrets and security around the offices and work areas."

She nodded again. "Well, lucky I'm here."

He knew something was wrong, but couldn't quite place it.

"And lucky Troy and I are friends, huh, Troy?"

His son smiled down into his bowl which was still half-full of bananas.

And he finally thought he might know what the problem was. "I'm sorry. I meant to ask you earlier if you'd be able to stay here with Troy. I call Beth and Alex most often. Even more often, I don't go in at odd hours. I'm still adapting to not being flexible."

She shrugged. "Yes, I would be happy to spend time with Troy tomorrow while you work."

Then she smiled and asked Troy if he was done, wiped his hands, and told him he could have more banana later if he got hungry. Which was a good thing because Troy's paperwork said he would sometimes eat too much and throw up and Andrew was quite glad he hadn't seen it happen. Then he worried he was underfeeding his child instead.

Delilah didn't know if she was doing the right thing in reading ten books, but she picked up the whole stack from the top of the low bookshelf and Troy had radiated pleasure at them all, following her finger as she read what were surely extremely familiar words. By the last two books, he was fighting to stay awake. After the tenth book, she lifted the sheet and blanket and he lay down. She stayed next to him on the bed until he was completely asleep, only then remembering Andrew had said Troy usually slept as a wolf.

Andrew had also said he usually slept next to the boy, also as a wolf. Andrew seemed to doubt his skills as a parent and worry about not knowing how to care for him, but he was bending over backward for the boy, who needed exactly that. They'd find their equilibrium eventually, she was sure. And maybe Troy needed a 100% serious and protective dad, especially right after losing his mom.

As she came out into the hall and closed Troy's door softly behind her, Andrew appeared in the archway leading to the living and dining room and gestured with his head for her to join him. She was mildly offended by the summons, especially after the assumption of babysitting earlier, but she went anyway. He watched her with those intent, piercing blue eyes and she felt both self-conscious and sexy.

His hand on her back as he directed her to the couch was fire to her nerves.

They sat close to each other, but not touching, and she looked around the room, trying to un-fluster herself.

"Thank you for reading to him," Andrew said. "You were in there a long time."

She grinned, glancing at his serious expression. "I wasn't sure if it was too much."

"I often end up reading him one book ten times. The Gruffalo is probably his favorite." He fidgeted slightly. "And I know you can tell he was happy. I worry I'm doing too much for him. Spoiling him."

She shook her head. "I'm firmly of the school of thought that unless he's never reprimanded for doing naughty things, you can't spoil him."

He nodded.

"I mean, I have noticed you're a big fan of rules, but he obeys them for the most part. He's only five and won't always remember and will test your boundaries and things."

Andrew fidgeted again. "He's never, um, never done anything naughty. Or not without reason. There have been times when he can't or won't control his shift, but he's usually upset about something and, like you say, he's only five. The last babysitter said he snapped at her, but she was…She was not friendly about us being shifters. She might have said or done something to anger him or frighten him."

"He was proud of himself yesterday because he hadn't snapped at another child, so it seems he internalized the rule."

Andrew smiled a surprisingly naughty smile. "He's going to need to know when it's the right time to bite people."

Del had one of those lightbulb moments. "I bet it's hard to teach a little kid with big teeth to not use them. My family had to teach me to not zap the other kids on the playground when they were mean. Eloisa and I call it the ballbuster curse now, but back then it was just a zap."

Andrew smiled again, more fond. She could picture him as a solemn five year old wolf cub, being a good boy and trying really hard to not bite someone who was bothering him. Or bothering a friend. "It's hard to teach them to not shift in public. Until recently, all shifter children were homeschooled until they could control their shift. Even now, many shifters don't trust the schools or don't want to be outed."

They sat in silence for a couple minutes, not awkward, but both thinking their own thoughts.

"I should go check on him," Andrew said. "He never sleeps well until I lie down with him."

She nodded. "Did he sleep in his mom's bed?"

He shook his head. "I have no idea. Possibly. The coyote neighbor told me, she would hold him while he slept, but it's not in any of the documents I have."

She could picture a kindly neighbor rocking Troy and realized after a moment that she had her hand on Andrew's wrist and the sentiment, possibly even the image, was coming from him.

Before she could pull her hand away, he turned his over and held hers. "Delilah..."

And before he could thank her for being kind to him or to his son, she leaned in and kissed his cheek.

And before she could back away, he turned his head and tilted it down and kissed her.

They both froze, his eyes narrow and assessing as he changed his angle slightly and pressed his lips to hers again. She could taste his toothpaste, then he turned toward her and she felt his hand travel up her arm and shoulder and to the back of her neck, holding her in place as her eyes closed and his mouth came down on hers again.

Chapter Fifteen

ANDREW GOT UP FROM his new desk in the research bullpen and stretched. He'd slept poorly the night before because Troy had been fidgety. They both needed to go out to Beth and Alex's house, which abutted a little state park, and go running in the trees. Unfortunately, current circumstances weren't conducive to making sure a cub got enough exercise. Or a middle-aged wolf. Alex's constant refrain that he was raising a wolf pup in a city apartment came back to him and he thought again of moving somewhere with a backyard or even someplace rural, though commuting would be a pain in the ass. He'd have to start all over again finding schools for Troy, but he suddenly had the urge to run through woods and mountains, teaching his son to hide and stalk and hunt.

He'd started taking lunch at his desk when his work life had been disrupted by Troy, while before he'd taken an hour or so almost every day to use the basement gym and shower before getting back to work. He used to go for hikes and runs that he couldn't do anymore. He'd thought about getting a jogging stroller and also thought about carrying his son. Then he'd wondered if his ex had enough friends and family around other than her mother so she could get exercise and have time to do the things she liked and he'd felt guilty. He'd been frustrated when she wouldn't let him see Troy, but she had full custody and Troy had special needs. He wondered if she'd really gotten past her dislike of shifters to love Troy the way he should be loved.

No, that was unfair. Troy had all the hallmarks, according to doctors and psychiatrists, of being securely attached to her. To Jasmine. He never thought her name, either, though it was through disinterest, which made him a rat bastard, didn't it?

Which made him wonder if he was a rat bastard for kissing Delilah the night before. She had responded eagerly, but after a minute, had pulled away, flustered, and wished him goodnight before disappearing down the hall.

The hum of other agents and civilian employees was a little louder now than it had been at seven when he'd arrived. A couple guys from the Organized Crime team he'd been seconded to stopped by his desk to say hello and to ask about Delilah's lawyers. Since there was no word from the lawyers – Andrew had asked Delilah mid-morning – they'd wandered off to do actual work instead of interrupting his. He had a chart of all the erased notes in the diary and the dates they were written on and he and the others were making headway on who they thought the initials were. He hoped the lawyers would release Serena Woods' full calendar with all the people and companies she'd worked for, because the planner, while detailed, often used initials or code words for the company names, too.

"Hey, we have a lead on this Shalonda from RFB," said Buho, an owl shifter and one of the few people he would call a friend. Though they never hung out unless working together, so maybe a friendly acquaintance. But then, Andrew didn't hang out with anyone, usually. He had the feeling Buho had also been seconded to this case because of Andrew and because the Serena Woods piece of the puzzle seemed to be bringing it to a head and they needed personnel ASAP. "She really is in Argentina, according to the airline. According to her work, she's visiting extended family and attending a wedding. Are we going to ask local authorities to go in and talk to her? Or keep an eye on her?"

"Do we have someone down there we're comfortable with sending in?" Andrew asked, sitting down again and clicking through a couple of pages to the info on Shalonda. "Can we have her surveilled just in case, but not spoken to unless we get some sort of break from the lawyers or the warrant comes through?"

Buho bobbed his head, sort of nodding, sort of not.

"I'll ask Quentin." Andrew sighed, thinking of the animosity radiating from Quentin, a lead investigator in the Organized Crime division and head of this Slovak mob project, toward him and the whole Shifter Task Force. Andrew leaned back in his chair and crossed his hands over his belly. "I'm more worried about Serena Woods. Her daughter seems to think Serena's in hiding right now, but we need to talk to her and we need to keep her safe."

"Let me check if anyone was traveling with Shalonda. The timing is right for them to both be in Argentina. I'll run her passport again."

"Good thinking." Andrew paused for several seconds, thinking about where else Serena Woods might be hiding. "I told the daughter we can't discuss it anymore, so someone should press her on where she thinks her mom could be. I'd bet though, that her guesses might be completely off. Serena has layers on layers of hiding places and security and Delilah is much too straightforward."

Buho's eyebrows went up. "Don't forget she is the same one the Ren Faire people called 'Daffy Delilah.'"

"Did they? That's rude. Though…" he scratched his head. "I mean, instead of saying she had an idea, she says the cards told her. I believe in magic, but I would bet she mostly has really good intuition and is good at reading people."

Buho shrugged. "I went over the Ren Faire file and she triangulated the place the Greys and Catellis were being held with no info except that she wanted to find her cousin."

Andrew nodded slowly. They'd been on the Ren Faire case together, too, another reason Buho was on this case. "Sadly, she said she can't see her mom now. Either her mom's blocking her or someone else is blocking her mom. But she admits she can't usually see the future for her family. Not sure how blocking someone would work, though I guess if some can see auras, others can hide them."

"Tell her to keep trying. Maybe something will shift. We'll have her in again on Monday unless something shakes loose between now and then."

"Hello Delilah," said the clipped, growly voice she was coming to love.

Love? Uh, it was sexy. Not that Andrew Miller was interested in her and right now, it would be really inappropriate for them to start something. Right?

But they had kissed and it was glorious, if all too short.

"Hello Andrew," she replied, just as clipped, forcing the heat out of her mind as she remembered how intensely he'd stared at her when she wandered into the dining room in the morning.

He paused, maybe taken aback by her efficient tone. He cleared his throat. "I have a problem. My car won't start. It's in the secure garage and I can't get it towed right now."

"Do you know why it won't start?" she asked.

He sighed. "No, I'm not, uh, mechanically inclined. One coworker says it sounds like the starter, another like an electrical problem." A short pause.

"I thought a starter problem was an electrical problem. Could you come and get me, please?"

Was this a ploy to get her into the FBI office again? She shook her head. He had to know she'd go back willingly. "I don't have a car seat for Troy in my car."

"There's an extra in the closet in his room. I got it for the babysitters. It's the same as the other ones. Do you know how to install it?"

"If there are instructions with it, I can muddle through. I've seen Eloisa and Mike install Daniel's seat, so I understand the concept. Tighten it down, lock the belt, attach the tethers. Kneel on it to squash it down while you tighten it some more."

Andrew chuckled. "Pretty much. If you want to send pictures for me to check, you can."

She smiled. "I might need to, yes."

A half hour later, she arrived in front of the FBI building and watched Andrew Miller exiting. He was standing as straight as always, wearing the same sort of navy blue suit as always, armed as always, but something felt different about him. "There's your dad, Troy," she said as she narrowed her eyes to focus on his aura. No, nothing really different, but her reaction was certainly different.

She stopped in the visitor lot and put the car in park to unlock the doors. He climbed in, nodded to her, then turned to greet Troy. "I see you've chosen to sit in the center."

"He did! I'm just glad the seat fit on the bump back there and there's a tether point in the middle. I'd like to say I bought the car with kids in mind, but my mom helped me buy the best used car I could afford and which would probably run the longest." She smiled as Miller turned back to the front and fastened his seatbelt. "You might want to check it's installed right when we get back."

She pulled back out onto the road, then had a sudden idea. "Oh! Maybe I should have made you drive. I don't know this area."

"You found it just fine, so we'll retrace the path."

"Ah, yes, well, I used the GPS and the maps on my burner phone. It's a good thing you got me a smartphone, that's all I can say."

He was silent for a moment and she darted a glance at him. He was thinking about if it had been a smart thing or not. "I doubt anyone has the info on your burner phone yet, so it's fine. I hope you turned it off again."

"Ah, no, I didn't think of it." She pointed at where it was in the cup holder, screen still on saying they'd arrived at their destination. "Go ahead."

He picked it up and squinted at it, dragging down from the top and up from the bottom and scowling so entertainingly that she didn't notice the light had turned green until the car behind honked.

"Ah sh...shoot," she said and waved in apology as she started up.

Miller set the phone back in the cup holder, the screen dark now. "Might have to get you another one. Who have you given the number to?"

"Eloisa, Aunt Moira, Beth, Joy the paralegal, you," she replied promptly.

"Hmm," he answered noncommittally. "I wonder if we can trust the lawyers."

"You can one hundred percent trust Joy. Her aura is very good and the cards said she's OK." She put on her turn signal when he said to turn left at the next street and stopped to wait for the light.

He gazed at her seriously when she turned to look at him. "We'll trust your instincts on her for now, but it's a big law firm and this number is probably in a report that others will see."

"True enough," she answered. "She said she would keep it to herself, but she's an underling and if they put a team on the evidence, the number will definitely get around."

"Which means your phone can be traced."

"Sure." He was as paranoid as her mom, but he had lots of experience to back it up. And her mom wasn't paranoid if there really was someone out to get her, right?

She didn't miss the light change this time, but as she glanced in her rear view mirror, she had a prickle of unease. "Is that gray car following us?"

The whole feel of Miller sharpened, his aura, which had been mostly content, but worrying on the question of tracing cell phones, drawing in tensely. He leaned forward to use the wing mirror on his side. "Hard to say. The streets are fairly busy, since it's early afternoon Saturday." A moment later, he said, "Turn right up here."

Since they were almost to the street he pointed out, she hit the brakes hard and still went around the corner too fast, her small sedan wobbling as she accelerated out of the curve.

"Is it still back there?" Miller asked, his voice growlier than before.

"Yes," she said tightly.

"OK, sharp left onto the one-way street. Don't signal the turn, just go."

She squeaked out, "It's one way the wrong way?"

"Yes," he replied.

She took a hard left and swerved into an alley on the left as the oncoming car slammed on its brakes and leaned on the horn. The driver rolled down his window to cuss her out.

"Keep going up the alley. It goes through."

"So we're doubling back?"

"Damn straight. Did you see this car following you on the way to the office?" He pulled out his phone and tapped on the screen a few times.

"I didn't, but it's a gray car and I wasn't watching." Her voice was squeaky, so she cleared her throat, trying to find some calm.

"It's not hard to figure out where I live, but it's not public information and we need to lose this guy before going back there." He tapped the screen a few more times and held the phone to his ear. "Buho. We're being followed ... Delilah's driving and my son's in the back. Can you track me? Find me a place to go to ground."

Delilah approached the exit from the alley onto the main road.

"Right, then get to the left and make a U-turn at the light," he told her. "OK, thanks, Buho."

He set the phone on his lap, but she was pretty sure he hadn't hung up. He leaned forward and used her wing mirror again before turning around slowly and scanning out all the windows. "I don't see the gray car or anyone else who seems to be trying to follow us."

The phone on his lap said, "Delilah, as soon as you do the U-turn, stay in the left lane. You'll turn left not at the next light, but the one after."

It was Special Agent Buho, whom she'd met briefly, but who she thought was strictly on shifter assignments, while Andrew was being loaned to the team working on this case.

"OK," she answered. "I've never taken evasive maneuvers before, so give me plenty of warning."

She swung a little wide on the U-turn, but luckily it was a protected one. A couple more turns and she was starting to recognize the area near the community college.

Buho said, "Take a right on Bishop."

She came to the corner and got a really bad feeling. "No, that's not a good idea."

"You're almost to the garage," Buho said, his tone as clipped as Andrew's ever was.

"I have a bad feeling," she said and went straight when the next light changed. "There's a white SUV down there. What's another place we can go?"

"God... OK." Buho took a deep breath. "It's not far from here. Take a left onto Chalmers, then an immediate left into the alley with the sign for the farmer's market."

She did as he said and saw the easy-ups and the crowd. "Do we need eggs and oranges?"

Buho grunted. So much for humor. "Turn right onto Bodega, pass the farmer's market and go one more block. Number 311 will be on your left. It's set back from the street with a lot of trees." He gave Miller the code for the garage door.

Chapter Sixteen

Once Del had pulled into the garage, Andrew walked in behind them and strode to the door into the house to push the button and close it again.

He spoke into his phone, conferring with Buho, as she inhaled deeply and got out, opening the back door to get Troy, who stared at the seat in front of him on high alert.

"Do you want to get out this side, Troy? Or on your usual side?"

"I wonder if we shouldn't always use the passenger side, since on the street that's usually safer," Andrew said. He opened the passenger-side back door and helped Troy unbuckle his belt. As soon as the boy was free, he scrambled into Miller's arms and clung tight. Miller supported him with both hands as the boy shoved his face against his dad's chest.

"Awww," Del said as she came around the back of the car. "That was maybe a bit too much excitement."

Andrew held his son flush against him as Troy whined softly. "Buho didn't give me the code to get in the house, so we're going to sit out here for an hour or so."

"Is it a safe house?" she tried to remember what it looked like, but she was probably going to forget the house number and the street as soon as they left. She'd be able to find the farmer's market, though, so it wouldn't be safe for long.

Andrew chuckled. "No, it's another agent's house. She's traveling right now, but she's Buho's friend. My friend, too. The place we didn't go was a mechanic's garage which has been for sale for a couple years, but Buho recently reprogrammed the alarms."

A beat of silence.

"So what sort of feeling did you have? What were the clues?"

She shrugged. "I don't know. I just felt it was wrong. I think it was more…it looked empty, like someone would spot us? And there was a white SUV which reminded me of the Escalade that tried to make me crash a few days ago. My feelings don't always mean anything, really, but I try to listen to them. Maybe my subconscious saw a gray car down there, too. Maybe my subconscious wanted to mess with me. Maybe it was a tiny premonition. Who knows?"

Andrew raised his eyebrows. "Without anyone to check down there, we will never know."

And…she felt stupid. It had been a real aversion to going to the garage, spoken into the same part of her that connected to the mystery of the tarot cards and sometimes to the crystal ball and tea leaves and a hundred other forms of divination.

But apparently it was all intuition to Andrew Miller. Never mind that he used magic to change into a completely different form with precision, losing and gaining teeth, hair, and mass with a thought. To him, her magic was unexplainable.

She sighed. And shivered, because like any normal person and unlike Aunt Moira's husband who worked on his custom antique car as a hobby, the agent friend didn't heat her garage. She unlocked the trunk and took out a blanket, then got in the driver's seat, wrapped like a burrito. Pretty soon, Miller – she wasn't going to think of him as Andrew until he trusted her magic, she decided - got into the front seat, arranging Troy's legs so as to not squash them.

"Let me know if you're getting cold and we can all sit in the back and share the blanket." She shivered at the idea of being squashed in the back with a car seat between them and the blanket only covering Troy.

"Wolves don't get cold easily, but thank you. We might have to take you up on that." Miller wriggled around to unbutton his overcoat and suit jacket and attempt to wrap Troy in them with him, but both were cut to fit with a slim line, so weren't voluminous enough. Troy solved part of the problem by losing mass and gaining fur. Instead of stripping him like usual, Miller kept him in his clothes. Troy's tongue hung out in doggy smile.

"Awww." Delilah pulled off one glove and poked her hand out of the blanket burrito and scratched between the cub's ears. "You are a brilliant boy, Troy."

He leaned into her hand and she kept rubbing his head, only after a minute realizing she was brushing against Andrew Miller's chest a little more often than she had anticipated. He had on a t-shirt and button shirt under the coat and jacket and heat was pouring off him. She paused, little finger pressed against his ribcage. She couldn't tell much about his physique from a glancing touch, but she had seen him in a t-shirt and knew it was a good one. And the thought of how he'd looked before and the heat from his chest now and the close quarters?

Well, it was probably pheromones. Definitely not magic. Nothing to do with compatible auras overlapping, oh no.

She wondered if compatible auras were in part pheromones and figured, OK, yeah, there might be more science to all of this than she liked to think. She was studying psychology, which meant she'd also taken a lot of classes in biology and chemistry just to get to the courses that include the nervous system and brain chemistry and so on. She wasn't against science, but she also knew it was only starting to really try to explain shifters and magic users.

Miller cleared his throat. "Would you mind holding Troy inside your blanket?" At her nod, he spoke to his son. "Troy, would you mind sitting on Delilah's lap for a bit?"

At Troy's short nod, Andrew took off the puffy coat caught up awkwardly around his wolf pup body and Del fidgeted to let him inside without letting out too much of her warm air. The cub's human pants fell off in the swap and he was left in a t-shirt as he lay down. Definitely warmer than she was. She peeked down at him and he had his eyes closed already, ready to take a nap. She adjusted his weight slightly and pulled the blanket more securely around them.

The windows were steaming up and, yeah, she had steamed up a few windows with former boyfriends, but somehow this felt more intimate. Maybe Andrew was thinking the same thing when she looked at him and he was staring at her with what looked like desire.

She swallowed and his lips quirked ever so slightly. When she looked into his eyes again, they and his aura were hotter than before.

"Do you ever go by Andy?" she asked, trying to ease off the tension with this man who didn't respect her powers and whose son was sitting on her lap, learning what pheromones smelled like firsthand.

He blinked and most of the heat was gone. "No. My mother insisted on Andrew. My dad went by Andy, so I had to be either the whole name or Drew or Junior."

"Or something else entirely," she added. "You could use your middle name."

"Faoladh," he said, his lips quirking again. "My grandmother's maiden name."

"Fa-what?"

"Fa-o-ladth. It is Scottish Gaelic for werewolf. Well, for the type we are, not the ravening beasts howling at the moon and attacking people in most legends, but people who turn into wolves."

She blinked. "That's not even a little subtle. And I know un-subtlety because my cousin-in-law's family name's Grey because they're grey wolves."

He smiled slightly. "Beth has a long list of shifter family names that are, essentially, the animals they shift into, but in different languages. I gave her mine when I found out about the list. But no, I couldn't be called Faoladh instead of Andrew or Drew."

"Yeah, I don't think most US-ian school children would understand Faoladh. Wait, say it again slowly for me?"

She practiced it a couple times until he nodded approval. "Andrew Faoladh Miller. Did your mother middle-name you when you were in trouble?"

His expression faded to a sort of blankness. "I...I didn't get in trouble. Or I was always in trouble with her, I'm not sure which. We couldn't afford anything after my dad left and it felt like my fault. She blamed Alex for being born and his mother for tearing apart the family, but they were distant people I'd never met."

She just bet he was 100% a rule-follower even as a child, but for his mother to have made poverty feel like her child's fault was some damaging shit.

"Her parents had been fairly rich and raised her expecting the best of everything, but the money ran out and she couldn't hold down a job. My father came from a law enforcement family and was certainly not getting rich as an FBI Agent." He shook his head and gazed out the foggy window at the dark, indistinct shadows of the garage.

"We all survived off the profits from Grandmother's magic shop. So in economic downturns, it was charity and food stamps and outside jobs when Mom and Aunt Moira were kids. When my mom got her degree and CFE certification, she started making more money than the shop ever did."

She stared blankly through the steamed-up windscreen, remembering the lean times when there was no profit. "Mom made the books balance at the shop, Aunt Moira managed everything else, Grandmother had the big, creative ideas and told fortunes in the back. I'm impractical like her, though without the big ideas."

"Does your family tell you that?" he asked softly.

She wrinkled her nose. "My mom does. Eloisa hints at it because she's so extremely competent, both magically and with her vet training, but she loves me anyway. Aunt Moira is never, ever judgmental, but is fondly exasperated with me most of the time. Grandmother wants me to dream bigger and to be more outlandish and creative than she ever was. So really, it's a mixed bag."

He looked at her, considering. "But it's your mom who tells you you're impractical."

She felt a rush of amusement, but tinged with a sort of thankfulness. "Right, well, she's one hundred percent practical. Well, maybe not, because she's strict about rules. She won't take bribes or work for a shady company and sometimes it sounds like that would be the most practical way to get rich."

He shrugged. "I'm willing to guess based on the files I looked in that she has a huge amount in the bank, taxes paid and everything bound by the rules. Not bending the rules has served her well."

"And she almost never takes a vacation or spends on anything other than necessities. She's ready to pay for Grandmother's nursing home and ready to retire. The job she has me doing is mostly unnecessary. I could do it part-time or remotely by internet and phone. But she wants someone she really trusts, not a virtual assistant. And it gives me money for school and time to study during the day."

They sat in silence for a while, both facing forward, staring into the darkness of the garage.

"So what are we going to do when we leave this garage?"

He sighed. "I'm going to see if Alex will go into my apartment and pack everything we need for the next few days. We can go to a hotel. Probably won't be granted a safe house just for this, but I'd like to be someplace unexpected and keep moving until the next steps come clear."

"And your work on Monday?"

He closed his eyes, a bit of pain leaking from his controlled aura. "I'm going to have to go in to keep the team updated on what you know and what we have. They haven't appointed me to be in charge of protecting you, so it's on my own time. Until we can get all the information your mom had from the lawyers and get warrants and subpoenas and do searches, you're going to be in danger. Even then, who knows what else your mom has hidden somewhere? She's going to continue to be in danger because she would make a good witness."

"And if I'm in danger, then Troy's in danger."

He nodded. "As long as you're with us, yes."

She shriveled a little. It made sense for him to ditch her to protect his son, but she'd hoped he would protect her, too. That wasn't fair of her.

"I'm trying to figure out where to leave you both so you're protected. Everyone I know well and trust is an FBI agent."

"Except Beth? And surely there are other people?"

He shook his head. "Beth is…She's wonderful for Alex, but she doesn't have any sort of protection skills. She's the first person I would hide if there were any sort of risk to Alex. But she wouldn't like it. She's a professor and dedicated to her students and her responsibilities. But Alex is still out in the field, though not undercover anymore. It's really rare that a threat to an agent spills over into their family, thankfully."

She nodded. "And even more rare that a threat to some rando like me spills over to an agent's family."

He shrugged again and pulled his coat more firmly around himself, finally re-buttoning it because it was getting damp in the car, which made it feel colder. When it was time to go, she would have to open the window and blast the defroster. She shivered. The warm weight of Troy on her lap, breathing slowly and rhythmically, helped center her.

"I should try to scry for my mother again," she said, suddenly realizing it. "Shouldn't I?"

Miller nodded. "You've had luck with it in the past."

"I found Eloisa based on nothing but a map and a good feeling. I haven't had much luck with other people."

"Maybe you need the emotional connection with the person to be able to find them, even if you can't read their future."

"Yes," she said, her mind going to her mother and their history together. "But so far, looking for my mom has been like running into a wall. She's everywhere or nowhere. Could you hand me my handbag, please? I've got my good cards in there. I used a few other things, too, when looking for Eloisa, so I'm going to need to go back to my house."

He reached into the back seat and gave her the hobo bag she carried everything and the kitchen sink in, but he held onto it when she went to take it. "Not back to your house, no. I'm not sure who we could send in there to get what you need. Maybe the paralegal."

"Joy? I guess that would be OK. Since she's standing between the FBI and my mom, and I guess I am, too."

Chapter Seventeen

Delilah contemplated the three cards she'd laid out on the drinks console between the front seats. "Still nothing. I need a paper map. Could we pick one up?"

Andrew pulled his gaze away from her pink nails and did his best to not sigh and instead asked, "Like a map of the world or a map of Cleveland or somewhere in between?" Because there was still a chance her mom was in Argentina with Shalonda. Or somewhere else in the world. They had a State Department request in to see if Serena Woods' passport had been used for travel, but he didn't know the answer yet.

She lifted her head and looked at him, eyes narrowed. "I don't know. Still working on the details, trying to get a sense of how far away she is. But since we're not exactly in a... I don't know, gas station? Bookstore? Who sells maps these days?" She waved the hand holding the deck of cards. "I'm anticipating our future needs."

She looked at him for a moment longer, until he nodded and she looked back down at the cards.

He heard his son's breathing change and a moment later, there was movement under Delilah's blanket and a little wolf head poked out and blinked blearily around, then glanced up at the weak dome light and down at the cards. He climbed out of the blankets and settled again on Delilah's lap, looking at the cards.

"I'm trying to find my mom," she told the pup.

His ears pricked up and he stared more intently at the ones face up on the console.

"It's not working right now, but I keep pulling the Eight of Swords and reversed Magician, so I'm getting more and more sure it's my thinking that's limited."

"I'm pretty sure your mom has a lot of secrets. Maybe once you know more, you can move past it," Andrew said and stretched his head side to side. The headrest on the seat hit him just wrong and though he'd tried to adjust it, his neck felt cramped. "Also, I need to get out and walk around and we should turn the dome light off so it doesn't run down your battery."

"True," she said with a sigh and gathered up her cards.

Troy gave off a slight whine and she said, "I think he needs to go potty. We should either drive somewhere with a bathroom or ask for the code to get into the house."

Andrew stood and held the door open for Troy to jump down behind him. He shut his door and heard the click of the key in the ignition and the windows whirring down.

"Gotta let the steam out," Delilah said. He blinked to let his eyes adjust to the darkness as the dome light went out, then willed his wolf night vision to the fore and made out the faint light from late afternoon, cloud-covered sun where it marked the door to Agent Strickland's side yard. If he remembered correctly - he punched the alarm code in and opened the door just a crack to be sure and yes - the door led to the fenced-in part of the yard. He'd only been here once a few years before, when Strickland had a housewarming party, so he had been hoping his memory was correct and she hadn't changed the layout significantly.

He looked up at the neighbor's house and saw there were only a couple windows overlooking the side yard and both had curtains closed. It didn't mean there wasn't someone behind the curtains peeking out or there wasn't a camera somewhere. He looked toward the front of the house and found Strickland's camera. She was a bit of a genius at everything with surveillance, so if he could spot her camera, it was meant to be spotted. It meant she had others he wasn't meant to spot.

Many FBI agents were moved from field office to field office, but everyone associated with the Shifter Task Force was rooted in Cleveland. Strickland, though not a shifter herself, had remained loyal to the unit and had been promoted from research and eventually to team lead. She'd finally decided to buy a house while most of them were still renting, the habit of being moved around still firmly ingrained. Andrew had bought his apartment when the previous owner, a retiring FBI agent, decided to sell. He'd decided it was easier than finding a rental place with equal or better security measures.

The weather had warmed slightly and there was a light fog rising from the frozen lawn. He crouched beside Troy and said, "The good thing about being a shifter is that you can pee outside and people don't get upset." He realized his son might never have lifted a leg like a dog when the boy didn't move, just whined softly.

He shut the door and strode back to the car, opening the door as he took his overcoat off. "We're going to go pee like dogs in the backyard."

Delilah stared at him in surprise, then looked away as he took off his suit coat and unfastened his shoulder holster. He hesitated at setting it next to her, since any responsible gun handler never left a gun outside their control. "Could you open the trunk? In case Troy gets back before I do. Also, do you have any towels for our paws?"

She pulled the lever to pop the trunk and he went back there to see that no, she did not have any towels. He'd have to give her some of his ratty, old ones he kept for mud and mess. To use for Troy, not because he'd be getting in and out of Delilah's car. Though he could sort of see her taking care of Troy for a while yet. And taking care of him?

Anyway, he finished undressing behind the barrier of the open trunk, slammed it closed and hoped it was dark enough that Delilah wouldn't get an eyeful as he crossed to the side door again. He checked the alarm was still deactivated, opened the door slightly, then shifted.

He'd been asked twice in his life what it was like to shift, once by Strickland, who was coming to terms with agents she'd called friends turning out to be shifters, and again by Jasmine, Troy's mom, when she was in a rare conciliatory mood and asked for his help to understand Troy better. It was a sort of electricity that tingled everywhere at once. There was no flash of light or of sparks, but he felt what he'd been assured was his aura flare around him and contract, then return to the size needed for the form he was in.

In the space of two seconds, he was wolf and shaking his fur out with four paws on the floor and seeing the world in high-definition black and white. He pushed the door open and nudged Troy out. The boy went through the door, but when his paw hit the first bit of slushy snow past the shelter of the house's eaves, he stopped, the offended paw in the air, a look of dread on his wolfish face.

Without being able to speak, Andrew wasn't able to reassure him. He realized with the kid growing up in Florida, he wouldn't have had any experience with snow before this winter, which hadn't been particularly snowy. Andrew also carried him a lot and the school Troy attended only had a small outdoor play area, which he bet they didn't use when it was covered in snow.

Andrew deliberately set one front paw then the other in the snow, then shook them off one by one. The boy mimicked his flicking motion, but his paw was still wet. And this was a kid who liked to run warm water over his hands. He whined. Andrew rubbed his face against his son's and pushed him to the right, where there was a leafless bush, cut way back for winter, against the wall and under the eaves, so there wasn't much snow. He went to it and lifted a leg, demonstrating dog behavior.

Troy wasn't convinced, but his bladder was apparently full, so he gave it a try, wobbling on three legs as he peed.

Strickland was going to be furious if her bush died.

The scent of Buho was all over the place, which, combined with how Buho knew Strickland's alarm codes and felt he had permission to send Andrew to her garage, caused Andrew to guess they were back together. Or still together.

They'd had a very private relationship for ten years: not-quite-secret and not-quite-allowed once Strickland had been promoted to lead. They occasionally seemed to have broken up, but Andrew certainly wasn't someone who would ask. Ten years already since the first Catelli kidnapping had brought shifters into the public eye. Andrew had been with Buho and Strickland and with Cassandra Catelli on the search for the center holding her husband and on the takedown freeing the shifters being held for experimentation. He figured part of why Strickland stayed with them on the STF was their relationship.

They were lucky to keep her around as it had to have scuttled any ambitions she had of further promotion and she was one of the best agents he knew. Her non-shifter humanity and no-nonsense skills also made her an excellent buffer against anti-shifter rhetoric and stupidity from their superiors.

Andrew figured Strickland was watching them on her cameras by now, so he trotted out into the snow and sniffed along the fence to the gate and back along the wall of the garage, then at the back corner of the house, lifted his muzzle and scented the air, listening hard for movement back there, though mostly he heard traffic and people talking out on the street. The sound was muffled and moving strangely in the swirling fog. After a few minutes, he turned around to see Troy, safe on the dry concrete by the back door, but sniffing the air the way he had.

He trotted the few steps back to his son and nudged him to go back in before staring directly into the camera and giving his biggest doggy grin. His wolf was apparently in a playful mood and if they hadn't been hiding, trying to figure out where to go next, and without dry towels, he would have explored the whole back yard and rolled in the snow to show his kid how it was done.

He was definitely going to do that soon. Maybe they could go out to Alex and Beth's house sooner rather than later.

And yes, he would use his half-brother and sister-in-law shamelessly if it meant teaching Troy how to be a wolf.

Chapter Eighteen

ON THE WAY BACK to the apartment - after drying Troy's paws with Andrew's undershirt and having him shift back to little boy and get dressed, shivering hard in the back seat - Andrew spent the whole ride liaising with Buho. Everything his friend said was correct: he'd do best to not go back to his apartment, but also Troy had things there he couldn't do without and Andrew wanted his secure laptop and a few other things. And Delilah had already packed up everything she didn't want stolen and moved it in boxes into his bedroom, so leaving everything behind seemed harsh. And no one was available to go in for them, so they were going in.

He also had paper maps and an old road atlas of the US and Mexico on a bookshelf in his living room. He knew there were better ones at the office, precisely for when they were out of reach of GPS or deliberately going off the grid, but the office was where they'd picked up the tail. Probably.

Seriously, though, without Delilah and Troy, Andrew would not have gone back to his apartment until the current threat was over.

Inside, he strode to his room and packed casual clothes for the next few days, then changed into jeans and a long-sleeve t-shirt, putting his shoulder holster back on before donning a zip-up hoodie.

When he came out, Delilah was waiting in the hall.

"This apartment is highly secure, but there's a slim chance someone will come here looking for you or your mom's information. There's no such thing as Fort Knox in private life. I don't think we can take everything you brought here, but please take out the most important things and we will make it fit."

She nodded her agreement and fifteen minutes later, as he was still sifting through Troy's books, having packed for him and rounded up some food from the kitchen, she was in the doorway with an office file box and her suitcase.

"What are you bringing?" he asked, eying the box.

She frowned slightly, her face only barely expressing the exasperation that the rigidness of her shoulders was telling him. "Just my and my mom's most precious things. And everything relevant about my mom's business."

"I hope your trunk is big enough." He looked at the box again, then remembered how much stuff she had piled in the corner of his room and sighed. Apparently, there were a whole lot of important things. He stood with the stack of books he'd decided to bring, which were all the ones Troy liked best, as far as he could tell. "I'll be ready to go in a few minutes," he said, "Just keep an eye on Troy for me, please?"

"Do you know how the warrant is going?" she asked behind his back. "And can we go by my mom's house to be sure everything's OK there?"

"We could drive by, but I'd rather not. And we're not going in, not unless you suddenly remembered the precise location and content of documents that will clinch the case and you wanted to hand them to the FBI."

She was silent as he pulled a flattened box from behind his dresser and carried it to the kitchen where he had packing tape to put it back together. He put the books in the bottom and layered in the maps and atlas, then his son's soft fleece baby blanket. He stuck a few more things around the edges, including a few bananas and a DVD of Troy's favorite movie in case wherever they stayed didn't have WiFi that could support streaming movies. He went back into his room to the desk in the corner and got the external CD drive to plug into his laptop, because the likelihood was low that a motel, especially one with spotty WiFi, would have a DVD player they could borrow.

"OK," he said, hauling the box to the front hall with the other luggage. "Are we ready?"

Troy was standing with his back against the wall in the living room, rocking from foot to foot and picking at his shirt. Delilah was not in sight anywhere, which didn't reassure him. He heard the toilet flush and water run in the hall bathroom's sink, then she came out.

"Now I'm ready. Oh wait!" She strode into his room and he heard her rummaging through boxes. She came out smiling. "The cards I promised Troy."

Troy whined softly, his head tilted to the side at the mention of "cards."

Then Andrew looked again at the pile of stuff and sighed. "I hoped to take all this down in one trip."

Delilah stepped next to him and looked at it. "Yeah, well. Maybe pile it all by the elevator, take it down, then pile it all outside the elevator and bring the car over?"

He nodded. It was the solution he favored and it didn't hurt to let her come up with it. She'd parked her car in his assigned spot, which was closer to the interior doors to the basement of the building. One of them could get the car and not be completely out of sight of the other.

Troy whimpered softly and they both turned to look at him. He was rocking harder and obviously in distress.

Delilah touched his arm gently, wincing as his emotions bled over to her. "Oh hey," she murmured, "of course you're coming with us. We're all three sticking together. Sometimes your dad or I will have to go off and take care of things, but you will be with one or the other of us or with your Uncle Alex or Aunt Beth wherever we go until this problem is solved."

Andrew decided to clarify, because that would be like a hard rule to stick to. "You will be with someone who cares for you at all times. Almost always with me or Delilah, possibly with Uncle Alex or Aunt Beth, with a small chance of having to stay with my other friends who will be kind and protect you."

Troy's rocking slowed, but Delilah frowned at him. "Which other friends?"

"FBI agents. There's a chance we'll end up with Agent Buho at some point. He doesn't have kids, but he will defend them to the…end." He didn't want to use the word "death" because it was becoming clear it was a triggering word for Troy.

Delilah still looked suspicious, as she had every right to.

Once downstairs, he asked for her keys and stopped briefly outside the locked basement door in the frigid parking garage, listening and watching for movement, sniffing for strange smells. Of course, any modern criminal worth their salt would have hacked into the cameras and not be sitting around in person, waiting for them to come out. He jogged to Delilah's car and got in, pushing the driver's seat back to make space for his legs and angling the mirrors before starting the car. He stopped in front of the basement door and left the car running to warm up as he popped the trunk open, then helped Delilah carry their things. He stashed the box with blanket, maps, and books in the back seat beside Troy and opened the top in case his son wanted his fleece.

He drove this time, checking all directions in a sweep as they left the immediate neighborhood, looping around a few blocks to see if anyone would follow, and shifting his eyes to wolf vision for short times to be even more aware of movement in the dark.

"East," Delilah said into the quiet of the car.

"Sorry?" he answered.

"Take the Turnpike east," she said and pointed to one of the signs reflecting in their headlights.

"I wasn't going to take the Turnpike at all," he grumbled.

She sniffed. "I know you don't believe any of the premonitory things about my talent, but maybe you could humor me."

He sniffed, too. "There's not a good reason to not take the turnpike other than their cameras record everyone going through the toll booths. One of the places Buho told me about is closer to Youngstown."

"Well, as long as you don't have a good reason not to." She was definitely mad at him.

Perversely, her getting mad turned him on. He'd steamrolled over girlfriends before, dictating the terms and duration of relationships, but Delilah was pushing back.

Not that this was a relationship. She was too young, too wrapped up in the fantasy that she could hear voices, too unsettled and unsettling. And her kiss was like fire.

He drove into the dark streets and entered the turnpike, wishing he had his EZ-Pass, but he hadn't thought to take it out of his malfunctioning car. He paid cash at the booth, wishing he could use his anonymous credit card, too. He did have an alternate ID in his wallet, but was pretty sure this gray area wasn't gray enough for him to call it official business. Maybe for the motel, though.

Chapter Nineteen

Troy hated the place. They all did, but poor Troy was having trouble holding it together. Of course, they had fucked with his routine an awful lot today. In the last few days. In the last few weeks.

Sure, it wasn't Andrew's fault the boy's mother was dead, but finding a school and childcare that could cope both with autism and shapeshifting had been rough. Even now, the teachers had been clear that if his wolf cub was a problem, he'd have to go somewhere else. Which reminded him to call the school and leave a message on their voicemail about a family emergency sending them out of town for the next few days. He paid them enough the spot should be held open.

Delilah darted into the bathroom, which smelled of bleach and mildew. Troy stood outside the bathroom, which he'd just used, rocking and whimpering in distress. Andrew dropped the last of their things on the desk and went to his son. He crouched down in front of him and held his son's skinny arms. "Do you want to shift? You can now if you want."

Troy hadn't shifted in his car seat in several days, even when distressed earlier as they were being followed and driving erratically through the city. Now he paused in his rocking and started to strip off his clothes. Andrew helped him and then once he was a pup again, offered to pick him up. Troy walked into his arms, so he guessed it was a yes and stood from his crouch, his left knee popping because he was old and because he'd messed his knee up so badly during a takedown he'd needed surgery a couple years before.

The bathroom door opened and Delilah's expression softened when she saw him cradling Troy. "Troy, could I hold you while your dad freshens up too?"

She took the boy and her aura sent a calm vibe to both of them.

"Freshen up?" he asked, replaying her words in his mind.

She smiled, just a little, sly smile which made her look sweet with an edge of mischief. "Isn't it a great euphemism? Troy, a euphemism is when you use a polite word instead of one that could be rude. I didn't even say the word bathroom and 'freshen up' could also mean wash or reapply makeup, if any of us were wearing it. I've only ever used it to mean go into the bathroom or to get away from everyone and give myself time to think. Maybe wash my face."

Andrew had closed the door while she talked and since she was addressing Troy, he figured it wasn't too rude. He really needed to piss.

When he was done freshening up, he came out and found Delilah sitting at the little table on the only chair, feeding Troy pieces of banana and talking to him soothingly about fruit. He nodded that yes, he liked mangoes, but no, he shook his head that he didn't like oranges or grapefruit. The dislike for oranges was documented, but Andrew didn't think the paperwork had mentioned mangoes. Of course, mangoes were messy and hard to come by in Ohio, especially in winter, so Andrew might have forgotten about them.

Delilah looked up at him and smiled, calm radiating off her and filling this dingy room with the noise of a state highway outside, the scent of other people, bleach, and mold inside, and a cold breeze coming from the inadequate window.

"I need to rinse the banana off my hands, then Troy and I are going to look at cards while I see if they can help me find my mom."

Troy's head swung toward her, ears pricking up.

Delilah's face fell and she stared at Andrew in shock, then looked down at Troy again. "Oh," she said simply. "Oh, Troy…"

"What is it?" Andrew said, alarm sharpening his senses.

"Um…" she licked her lips and took a deep breath. "Troy, I can't find your mom. I could help you find…closure. I think." She looked up at Andrew, distress in her face.

Andrew's heart broke. He picked Troy up off Delilah's lap and held him close, closing his eyes tightly so they wouldn't leak. The cub stiffened against him and whined, then collapsed into him, continuing to whine and whimper.

"Children as young as he is typically don't understand death," Delilah said softly. "I had wondered."

"God, Troy," he gasped out. He'd understood on an intellectual level about Troy not understanding death, but hadn't realized that no one had tried to explain it. "Your mom loved you so, so much." His manly attempt to not cry was about to leak. He didn't know what words to say. "She wanted you safe, which is why you're with me."

The shrieks of his ex's mom came back to his memory, her accusations of devils and demons and witchcraft. She'd hired a lawyer and even now was trying to get custody, presumably to do exorcisms and force Troy to be regular human and neurotypical. How baffling it must have been to be picked up from a trusted babysitter by strangers and taken to a hateful stranger, then picked up again by him, another stranger who had held him close, but not offered the comfort he needed.

Or, apparently, adequate explanations. The friendly neighbor had been sad and talked about how Jasmine had passed on, but what sense would "passed on" make to a scared five-year-old? He didn't think he'd ever said Troy's mom was dead. But right now, in this place with the stress they were under, he just...couldn't.

Delilah escaped into the bathroom, leaving the door open, and he heard her washing her hands and probably her face. Freshening up. Troy struggled to get down, so Andrew set him on the icky carpet and the boy trotted to the bathroom, then shifted and walked in.

"Do you want to wash your hands?" he heard her ask and the water came back on.

Andrew took three deep breaths and picked up the pile of clothing, changed his mind and opened Troy's suitcase to take out pajamas. He followed into the bathroom and found Delilah sitting on the closed toilet, projecting calm again while his son ran his hands under the warm water of the sink. He interrupted long enough to put warm pants on the boy, but left him shirtless for the moment, mostly so he wouldn't get his cuffs wet. He would shift to sleep anyway.

"Do you want to get started on the maps?" he asked Delilah, who agreed and left the bathroom with a soft pat on Troy's head. He stepped out of the bathroom to say, "Thank you. I...I mean for the calm. We're going to have to grieve at some point, but maybe not tonight?"

She smiled, her eyes sad. "I get it. It's a lot to think about for anyone."

He went back and sat with his son, brushing his teeth while they were in there. His fingers had pruned up by the time Andrew turned off the water.

He dried Troy's hands on a thin, shabby, bleach-scented towel, so he could at least hope it was cleaner than anything else in the room. He was going to tell Buho...he was going to tell Buho what? That the place sucked and yet no one was going to look for them here? Which was the point after all. He wondered why Buho had chosen this place or if someone had just come across it and recommended it to him.

He helped the boy into his shirt so he wouldn't get cold. "Let's go watch Delilah use the cards. Or would you rather I read you a book?"

Yeah, he knew better than to ask either/or questions, but Troy pointed at Delilah, so he carried Troy to her and she took him and set him on her lap and began to explain how she was leafing through the atlas, hoping inspiration hit. She had a feeling her mom wasn't too far away and hoped it would be an easy drive.

Andrew sat on the bed again and dropped his face into his hands. He'd need parenting advice on what to say to Troy and how to help him understand and process the loss. He supposed there were books and online articles about the subject and so pulled out his phone and started searching.

Maybe half an hour later, he'd read several articles with sometimes contradictory advice and yet he knew he'd wait for another day to really sit down and talk to Troy. The poor boy had been dealing with the loss of his mom all this time, but he hadn't known this would be permanent. He probably thought one day Andrew would take him back and drop him off with his mom.

Delilah was setting her cards face down on the atlas, so Andrew approached and saw it was the map showing the entire world and she had cards spread across the continents, almost completely covering the map. She turned up the cards on Australia, then several cards on Asia, then all over Africa, then Europe. She paused, humming softly over each one, touching each card. She touched the two cards still face down on Russia and breathed in and out several times before turning them up.

"Is it a Russian gang?" she asked, eyes still on the cards, but the question directed either at Andrew or at whatever spirits she was talking to. "Or maybe Armenian or…another former Soviet Republic?"

Slovak with several members from other parts of the former Eastern bloc, but he wasn't sure how much he could tell her. His silence made her glance over at him and she nodded. "My mom isn't there, but there are ties to something here in the western part around Russia."

He didn't budge and she rolled her eyes and turned back to the map.

OK, so maybe there'd been a mention of something in some of the papers and stuff she'd seen and only vaguely remembered, but still, it was impressive.

South America got a little hesitation and a murmured, "Don't cry for me, Argentina," which made him smile in spite of himself.

Then Central America and a head shake, then Canada, working from west to east, with increased humming over Toronto, but she moved on.

Finally, the USA, again west to east. She paused to tap Wyoming and say to Troy, "My cousin lives there. She's like a big sister to me and I love her."

So easy with the admission of feelings. Her family seemed more than a little odd and even spooky and her mom was apparently severe, but love seemed to flow among them. His mother had taken a long time to get over his father's betrayal and departure and even now his resemblance to his dad, everything from his blond hair to his FBI job, made her sneer.

She skipped over the card lying over Ohio and most of the states bordering it, working around it. She pointed out Florida, where Troy had lived before, which drew his close attention.

Finally, she set one finger on the last card. She said to Troy, "The rest of my family is under this card. My aunt and grandmother especially. But also my aunt's husband, a few second cousins, most of my friends from high school. And you and your dad. But it's still too hard to say if my mother is here."

She closed her eyes and started humming again, a low, tuneless sound that resonated in Andrew's chest and seemed to electrify her aura as it brushed against his, calming Troy. He wondered if she stopped using some of her energy to calm them and focused hard on the cards, she would have better luck.

Finally, she stopped humming abruptly and her eyes snapped open, every particle of air in the room somehow magnetized toward her and bending outward from where her finger touched the map. She lifted the card without turning it over and turned to a closer map of the Midwest, holding the card over it like she was looking through a magnifying glass. Then she turned a few pages until she had Ohio, Western Pennsylvania, and West Virginia and began humming again.

The hair stood up on the back of his neck. Whatever power she was using was strong. He felt the surge of it through his body, asking him to shift, but he resisted. Troy did not, popping to his wolf form and sitting up straight in his PJ pants to watch what she was doing just as intently as before. She pulled the card away, flipping through the pages until she came to West Virginia filling two whole, large pages, then she swayed slightly from side to side as she hummed and seemed to look *through* the card in her hand, until she set it with one corner on the narrow strip of the state that reached up between Ohio and Pennsylvania and set her finger on the card. She leaned down, carefully moving Troy out of the way so she didn't squash him, her nose almost touching her finger on the map.

Finally she sat up and the electrical magic faded from the room. She took a deep breath and looked over at him, her pupils huge, but rapidly returning to normal.

"She's in or near Wheeling, but I can't tell where. If you can get a more detailed map or we can go there, I think I can find her."

"She's not blocking you anymore?" he asked softly.

She shook her head. "No, something changed. Someone found her before we did. She's calling for help, but her signal's fading in and out."

She wiped away tears with one hand as she pulled Troy back to the center of her lap. "She's in trouble. I need to go to her." She swayed on her chair.

Andrew got up and lifted Troy from her. "You need to sleep first. We'll leave early in the morning."

He'd have to call Buho and figure out what backup he could have on the ground in Wheeling and environs. Maybe another horrible motel. And he'd have to convince the non-shifter team in Cleveland he was following a viable lead. They weren't expecting him in until Monday, so he would be OK for another thirty-six hours, he supposed.

She nodded and blinked a few times.

"Go get ready for bed," he said softly.

He pulled back the bedspread on one of the saggy double beds and the bleach smell wafted up. He set down Troy, who pawed at his nose. "I know it smells and we should have aired out the sheets, but the bleach smell means they're clean." So yeah, Buho had chosen the motel for its relative cleanliness. Good job. Maybe also because bleach would cover their scent if shifters were looking for them. Though it messed up his sense of smell so badly any advantage was lost.

Delilah got up and wandered to the bathroom, only taking her bathroom stuff when he pointed it out. He heard her brushing her teeth and freshening up, then she came back out in her flannel pajamas, looking exhausted and strained and adorable.

He took Troy into the bathroom where they both peed and he stripped down and opened the door slightly before they shifted to wolf. Delilah was already in the other bed, but when he helped Troy hop onto the bed before climbing up himself, she smiled and swung her legs out.

"Let me help with the covers," she said and he nuzzled her hand in reply as she pulled the sheet and blanket over them.

Chapter Twenty

TROY WENT TO SLEEP first, his small, warm, fuzzy body shoved up against Andrew's. He was going to have to figure out a way to get Troy to sleep alone if he was ever going to be able to sleep with a woman again.

To sleep with Delilah.

Her breathing evened out after she tossed and turned for a few minutes in the sagging bed. He didn't envy her having to sleep as a human, unable to curl up tight in the saggiest spot like the terrible mattress was a hammock.

It took him a long time to fall asleep, his body restless after a day without any sort of workout and a good deal of tension and thoughts and regrets and questions.

Finally, he closed his eyes and went through his insomnia relaxation routine, emptying his mind as best he could until he drifted off.

It felt like no time at all when he woke to uneven breathing. He froze in place and tipped his muzzle down to see Troy still breathing slowly, still deeply asleep. He swiveled his ears toward the door, thinking maybe someone was outside it, sneaking up on them. He would hear it open, he hoped, if someone came inside.

He swiveled his ears back when the breathing - Delilah's breathing - got jagged again.

She was crying, maybe in her sleep.

He eased himself off the bed and to the floor by the motel room door, shifted, and pulled on his sweatpants, then walked to her bed. He bent over her and set a hand on her shoulder, bringing her immediately to wakefulness with a jump.

"Bad dream?" he whispered, not sure she could hear him.

She nodded and wiped her eyes on the edge of her shirt. "My mom is calling out again and sending pictures, but it's dark and there are circles and guns. Or my dreams are dredging up every bad thing I can imagine could be going on with her."

He wanted to tell her it would be all right, but he really couldn't. If her mom was really in danger now, the people she had information on were ruthless and had a long reach and many loyal employees. It wasn't called 'organized' crime for nothing.

Besides, he already had one person to take care of whose mother was dead, and he didn't want to help Delilah grieve, too.

He hoped the warrants and subpoenas came through and wondered where Joy the paralegal was on deciphering everything she'd taken out of the office. He hoped Joy was honest and working for justice.

He also hoped Delilah was right and they were going toward her mom and not roaming aimlessly around while her mom sipped cocktails at a wedding in Argentina.

He was still touching Delilah, who could probably read his worry.

She proved this when she said, "You're not sleeping well, either."

"An excess of caution." He sighed and admitted the deeper truth. "Too many things in my head and not enough physical activity."

"Yeah, me too. I mean, I don't workout most days, but I at least go for a walk or take the stairs a few times to get my heartrate up."

Silence as he absently patted her shoulder.

"Do you want to lie down?" she asked out of the blue. "I mean, not in a seductive way, but to fall asleep. I can't guarantee I won't have more nightmares and wake you up again."

He glanced over at Troy, then went back to his spot closest to the door and took his gun out from under the bed where he'd set it on the floor within arm's reach. He transferred it to the nightstand between the beds, leaving the drawer open an inch. He didn't like not locking it up with his son in the room. At home, he kept it in a gun safe and changed the code once a week.

He didn't like leaving Troy closest to the door, either, but Andrew would stay alert and in human form and could draw the gun before the door even opened.

Delilah scowled at the gun. "I know you need it and I guess it makes me feel safer, but I don't like it."

"Yeah," he said. "I don't like it either, but in my whole career, I've had to draw it four times and only discharged it once. I mean, there were a few other times I was on a SWAT team and carried a long gun. There was shooting."

She shivered. "So anyway..."

He double-checked the safety was on, then slipped under the disinfectant-smelling covers next to Delilah and lay on his back. She moved over and shivered again.

"Sorry," he said. "Now I have the warm spot."

She wiggled a bit and he felt her warm feet brush against his colder ones.

They lay in the dark and silence for a while. The people next door flushed the toilet. The cars on the highway, though rarer than earlier, whooshed by with the occasional truck vibrating the windows.

"This place is pretty shitty," Delilah whispered.

Andrew stifled his surprised laugh with a hand over his mouth, mindful of Troy and his sharp ears sleeping five feet away.

"Even nearly silently, it's good to hear you laugh," she said. "Everything is grim right now."

He slid out a hand and found one of hers and squeezed it. "My job is grim."

"Yeah..." she sighed.

There were a few seconds of silence before she said, "I'm glad you're here with me. I don't know what I would have done if I'd had to navigate this by myself. Thank you."

"You would have figured it out. Maybe called in your mom's lawyers sooner."

"Yeah..." she sighed again. "I wonder if Joy is done looking at everything."

"Depends on if they pay her overtime to work the weekend. It's urgent, so I'd guess they will."

"Billable hours," said Delilah. "My mom's going to faint at the bill."

"Better to pay the paralegal rate rather than the lawyer rate, though I assume the lawyers will consult."

"So what do you do with your free time?" she whispered.

He breathed in and out twice. "Take care of Troy. Read about autism."

She smiled, just a flash of teeth in the dark and he realized he was watching her and not paying any attention to the rest of his surroundings. Yeah, the security bolt was on the door and the chair under the knob, as if that would make any difference if someone got past the bolt. Maybe they'd trip over the chair.

She looked over at Troy, then Andrew felt a rush of magic. "Cone of Silence," she said. "I don't want to wake Troy up." She paused for a few seconds and he felt another flare of magic, as if she was adjusting her cone.

Then she asked, "What did you do before you had custody of a child and what will you do once you and Troy settle in together?"

"I used to go running. Most of the time on a treadmill at the office gym. Now, I work straight through for eight hours and hope I don't get a call to come pick Troy up from wherever he is because someone can't deal with him."

"And you used to get sent all over the country. I think you miss that part the most."

"That might be gone for good, so I'm trying to not think about it too much."

She laughed so softly it was more like breathing. "I bet you get some of it back. Maybe not the 24/7/365 agent thing, but some of it."

"They expect 24/7/365. There's comp time and down time and sometimes vacations and sick days, but it's all-consuming. It's what we sign up for."

They lay in silence, each thinking their own thoughts. His were about his doubts that he wanted to be an all-consumed agent anymore.

"Do you want to be signed up for 24/7/365 still?"

Or maybe they were both thinking about the same thing.

"I don't know," he said. "I have no regrets about putting Troy first, but it's been a hard adjustment. And being a shifter in the current political climate means they're looking for reasons to push me out."

She squeezed his hand this time. "I've never had a long-term regular job except with my family. So I know a lot about retail and a lot about being a receptionist, and even more about being a temp. And I know how to tell fortunes, which is not really a viable career path, not without the retail part, and even then it's a tiny store in a mall where they raise the rent every year. And you need family members at poverty wages to keep it afloat."

He nodded.

She rolled onto her side to face him, bringing her much too close. "When I get my Psych degree I'll have to figure out how to get a master's. Even then, there are better opportunities for people with a PhD. I don't know if I can go that far, but I don't know what to do with any of it."

She sounded so young and so unsure and he felt so very old.

"I always knew I was going into the FBI, so I got in as soon as I could," he said. "I was going to be just like my dad. Even when my dad was less than optimal as a father, he was my goal."

"Because they divorced?" she asked in a whisper.

"Because when he left, he left me behind, too. My mom was bitter, so I idolized him. He didn't visit because he was traveling on a case. Then he was transferred away from us. But I kept on thinking he was better than my mom. And..." He took a deep breath and she squeezed his hand again. "She blamed it all on Alex and his mother, but he was even more horrible to them, apparently."

The silence rested heavily under his words.

"I'm glad you're friends now. You and Alex, I mean."

"I am too," he replied without thinking. "I mean, we're trying to be. And Beth wants us to be and she's the person with emotional intelligence, so we're both doing it for her, I think."

She let his sort-of-joke, sort-of-truth pass with a slight chuckle and a minute of silence.

"Can you get retirement now? You sound like you might be ready to think about changes. Especially with Troy depending on you."

"With partial pension, sure. I've always planned to do my full twenty-five years and retire at forty-eight."

"And then what?" she asked.

"I always thought I had time to think about it. But now I'm most worried about leaving with honor and under my own steam. I have savings and have almost paid off the mortgage on my apartment, so I have a cushion."

Her hand drifted to his wrist and stroked. He wasn't sure she was aware of what she was doing or if she was falling asleep. It was certainly waking him up. He rolled to his side and scooted his body around to fit into the dip in the mattress and brought his knees up so he wouldn't spring a pup tent.

She yawned and used her other hand to cover her mouth, then brought her hand back under the covers and caressed both his hands. Then her top hand drifted up his bare arm to his shoulder and down again to squeeze his bicep.

She had to know what she was doing to him unless she was asleep. She moved slightly, sliding her legs against his and he smelled her arousal.

"Delilah," he murmured.

She froze and opened her eyes. "Shit, sorry. Sort of drifting. You have very nice skin."

"Thank you," he said. He wasn't sure what she meant because skin was skin, but he didn't want her to stop touching his skin.

She slid an inch closer, their knees bumping, sweatpants catching against flannel until he straightened his legs part way and she did the same.

She tilted her head back and her face was so close in the dark. He wondered how much she could see. His night vision showed her pupils huge as her eyes traced over his face. He took her hand and set it on his bare waist, both of them catching their breath as her slight callouses traced across his vulnerable skin.

Delilah held her breath, feeling the play of soft skin and warmth and muscles. He wasn't super buff, but was lean and - she traced her hand up to his rib cage and he squirmed slightly - and ticklish.

She cleared her throat. "Do you mind if I…"

"Go on," he whispered, his gaze and aura intent on her. "Whatever you want."

She could feel her hot blush as she traced her hand through the coarse chest hair and over his pecs. Not huge like a body builder, but solid. And down the centerline of his torso, again with a little wiggle of ticklishness, and the slight scrape of his chest hair ended before starting again just above his waistband.

There, she paused. She couldn't see his arousal in the dark, but his body was throwing off waves of sex and of restraint.

She glided her fingers back up and through the chest hair and over to one nipple.

Andrew grunted. Or maybe growled?

She circled the nipple with one finger.

"You're killing me, Delilah," he definitely growled.

She pulled her hand away, but only to take his hand and set it on her waist. He eased her floppy pajama shirt up - she was going to have to dig her sexy nightwear out, at least her camisoles, because the flannel was unsexy as hell. But he finally found skin and paused, making tiny circles.

He cleared his throat softly.

"Whatever you want," she echoed his earlier words. She used her last bit of rational thought to reinforce the cone of silence over the bed. She was better with bespelling some sort of barrier, but could hold the cone as an umbrella for a short time.

She went back to his nipple, maybe a hint for him to search for hers, maybe just a way to make him feel good. Maybe both.

His hand slid up her side, brushing along the side of one breast, which sent fire down between her legs. He didn't take her breast in his warm hand. Instead, he slid down to her waist and teased his fingers under the waistband in back before pulling her forward and easing his hips forward until they were groin to groin, his erection against her lower belly. She fought against the sheet to lift her upper leg and drape it over his hip until she was open to him, hampered only by their pants. He was between her legs. Finally.

Then he was kissing her. Each separate kiss a pressure and a slide on her cheek, down to her neck, up to her ear. He lingered there, breathing softly into her ear, sniffing her hair.

Then he moved back down, going to her neck and breathing her in before licking under her chin.

She wriggled her hips against his hardness, wanting more. He pulled his head back to look at her. He maneuvered the arm he had been lying on under her so she was surrounded by him while she held him with her leg.

She was going to come from dry humping and they hadn't even kissed on the lips.

He eased his hand around from her back and cupped one breast. She had a momentary twinge of self-consciousness. Her breasts had been too much since she was thirteen.

He groaned, though, and squeezed gently, filling his hand and rubbing his palm against her nipple. And she didn't care about her teenage body image anymore, she just wanted more of this.

He set his mouth against her neck and began to thrust gently, rhythmically, his cock pushing against her exactly where she needed it, his hand moving in time on her nipple.

And finally, she couldn't stand it anymore and grasped his short hair to tilt his head back and kiss his mouth.

Andrew Miller was bossy in all aspects of his life, apparently, and took charge of her mouth, opening it wider with the force of his tongue and lips, moving against her, the heat pouring off of him, the lust filling the air, electrifying them both.

She went somewhere in her head, somewhere beyond the dingy motel room and bleached sheets. Somewhere with just the two of them in a place very much like where she had her visions, but just Andrew and her and this moment stretching on into the future.

He thrust against her again and stilled for just a moment. His hand which had been busy shaping and caressing her breast came to a stop on her hard nipple. He pulled his head back a fraction of an inch, heavy-lidded eyes staring into hers.

And he pinched her nipple, rolling it between his fingers until she bucked against him and came, barely remembering they needed to be quiet, making muffled groans and a squeak when he kissed her again, long and languid as he thrust frantically, sliding his hand out and grabbing her ass to pull her tighter against him as he came with a grunt.

They lay there, panting as the world came back into focus around them.

He breathed in deeply.

"So much for staying vigilant," he whispered, but he didn't let go of her butt.

She laughed, more of a breathy huff and stretched to kiss him again. He was soft and gentle and lingered over her mouth and down to her neck, where he sighed against her skin.

She held his head against her, petting his tousled hair, feeling the softness of it against her fingers.

He grunted, but didn't pull away. "Troy OK?"

She lifted herself up slightly to look over him and over the pillows to where the little wolf pup lay still. She squinted to see his aura and it was calm with a few flashes of dreams. "Still asleep."

He sighed against her neck again and pulled away. "I need to go clean up."

"Me too." She'd have to change her underwear and hope she hadn't gotten the crotch of her PJs wet. At least she didn't have her pants full of jizz like he did.

He eased away from her, sliding his hand down her leg as he moved it off of his hips. He stared into her eyes and kissed her again before rolling to his feet. He leaned over Troy, checking for himself that the boy was all right and pulling the blanket over him again.

Delilah released the shreds of the Cone of Silence and watched as he dug with barely a rustle through his suitcase and carried something, probably clean pants, into the bathroom. She heard the water run and he came out a minute later and went over to look at Troy, who twitched.

Delilah got up and dug, probably not as quietly, and took out a clean pair of panties. She shivered as she took her pants off in the bathroom to use the toilet, then pulled her clothes back on as quickly as she could. She washed her hands and face - freshened up - and slipped out of the bathroom and back into bed, searching for a warm spot.

She didn't expect Andrew to scoop up a barely-awake Troy and for them to both climb into her bed, Troy in the middle. The pup yawned hugely and glanced at her out of the corner of his eye before digging his face into his dad's chest.

Andrew reached over him and brushed her hair with his hand. "Good night," he whispered.

She whispered it back, closed her eyes, and immediately fell into a deep, restful sleep.

Chapter Twenty-One

DELILAH WOKE UP TO the weight of a small, warm animal clambering over her and the sound of four paws hopping to the floor. For a moment, her body remembered the cat she'd had from when she was eight until he died when she was nineteen.

The mattress shifted and shook as a much larger form grunted and sat up.

Oh yeah. Cheap motel outside of Youngstown. Mind-blowing almost-sex with an FBI agent. A small wolf shifter pup climbing over her to get to the bathroom.

She opened her eyes all the way and smiled as the FBI agent pulled his eyes from the bathroom door where the sink turned on with a rattle.

He smiled back, a small, contented, sleepy smile, then looked away to pick up his phone. "Five twelve AM."

She sat up and stretched and noticed he watched her body as she did. Which, OK, because if his son weren't ten feet away in the bathroom, she would have pulled him back down, because that smooth skin and delicious chest hair were right there.

Then she remembered pinpointing her mother's location not too far away and thinking her mother was now in distress and she got serious quickly. "How soon can we get to Wheeling?"

Andrew rubbed both hands over his face. "A couple of hours driving. Breakfast, quick showers, some evasive maneuvers. Let's say three to three and a half hours."

"Mom needs me."

They were out of the motel in thirty minutes and had driven half an hour with no one behind them before they stopped at a chain diner.

"It's a toss-up if Troy will want bacon and eggs or a burger," Andrew said softly, looking at his son in the rear view mirror. "This place serves both."

And they were studiously not discussing their relationship or what happened the night before. Having a small child in the car with them kept them from dissecting it, Del supposed. Maybe it was the dissection that had killed her past relationships. No one was currently needy with *What Does It Meeeean?*

And it might have been a relief if she hadn't been wondering what it meant.

Troy had the burger with a side of fries and Andrew and Delilah had breakfast food, heavy on the protein for him, light on the saturated fat for her.

By the time they took a right onto the scenic highway heading south toward Wheeling, the sun was up, though it was another gray day and other cars were showing up more frequently. She opened the atlas on her lap and tried to connect with her mother again, but couldn't get into the trance the way she'd done the night before.

On the approach to the city, just after Andrew asked if they were crossing the river or staying on the Ohio side, her phone rang.

"Sorry to call so early," said Joy's abrupt voice. "I finished sorting through your mom's data at about three this morning. I made a backup of it before I started and secured the backup and used a non-internet computer in accordance with what you believe your mom's wishes were. I discussed it with Reynolds, your mom's lawyer, and she and I both believe the FBI will be very interested in what was on the external drive. We want to turn it over to them."

"Do you need my signature or anything? Because I'm out of town in a moving car in an undisclosed location."

"I will need to record the relevant part of this conversation." Joy paused for a moment, then there was a beep and a tinny voice announcing the conversation was being recorded.

Delilah identified herself and gave the date and time and permission.

Joy asked a few questions and eventually thought she had enough and ended the recording. "The FBI was calling all day yesterday asking about our progress, but still no subpoena. Apparently the judge doesn't believe in them on the weekend unless someone's in danger."

Delilah shivered. "My mom's in danger now, but I don't have evidence that will hold up in front of a judge. I also don't know if she'd be in less danger with the info in the FBI's hands or if the gang's interested in keeping her from testifying."

Andrew glanced at her sharply as he pulled off the highway and into the empty parking lot of a hardware store. He drove through it to a little gas station and turned off the car, got out, and started to fuel up.

"We've stopped for gas," she said.

"Good," Joy said. She cleared her throat. "Can I...ask you something else?"

"Of course," Delilah said.

She heard the rustle of Joy walking and a door closed. "OK, so, one of the junior partners has taken an interest in this data and in this case. I've had to get Reynolds to shoo him out a couple times. I've kept the drive and the copies with me at all times because I didn't want to leave it anywhere Phil could get it."

Delilah had a feeling wash over her. Something her mom had said about Phil. Something in the notebook. Something the ether was putting together for her. "Did you sleep at the office for the last two nights?"

"Yes. There's a couch in the shared paralegal office and I ordered in food and there are showers in the weight room."

"Joy. Thank you. I'm pretty sure my mom had suspicions of Phil. Of someone named Phil. I can't quite remember, but thank you. Please get the data to the FBI as fast as possible. I'll have Miller's friend Agent Buho meet you at the field office. I know we can trust him."

Andrew swung into the car again. "I couldn't help overhearing," he said. "I'll give Buho a call."

"Joy?" Delilah asked. "Will you be safe on the way there?"

Joy gasped slightly. "Now you're freaking me out."

Andrew was dialing his phone. "I'll have Buho meet her there. Let me send you a photo of him and you can send it to Joy."

"Are you alone in the office?" Delilah asked Joy.

"Now you're really freaking me out," Joy said, her voice shaking. She sounded like she was jogging.

Dread crept up Del's throat. "Take the data and the copy of the data and all your files about it and get in your car and go now."

Andrew was talking softly into his phone, then turned and said, "Buho says there's someone on the team already at the office. He's on his way in." He went back to the phone. "Can you trust them? ... OK ..." He turned back to Del and put his phone on speaker as he flipped and scrolled.

"They've got a guy watching the law offices and he'll follow her. I'd say she should ride with him, but I don't know who it is."

Del relayed that as her phone pinged and she looked down at a picture of Agent Buho smiling slightly at someone just off the screen. She forwarded the message to Joy. "I just sent you a picture of the agent who's meeting you. Are you in your car?" Her phone pinged again and it was Andrew sending a text with Buho's phone number. She forwarded that, too.

"Almost out of the building," Joy said as there were beeps in the background with the alarm code, Del assumed. Then more jogging and car locks beeping. "The parking garage is well-lit and I know there are cameras, but there are only two cars in here and – Oh, goddamn it. Phil's is the other car. At least I think it's his car."

Joy's car door slammed, then Del's phone pinged with a picture of a red sports car in a dim garage. "He's not in it, I don't think, but I'm going now."

There were sounds of a car engine and then acceleration. "OK, I'm out and there's some guy in a beige Honda who pulled out behind me. Please tell me he's your Fed."

Del asked Andrew, but neither he nor Buho were sure. She closed her eyes and focused on Joy, on the cards she had pulled for her, on the feeling of frustration and stifled career and stifled life. "I think you're in the clear now, Joy. Keep going. Pull up out front of the FBI building and ask to see Agent Buho's badge. He'll take her inside, right?"

Andrew listened to his phone for a few seconds. "Absolutely."

"Then you'll be safe," she said to Joy. "Keep being careful."

Joy's breath was starting to even out, then there was a little blip and a moment later she said. "Phil just texted me."

"Ignore it and watch the road. You're almost there. Buho just arrived and he sees you coming," Andrew said. "At least if you're in the dark blue Subaru, maybe five years old, that you were driving the other day."

Del relayed it and Joy laughed tightly. "Seven years old, but close."

Del's skin tingled and tensed. A little bit of Sight hit the back of her eyes. "Shit! Once you're in the gate, go around and use the side entrance with the big doors. On the other side of the building," Del said.

"The loading dock?" Andrew asked.

"Drive right past Buho and around the back to the other side. Go fast. Go in that way. Buho, I know you can hear me, follow her around there."

Tires squealed and there were bangs and shouts. Then acceleration and tires squealed again and Joy's car door opened and there was more running and more tires and car doors.

She could hear Buho shouting and a door scraping open.

"Holy shit, you weren't kidding," gasped Joy.

Del gasped, too, her heart racing. "Everyone OK?"

"I'm fine, someone shot at me before I got around the corner. Hi, Agent Buho, I want to see your ID."

Buho's voice clipped out orders and then he came on the line. "I wish I knew how you did that, Ms. Woods. We've got people after the shooter and Ms. Joy's safe. We're going to hang up now, though."

The phone beeped off and Del touched the red button and set her phone in the cup holder, hands shaking.

Andrew talked for a couple seconds to Buho, then hung up, too. "Good job. That was close."

She drew in a big breath. "I had a bad feeling about the parking lot when I picked you up. Like there were too many sight lines for what's basically a cop shop. A federal, secure cop shop shouldn't have so much, I don't know, other businesses and parking right by it."

"It's got a perimeter fence and guards and all the best tech," he said. "But no, none of that stops bullets. I mean, there are other protections once you're inside."

A whine in the back seat told them Troy had woken up again.

Andrew turned around. "Are you all right?"

More whines.

"Do you need to pee?"

He must have shaken his head.

"Delilah is going to get her maps out and decide where we're going next. Del, do you want me to park off to the side and we can get out and walk around a bit while you focus?"

"Yes, that should work."

"We won't go far," he promised, his voice a bit growly, which made her look at his blue eyes and think about the night before. And think about making love with a light on. And suddenly the only awkwardness was about lusting for each other in front of his son.

He sucked in a big breath and let it out slowly. Then he leaned in and kissed her quickly on the lips before driving the car across the potholed parking lots of closed stores and up to a gas station and climbing out, handing her the keys and locking the doors after taking Troy out of his seat.

Andrew carried Troy around the parking lot for a few minutes in the wet, gray cold, then took him into the grimy convenience store to look around. Troy was hyper-vigilant out of the corner of his eye, checking out absolutely everything while Andrew kept an eye on the teenager who was behind the counter.

A couple minutes in, the teen said, "You gotta buy something. You can't just hang out."

Andrew raised one eyebrow. "Already bought gas."

"Where's your car, then?"

Andrew pointed at the car half-hidden by the pumps. "My wife wanted privacy to make a phone call." Why did it feel so good to call her wife? Like it was right.

"Heh," the teen sneered. "You shouldn't let women have privacy. They need to be controlled or their weaker nature will get them in trouble."

Andrew raised the other eyebrow. "How old are you?"

The kid stood up straighter and flexed his arms back like he was ready to start a fistfight. At his job. Against a man holding a child. Obviously a super cool dude. "Nineteen."

"When I was nineteen….no, even then I knew women were rational human beings." Unlike this teen. The country was going to hell and this was definitely one person who was driving a pickup on the expressway there.

But he shouldn't have said anything.

The kid's posture got even more aggressive. "You some kind of liberal? Some sheep?'

Andrew thought about it. He wasn't very political. The job didn't allow much political expression, at least. "More centrist, really. I mean, I believe in the equality of human beings and hold respect for them."

He tried to keep an easy posture like this was just a conversation, but Troy was obviously feeling the tension and whined.

"What's wrong with your kid. He a retard?"

Andrew, who'd just glanced out at the car again turned his head slowly back. "My son is brilliant and is different from you and me. And he is a child."

He looked the teen up and down and didn't say anything else.

The teenager must have had a few extra brain cells he hadn't displayed before or else good instincts, because he drew back, wary.

Andrew knew better than to turn his back or to approach. An animal backed into a corner will come out fighting. A frightened predator will attack from behind.

Troy whined once more and electricity ran through him and he shifted to wolf form. Andrew bobbled him slightly and caught his sweatpants before they hit the floor.

"Holy shit!" the teen cried, pointing at Troy. "That's one of them demon spawn. A Satan shape shifter."

Well. Time to go. Andrew glared at the kid all the way to the door. The teen was trying to get a picture, but Andrew kept Troy covered and turned his face away before the teen could point his phone. He'd spotted one surveillance camera, but thought he'd been out of sight of it most of the time. He jogged to the car, face still averted, and hastily stuffed Troy into his dog harness and latched him to the seatbelt in the back passenger seat.

Delilah watched them, blinking, her pupils still dilated from magic, but growing smaller.

"Kid in there appears to have several biases and misconceptions about human beings who differ from him, especially shifters," he said calmly as he pulled out of the parking lot and back into the hardware store lot. He glanced into his rear view and hoped the teen didn't get a picture of the license plate. "Where are we headed?"

"Into Wheeling, then south," she said promptly. "It's all I could get, but I have a vague sense of direction. The river is throwing me off."

He drove back onto the highway which would take them across a bridge and entered West Virginia. He'd been in the state a few times, but never for anything good. Of course, most places he'd been hadn't been because of something good. And he'd never been in the little point that ran up between Ohio and Pennsylvania. Blink and you're out of the state again.

"Take 250 south," Delilah said. "The junction looks hard on the map, but the signs seem pretty clear."

He wondered if it was even a city, because it looked like a small town crisscrossed by interstates. He wondered if more of the residents were as ignorant as the kid in the convenience store. Probably the kid's immediate family and peer group, but he wouldn't make assumptions about anyone else.

It burned his gut, though. He was an adult and had already been a wolf in secret, then a wolf at work, then a wolf in public. And yes, there was constant pressure building as the hellfire preachers and conspiracy theorists and various hate groups decided shifters were evil. But his son was vulnerable - more vulnerable than most kids. He couldn't carry him forever, couldn't protect him from every bully. He wondered if trying to cover up his son's nature was wrong. Then he wondered if he wanted to cover up the shifter nature or the autistic nature, because both were parts of his son. And he loved his son.

"Are you all right?" Delilah asked and Andrew realized she was talking to Troy.

He whined softly, but when she held a hand out to him awkwardly between the seats, he stopped.

"Yeah, you can shift next time we stop and we'll get you back in your clothes and in your car seat."

Andrew took the exit for 250 south and curved onto the smaller highway.

Delilah turned back to the road atlas in her lap. "OK, before we get to 470, there's an exit onto 26th Street. Then take a left onto Jacob."

"And boom, we're already out of the city," he said, pointing vaguely at the trees and hills rising to their left.

"Mostly," she agreed. "There are houses up in the hills, too. And South Wheeling along the river."

They rode in silence, even Troy settling in to look out the window. He hoped his boy wouldn't remember anything the hateful teenager at the gas station said. He'd probably hear it again and again and Andrew didn't know how to stop it from happening.

He took the 26th Street exit and turned left onto Jacob, which started out with cracks and potholes and only got worse after they passed under the interstate.

"They never recovered from the whole Rust Belt thing, did they?"

"No," he said on a sigh.

"There's these cute little houses, perfectly done up, and right next door is an empty shop with graffiti. It's a lot like Youngstown."

"Yeah," he said. "Imagine Youngstown, but remove most of the Black people and other people of color." He knew the basics of the population because he'd looked it up the night before. He hoped like hell they were in the right place and still didn't understand how they could be. Most of the time, her psychic readings could be put down to putting together clues, but unless her mom had mentioned Wheeling and specifically South Wheeling, she was definitely getting her ideas from elsewhere. The warning to Joy the paralegal had been precise, but could have been based on intuition after seeing the layout of the FBI building.

They rode in silence. "The hills are pretty, though," she said.

He chuckled. "They are." He slowed down suddenly because there was no one behind them. "And look at that house. Recently fixed up, I'd guess."

"Someone loves that house," she murmured. "I could live in that house. I wonder if they have a magic community of any sort."

He sped up to the speed limit again and didn't answer. He had friends who came from towns like this one. Some had left seeking school or work or just a way out of a small town. Not many went back.

"Let me know where we're going next," he said.

"I'm hoping to get inspiration," she said and leaned down to pick up her big handbag and take out the box with her cards. She took them out and cut them several times. She fanned them out and picked one seemingly at random. "Justice," she whispered. "She's close."

She set Justice on her lap and took another. "Eight of Swords."

She lifted the card and held it to her eyes like she had done with a card over the map last night. The electricity of magic gathered around her and through her, making the hair on his arms stand up.

"There," she whispered. "There. Across the side street from the funeral parlor with the green trim. In that closed shop. Is it closed because it's Sunday morning?"

"I don't know," he said.

"No, it's closed closed. Half the windows are boarded up. Why aren't you stopping?" she asked, turning to glare at him.

"Because I'm not leading an assault on mobsters or going into god knows what with one handgun, a psychic, and a five year old," he answered. "We'll go to the local Bureau and I'll call in backup."

"Oh, sorry. That makes sense."

"Any idea of what we're going into? How many people? What sort of weapons?"

Out of the corner of his eye, he could see her shake her head. "I'll have to think about it. She's being hidden now and not hiding herself, but it feels weird. Mom's fading in and out, but she's healthy. Something's interfering with her magic."

Chapter Twenty-Two

"WITHOUT GOING INTO TOO much detail, Miss, the two offices in town have different purposes."

Ferguson, the agent from the local Bureau - sorry, *one of* the local Bureaus - had latched onto Delilah with near-ferocity as soon as they came in the door. He had a drawling accent about like her cousin-in-law's when he was talking to family and friends and locals, so she'd asked and he'd said he was from Montana. But he kept addressing his questions and asides to her and not to Andrew, which while it made her an equal in the investigation, also felt a little creepy, especially as he followed her around the conference room and kept glancing at her chest.

She sidled closer to Andrew and set a hand on his arm as she set a cup and plate for him on the long table. They'd been there almost two hours and the need to reach her mom was burning only slightly brighter than her need to stay away from this Ferguson guy. He was untrustworthy, but she couldn't tell if it was his stalker vibe or if there was something else.

The other agent who'd been called into the office on a Sunday morning, Gaines, was an older man and completely taciturn, but his aura felt like he was weighing everyone up and they were all a great disappointment.

"Got one more agent coming in," Gaines said with a scrunching of his eyebrows at his phone. This time, Del heard the New York/New Jersey accent loud and clear.

"And some local police, if-slash-when we go into the building?" Andrew asked, finally sitting down and settling Troy, thankfully back in boy form, on his lap.

Ferguson shrugged, very aw shucks. "Aw, we can take care of it."

Andrew opened his mouth, probably to point out again that this was organized crime and not a couple of guys on a tear.

"How do you know your mother's in there and is being held against her will?" Gaines asked.

Delilah narrowed her eyes and focused on his aura. Definitely suspicious and didn't believe in any of this. She closed her eyes and thought for a moment. Full psychic? Or the rational explanation? Though she didn't have a rational explanation because pinpointing her loved one's location using tarot cards and a twenty-year-old map didn't have a rational explanation.

She opened her eyes to see Ferguson watching her with a little sneer. He was trying to flirt. Or to creep on her. Maybe he didn't know the difference.

She decided to go full mystic. "I read it in the cards, of course," she said airily.

Ferguson looked confused for a moment, then the flirt was definitely gone as he said, "Miller said you were a psychic. I don't believe in any of that."

Andrew took this as his opening into the conversation. "Do you believe in shifters? And did you read about the op a couple years ago where the perps were identified because an aura reader saw them at night? I know there was a white paper on it and similar incidents."

Del thought of Aura, Lac's girlfriend, who was a powerful aura reader and wondered if she'd been the one he was mentioning.

"It's all magic," Andrew went on. "All on the same spectrum. Some of it is instinct and putting together half-remembered hints and context clues, but there was no way for Delilah to know yesterday that the paralegal looking at her mom's evidence was unsafe in her own office or the loading dock at the opposite side of the Bureau in Cleveland was where the paralegal should enter. Maybe some of it was context, but even if you can call it intuition, it's damn good intuition. Because there was someone from this same gang we're going against today who fired into a federal compound this morning. I bet you already had word about that."

Gaines sighed wearily.

Miller sat forward, sliding Troy to one side. "So One: you need to believe Delilah, and Two: we're going to need more than the three of us and one agent who is on their way in."

Her sense of rightness with this man was glowing inside her. He'd defended her. Sure, he thought some of her insights were from context clues, but he believed intuition was a real thing.

Her phone rang, which surprised her, since no one had called this phone since she'd gotten it. She looked down at it and saw it was a Cleveland number, but since she hadn't programmed numbers into it, she couldn't remember who it was. She hoped it wasn't about her car's extended warranty or someone asking for donations, but she answered.

"Delilah, this is your Aunt Moira."

She smiled at Andrew. "Just a minute, my psychic family is contacting me."

Andrew looked suspicious, but she had been up front about giving her family this number.

"I have to take this," she said and got up to walk to the other side of the room. The shifters could hear her. Probably the others, too.

"Aunt Moira, is something wrong?"

"Not with us, dear. We're safe. Someone broke into Serena's house yesterday and got past the alarms. Not much was taken and it doesn't look too bad, but we'll have to talk about it later. Your grandmother has a message. She's staying with us until this blows over."

Her grandmother didn't like telephones of any sort and made any nearby family members make calls for her. Del had never been sure if it was a phobia or an affectation that had taken on a life of its own. "Go on, Aunt Moira."

She heard her grandmother talking in the background, but the sound was muffled.

"She says there are five men and one woman with your mother, but to go in soon or they will move her. It's one of the men who's the magic user."

There was a magic user? Sure, she'd thought there might be, but Grandmother was seldom wrong.

More muffled speech.

"You have to go with them to contain his magic. Serena's been shielding herself over the last few days and she's too tired."

"But someone has to stay with the boy," Del said.

Andrew had clearly heard every word and looked grim.

A knock sounded at the door and in came Agent Buho and a small, blonde woman in khakis and an FBI windbreaker who was clearly very powerful in non-magical ways and also clearly bonded with Buho.

Andrew suddenly looked less grim.

"Mother says Strickland can organize this. And I should speak with her," Aunt Moira said.

The shifters in the room turned their heads toward Del in confusion. Strickland looked over as well, probably following their lead. Ferguson looked pissed off and Gaines looked resigned, but nearly catatonic. She thought it might be rude to ask why he didn't just retire.

"Delilah Woods," Agent Strickland stated, holding out her hand to shake. "Agent Strickland from the Shifter Task Force. Miller's friend."

Delilah took her hand and confirmed the strength and the friendship with Miller. "My aunt and grandmother want to talk to you," she said and held out the phone. "Well, you'll talk to my aunt, but my grandmother's telling her what to say."

Strickland's eyebrows went up, but she took the phone. "Moira Woods," she stated, once again not surprised by who was turning up uninvited. "I met your daughter Eloisa a couple of times. How can I help you?"

"I don't see why all these agents turned up here." Ferguson had started bitching. "We had it under control."

"Shifter Task Force," said Buho. "Our mandate covers magic users."

The door opened again and in came Beth Ogden and a dark-haired man Delilah had last seen in the chaos of a scrub forest in Nevada during a wild battle between shifters and kidnapping bigots, though he'd been bald then. There were swords and guns involved and a great deal of protective magic. She remembered his name: Alex Three Feathers, FBI Special Agent, previously undercover, now on the Shifter Task Force with his half-brother, Andrew Miller. Oh, and cousin of Lac Three Feathers, who walked in the door right behind him.

Beth waved at her, but crossed to where Miller was getting to his feet and greeted Troy first. She held out her arms and Troy leaned toward her. She caught him deftly and gathered him close. He wouldn't allow hugs, but was happy to be carried around. Alex followed her, greeting Andrew with a firm handshake. Andrew didn't allow hugs either, not even from his half-brother.

Lac, though, made a beeline for the corner where Del stood with Strickland. She gave him a quick hug, conscious as before of how attractive he was, but how he was not at all her type. "You just left town a few days ago."

"I came back and they let me tag along," he said with a smile, but there was anger below it.

"Let's talk after this. I'm getting a feeling of urgency and Grandmother is too, apparently."

Strickland was listening to Delilah's phone while taking notes on her own phone.

Ferguson's voice was raised in a whine when another agent entered, a woman of maybe twenty-five with short, choppy dark hair, apparent muscles under her dark dress pants and FBI windbreaker. Not magic, but strong like Strickland with a great hunger to prove herself.

"Katie, it's about time you got here. These assholes showed up and are taking it out of our hands and want us to be their backup."

'Katie' winced as she scanned the room, clocking the groups of agents and civilians and the small child. Her eyes fixed on Strickland who was just hanging up and who nodded a greeting. "Agent Kaitlyn Trent, good to see you."

Agent Trent was a much better name. She came to them and shook Strickland's hand. Strickland introduced them with, "This is Delilah Woods, the vic's daughter. She's got major premonitory skills and pinpointed the location where her mother's being held."

Agent Strickland clapped her hands and raised her voice, "There's a strong magic user inside messing with the vic's powers, so we need Ms. Woods along to push back. We need everyone suited up and armed in five minutes. Unless you're not an FBI agent, in which case, you get protective gear and no weapons." She glanced at Lac and said, "Teeth and claws only if necessary. You're backup, not an agent."

He nodded, sour anger rising.

Gaines, for all his apparent catatonia, had already brought in bulletproof vests and helmets for anyone who hadn't brought their own.

Strickland looked at Beth, who was speaking softly, but animatedly to Troy. "We're going to leave Dr. Ogden and Troy here." She looked around the room. "We don't have enough people as it is and we'll be bringing in two civilians who need backup. Sorry, Lac, but you're still a civilian no matter how much school you've had. But I've been told we need to leave them a guard. Shit."

Agent Gaines handed Delilah a heavy black vest and Agent Trent demonstrated how to put it on.

Gaines cleared his throat. "As much as I would enjoy sneaking around an old, empty building with gangsters shooting at me, I might let you convince me to stay behind."

Strickland considered him for a moment. "Are you sure? You've got a talent for keeping a team together."

Gaines shook his head. "Yeah, well, I used to be an adventurer."

Strickland blinked. "When do you retire?"

Gaines smiled for the first time since Delilah had seen him and he looked younger, but not by much. "Couple months. And I hate the thing in movies where the guy's about to retire and he gets killed. I mean, I'll go in if you need me, but making friends with a small child seems easier on my nerves."

Del had the feeling the older man had grandchildren and would lay down his life for Troy. Loyal all the way through, but tired.

"Take your cue from Dr. Ogden with him," Andrew said from behind Del's right shoulder. He turned to Strickland and said, "Dare I ask why the organized crime squad isn't here?"

She wrinkled her nose. "They've got the data from the paralegal and say there's no proof anything's wrong other than Serena Woods not wanting to deal directly with them."

Andrew tipped his head. "Yeah, that sounds like Quentin all right. Some of the others were intrigued by the magic aspect and wanted to investigate it. But no one else on his team was consulted, I bet."

Strickland glowered. "You'd win that bet."

She clapped her hands again. "OK, anyone who's not ready better scramble. One minute and we're in the cars."

Luckily, they were all nearly ready and Gaines was signing out firearms. "He's really good at this," Del murmured. "His aura says he's tired, but he's on top of this stuff."

Strickland nodded. "He's a bit of a legend. He's got an instinct for the work. Now that I think about it, it's a sixth sense sort of thing." She smiled. "Maybe not quite to magic levels, but definitely there."

Ferguson got loud at Buho about civilians and people who don't take orders.

"That one is not a legend," Strickland said and rubbed her forehead. "Thinks he runs this place, stares at women's boobs, generally a pain in the ass sort of guy. They warned me about him when I said I was coming to Wheeling."

"Yeah, he stared at mine. I get a creepy vibe. He also gets people's names wrong," Del said.

Agent Trent strode up to them again. "Do you even go by Katie?" Del asked her.

Trent rolled her eyes. "My dad is the only one allowed to call me that. And I'm sorry I'm late."

Del snorted. "You're not late. You got a call twenty minutes ago and I'm impressed at your speed."

Strickland took Agent Trent's arm and they started toward the door, talking with their heads close together. Trent's aura said she was serious about this job, but also dancing around inside her head that she got to work with Strickland, who, Del guessed, was a legend as well.

Andrew set his hand on Del's back and spoke softly into her ear. Over her own shivers and melting, she heard him say, "I've got a good feeling about this. I think we're going in together, you and me and someone to guard our backs, as we break through to your mom."

"Who do we get at our back?"

"Not sure. Since I'm FBI and you're the witch, it could be anyone. Strickland will do the teams, if you have any preferences, ask her."

"Hmmm. Well. I'd like Lac to do it because I know him, but you probably want an armed agent with us and I get good vibes from your friends and brother. In a nutshell: anyone but Ferguson."

"OK, does everyone have the pictures of Serena Woods? And does everyone have an earpiece?" Strickland asked as she strode out behind them. Gaines hustled to keep up, little bags with transponders and earpieces in them. He handed them to all the FBI agents and Strickland gave the channel.

"The core of the gang, the bosses and a lot of the members are from Slovakia and Czechia. There's a significant number from other East European countries, so the older ones especially speak Russian as their lingua franca. Anyone speak Slovak, Czech or Russian? No? A little bit?"

Miller and Ferguson's hands went up and they both muttered "Russian."

"Alex with Miller," she said. "No bickering."

Alex grinned and rubbed his hands together.

"Non-Bureau stay with your Bureau companion. Non-shifter stay with your shifter. Delilah, that means you and Miller, Three Feathers is second string."

Alex grimaced. "Why do I always have to be second string?" But his eyes and aura told her he thought it was funny and he wiggled his eyebrows at Del. She knew he would back them up one hundred percent.

"Lac with Ferguson. You stay with Ferguson, Little Three Feathers."

Snorts from around the room and a guffaw from Alex who was, she supposed Big Three Feathers. Lac covered his face. Ferguson looked disgusted, which had become his default now he wasn't trying to look down her shirt.

"That leaves Buho with Trent. Trent, take Buho's lead. We've done a lot of these together and you're fairly new. And Buho's a shifter, so rely on his vision and hearing. If he needs to shift and fly, gather up his earpiece and sidearm."

Agent Trent nodded seriously. "Keep control of communications and weapons. Yes."

"Exactly." Strickland favored her with a strained smile, then she and Buho shared a long look. One that said, *Be careful, be safe, I love you.*

Del wondered if everyone knew about them being together and if there were rules in the Bureau about it.

"Ferguson, same goes for you and Lac. He doesn't fly, but he might need to shift."

Ferguson gave a tiny, disrespectful jerk of his head in acknowledgment.

"Ms. Woods?"

Del nodded and gave Agent Strickland a thumbs-up and went to pet Troy one more time and give him some calming vibes before they left him behind.

"Each team in a separate car." She assigned them doors to the locked building - a fire escape and a door on the top floor for Buho and Trent – and wished them luck.

Chapter Twenty-Three

DEL WAS GLAD FOR Andrew's solid presence beside her, driving her car, but was also glad for Alex's jokes from the back seat. She could feel he was gathering his intensity around him and was taking this seriously, in spite of his light tone. She remembered glimpsing his aura and hearing stories about him from a few years before in Nevada and realized he'd been at the end of his rope back then. He probably had been burning out until he met Beth.

She pulled out her deck of cards and flipped a few idly. Justice again, and some minor arcana. She closed her eyes and hummed softly to herself, finger on the Justice card. Visions came in waves, tracking through every possible outcome in her mind and watching the assault end with blood and without, with her mom free and with her in the back of a van being driven away. Always, there was a dark space, an unknown person who was at the center of the mobsters.

The witch, Andrew had called this unknown person. Her family preferred magic user or some other slightly euphemistic name, but yes, witch was fine, especially when talking about a psychic person who was doing evil. She was trying to not think of him as a warlock, which was a huge insult for normal magic users. She had a sense of maleness from the witch, but no more. Even magic users could conceivably sub-contract their services, but she felt she would draw the line far before mobsters and kidnapping, but that was her. And she had a sense this guy loved his work.

She took a deep breath and dug deeper into the scenarios scrolling through her head. She flipped up the Magician card, reversed. Yes, evil wizard. It had been literal all along. She closed her eyes again.

"Tell them to stick together like glue," she said, then opened her eyes and realized she'd interrupted a story Alex was telling about home repairs.

"All right." Andrew, definitely in Agent Miller mode, clicked on his earpiece and told the whole team.

"The only way we're going to win this is if everyone stays with their partner. The three of us together, of course."

Andrew relayed the information, then muted his mic. "No jokes about threesomes, Alex?"

Alex snorted from where he sat in the back, wedged between the empty car seat and the passenger-side door. "Nah, you're too newly together for me to joke about it. We've got work to do and I'll tease you after."

Del put all her cards except Justice back in their silk scarf and back in the box and latched them in. She handed Alex her handbag to stow under her seat because she couldn't get it there past the little bar to adjust the seat.

She tucked the card into her bra where it dug into the side of one boob until she adjusted it just right. She hoped her sweat and body oils wouldn't ruin the card, but she was holding it as a talisman. *Mom. Andrew. Justice.* She took a deep breath and visualized the outcomes she wanted, holding them close and planning out what spells she might use. She touched Andrew softly, giving him a layer of protection from magic. Then she turned around and asked Alex to hold out his hand and she gave him the same.

"Can you give us that silence and look-away that your cousin did for me?" Alex asked. "I walked right out from under ten people's noses in Nevada."

She shook her head. "I do silence well and look-away moderately, but I can't specify that I'll still be able to see and hear you. We could lose touch with each other, which would be a mess."

"Yeah," Alex sighed. "My mom mostly does premonitions, but she handles the emotional spells well. Like projecting calm and fear and a sense of awe of her power. Though the latter is maybe a combo of the first two. Sort of: 'Fear me, for I am your goddess.'"

They pulled up into the funeral home parking lot across the street, just a family coming to pay their respects to the honored dead, right? She shivered and shoved the thought out of her head. No one was going to die.

Andrew parked the car on the opposite side of the funeral home from the building they were going into, sliding between a pickup truck and a rusty hatchback. It was a gray, gross day and felt like it was going to rain or snow. Or sleet, which would be fun. It was still daylight, though, and anyone looking out a window would see them strolling across the street.

"Buho's in with Trent," Andrew relayed from the earpiece. "Let's get in position."

They waited with their backs against the wall of the funeral home.

"Earpiece off," Andrew whispered and he and Alex hit a button.

There was a muffled boom and the rat-a-tat-tat of fireworks from the dingy brick building across the street.

"Distraction ongoing. Earpiece on," Alex said.

They ducked behind another parked car in the lot, probably a mortician's or maybe a grieving relative's. Del silently apologized for disturbing their peace as they scurried across the street.

Andrew had never, ever liked taking civilians into a crime scene. He'd had enough experience with expert witnesses and CSI teams, some of whom had no fighting skills or even much situational awareness.

It was completely different in a really bad way when it was his own... His own whatever Delilah was to him after a few days together, a few kisses, and one blissful make-out session.

He pushed thoughts of how vulnerable and soft and warm she was out of his mind and considered her like any other civilian magic user. He was glad they'd put a bulletproof vest on her, but wanted her in full armor. And bubble wrap. And whatever it took to ward off bad magic. He had wanted to ask what card she'd put in her shirt and why, but they'd run out of time. That was a conversation for later. Because there damn well would be a later.

Alex unlocked the back door and they slipped in. There were distant running footsteps, hopefully going upstairs to be stopped by Buho and Trent. The plan was to lock as many mobsters in the little store rooms upstairs until the police backup showed. They needed a lot more people and they were all in a lot of danger.

Right. Delilah's grandma had said there were six people holding her daughter hostage. Two or three upstairs. Three or four left down.

The next boom and crackle meant Lac had set off the fireworks inside the front door and that fucker Ferguson hadn't warned them to turn off their earpieces. Strickland scolded him in a whisper as Alex and he both grabbed their ears.

Delilah had startled, but without an earpiece and without shifter hearing, she was fine. Andrew's left ear was deaf for the time being, which sucked.

Delilah, though, reached up and touched his temple and pulled some of the pain out, though his ear was still ringing slightly. She touched Alex's temple, too and his half-brother nodded his thanks.

There was shouting in what he assumed was Slovak. Footsteps pounded, then the dreaded gunfire sounded from the front of the building.

A door banged upstairs and Buho whispered. "Got two of them cornered."

Trent said, "Pulling the tables in front of the door. For what good it will do."

"It might hold them for a couple minutes," said Buho. "This place has flimsy locks."

Ferguson reported he and Lac were OK, though they were cornered in a stairwell. Two men and a woman were pounding on their door, which they had wedged shut and were holding.

As Strickland told Ferguson and Lac to go upstairs, their small group proceeded down a narrow hallway, past the back office and restrooms and broom closet of the lamp shop that had once been in the building. Not for a long time, judging by the dirt and bird nests.

If Andrew had a hostage, he'd hold her in one of these smaller rooms, not out in the open shop space, surrounded by windows, albeit windows with bars and boards.

He held up a hand and they stopped. He whispered to Delilah, "Why would they hold your mom in the store and not in an office? Is it a magic thing?"

She shook her head, looking worried. "Could be. But other than protective circles and the like, I don't know why they'd choose the open space."

A distant door banged open and a woman shouted in what sounded more like Russian than Slovak as footsteps pounded up the stairs at the front of the building.

"OK, so you should have just one kidnapper and our vic downstairs," Strickland said, her voice as calm and steady as every other op they'd done together. As long as she didn't get pissed off or someone got hurt, she always sounded perfect and direct and serious.

"Witch?" Alex asked.

"Don't know," Strickland answered. "I'm assuming the witch is guarding the hostage, but for all I know, she's throwing spells at Lac and Ferguson. Ferguson, report."

Silence on the headsets.

"Ferguson."

Still silence.

There hadn't been more shots, so the other conclusion was that Ferguson's mic was off or he wasn't able to talk. Since there weren't background noises or voices, they were going with mic off. That fucker.

"Lac had better be OK," Alex murmured.

The whole building was silent.

Way too silent.

Andrew pointed his fiber optic camera around the corner and checked out the room, sweeping from left to right and watching it on the tiny screen. The picture was blurrier than it should have been and there was a large rectangular object blocking most of the view, but two people were visible, one sitting and one standing nearby.

"Two in the main room," he whispered into the mic, but he got only static in reply.

Alex touched his arm and when he turned, he saw Del holding onto Alex's sleeve.

She mouthed, "Silence spell."

Yeah, that made sense, now he thought about it. He couldn't hear footsteps or doors or cars going by. He only heard the tiny, soft whistle of tinnitus in his left ear that he only ever heard late at night when he was trying to sleep. His own whisper was inaudible to himself when he said, "Fuck."

Delilah was almost surprised she could move, given the completeness of the silence around her. She supposed the good thing was that the person who was throwing this spell wouldn't be able to hear her, either, though with a bit of a look away, he would be hard to find.

This was definitely a masculine spell, it had the feeling of maleness about it. And no, she could never explain what she meant by that. Hell, she'd known friends were trans or non-binary before they came out to her. She'd told a few customers and some had been relieved while others had been immensely offended.

Anyway, whether born male or female, the inside of the witch in question was male.

She held onto Andrew and reached behind them to Alex. She said, "The witch is a man," slowly and clearly. The words were inaudible, but she enunciated them again, pointing toward the closed door, until both men with her nodded.

"Good," she said and winced because being completely deaf was extra annoying when the people around you were, too. "Hold hands and I'll lead."

Well, they understood, but weren't happy. Andrew shook his head and pointed at himself. Alex shook a finger and pointed at himself. Andrew pulled out his little camera and she nodded. Yes, he could look, but she had to enter first.

"Magic," she said. "It has to be me."

She pumped more protection into their arms, but didn't have a specific thing for magical protection. She supposed it was all she could do and she felt it draining her energy, so she stopped.

She led the way, holding Andrew's hand. She looked back when she reached the door and waited until Alex and Andrew were holding hands, too, before reaching out, putting a look-away spell on the door, and swinging it open.

Nothing happened. Nothing she could hear, anyway.

Andrew tugged at her hand and she looked back to see him crouching down. He duck-walked to the door and pulled out the camera to look around the corner. He frowned deeply, then scowled. He held his viewer up and it showed only static. He tapped at the screen, but still static.

He pointed two fingers at his own eyes and then through the door from a crouched position and she crouched too. Her thighs and knees couldn't handle much of this, so instead of duck-walking over, she stood again, feeling the burn, and crouched right next to the door. She went down on one knee because honestly, she was about to fall over. She put a look-away on herself, leaned her head out, saw her mom on a chair looking right at her, then pulled back.

"Mom," she mouthed.

The men nodded. Andrew did the look gesture again.

She hadn't seen anyone else, but she hadn't looked around the whole room. She stayed back from the door as she looked as far to the right as she could, then whipped out and around, still not seeing anyone in the semi-darkness other than her mom, who waved for her to get back and looked pointedly over her shoulder. Del completed the circuit and no one was to the left along the wall. There was a ten foot long checkout counter and she couldn't see much of the room past it. For all she knew, there was someone crouching right behind it, waiting for them. Except her mom had looked over her shoulder.

She pulled back. "I can't see him," she said, still silently. Then took the look away off herself because Andrew and Alex were staring blankly at where they probably could barely tell she was and certainly weren't reading her lips. She repeated herself. "Mom is out there and looked behind herself." She accompanied this with hand gestures they might or might not have understood.

She'd never been good at charades. *First word, sounds like the kidnapper is behind me.*

She mimed, Don't let go, and put a look-away on all three of them as she held Andrew's hand tightly. She could sort of see them, since it was her spell and she knew where they were and it looked like they were holding hands with each other, so she inched forward.

Her mom waved at her to go back again, but she shook her head.

They bobbed through the door, still down near the floor and she pulled them toward the left side of the checkout counter, where they ducked down. They weren't much better off, but they were in the room.

She looked at the others and realized Alex had dropped Andrew's hand and had a gun out. He shook his head and mouthed and gestured, "I see nobody."

She blinked. Maybe her mom had a look-away on her, but since it was her mom, she was the only one who could see her? She pointed at Alex. "No gun. You might shoot Mom."

He nodded, but didn't put away the gun.

She looked at Andrew in alarm and saw he had his out, too. "I see nobody."

She narrowed her eyes, trembling slightly, afraid they might shoot her mom. She realized she could see their auras as clearly as ever in this shadowy place. Which probably meant she could see the witch if she focused. She crawled to the end of the counter and peeked around, feeling Andrew's hand on her leg, trying to pull her back. She took her scan more slowly, this time, looking for ripples and auras that could indicate a hidden person.

She saw her mom, who turned her head toward her again and glared with exasperation, which was her mom's default expression around Del. She felt a great rush of affection. Her mom pointedly looked behind her toward the opposite corner and Del narrowed her eyes to slits. Yes, there was the man. He wasn't very tall and was rather thin, but otherwise, she couldn't really tell anything about him at all. But yes, he was radiating power, but pulling it ruthlessly toward himself.

Surely, all this silence and invisibility was wearing him out. Maybe they should sit tight and let him exhaust himself.

But then, her mother pointed at the man and mimed him pulling something from her chest. She looked like she was about to fall over from exhaustion and was having trouble breathing.

Del pulled back and grabbed Andrew's arm. "He's pulling her life force."

Andrew shook his head, looking at her mouth, not understanding. She copied her mom's movements and he looked shocked. Alex swore. He must know about people sharing magic. Eloisa said Aura had shared her magic to help heal Alex, so he had firsthand experience, at least on the receiving end.

She peeked out again and the witch hadn't moved, but her mom slouched sideways. Del hadn't noticed her mom was tied to her chair and wanted to go smack the witch for it.

"He's going to kill her unless we do something," she said and her voice sounded like a distant echo, but at least it had sound. "He's draining her. He's not even touching her and he's draining her life out of her."

Andrew leaned over and conferred with Alex now that they could hear each other.

"He was in the back corner, but he might have moved," she said and crept over to peek again.

Then with a suddenness which made them all startle, the sound came back.

"Mom!" Del cried out, thinking maybe her mom had died.

She started to stand up to check, but Andrew grabbed her arm and pointed above them to where a handsome, blond man in a blue, fuzzy sweater leaned on the checkout counter.

"Not your mother," he said with a thick accent. "She is alive, but asleep for now. I still control her and have access to her powers. There is only me."

Chapter Twenty-Four

Andrew pointed his handgun at the man and he saw Alex out of the corner of his eye, also aiming at the man's head. The man rolled pale blue eyes and uttered a few words in Russian and Andrew felt his hand freeze as his pistol grew hot. He managed to unclench his fingers and drop the weapon before it burned him, but his skin was red and he had a blister coming up on his right thumb.

Alex swore loudly and cradled his hand to his belly.

"So vulgar, these shifters," said the witch with disdain and with that particular way of pronouncing all the Ls and Rs in the back of the throat that so many Russians and Eastern Europeans had. "Wolfs, no?"

They didn't answer, but Alex cussed again and bent over his hand as if he'd gotten a lot more than a blister and some discomfort.

The witch looked at Delilah, appraising her body, and Andrew wanted to murder him.

"I think you have power not so good as your mother? It has been watery, no? Watered. Thin."

Delilah frowned and her eyes cut away from this asshole, looking hurt.

"I am from long line of witches and wizards, men and women. We do not water down. We know each other and when we have baby, we have baby with other witch." His gaze dropped to Delilah's breasts, though she had her bulletproof vest on, which was also leer-proof, luckily for this asshole's eyes.

Andrew slid closer to Delilah. Or tried and failed, because his legs were frozen in place.

"How did you do this to my mother?" Delilah asked. She blinked several times and came to some sort of decision. "It's very impressive magic."

The witch shook his head. "Is simple. Very basic magic of protection, only also of control. You have very poor training. Of course, you have only little magic. You are little hedge witch."

Delilah leaned out and looked at her mom and whatever she saw both satisfied her and pissed her off. "A salt circle? Really?"

"Is more than salt, but yes, salt is part." The man see-sawed his hand in a so-so gesture.

"The silence was very impressive," Delilah said, going for flattery again.

The man smiled and preened. "Is one of my special spells. I am very good with silence and with freezing."

Yeah, Andrew could attest to that.

"And with sharing others' power. I mean, sharing them with me, do you see?"

Delilah leaned out to look at her mother again, so Andrew supposed she did see. He still hadn't seen what state Serena Woods was in, but based on Delilah's grim expression, it wasn't good.

"I do not want to use her power to stop you from saving her, because she will be dead and I am not necromancer." He laughed at his own disgusting joke.

Delilah blinked several times, but didn't even smile. Perhaps she hadn't heard of any real life necromancers, either. Andrew shivered.

"I think I put you in circle, too. Not so powerful, but enough power. Shifters are less good sources of power, and they beat themselves to death on the walls when you cage them. Is not worth effort, I drain them fast if I am working on a project."

And the dude was talking shop with Delilah about how he murdered shifters for their magic.

"If I have all four of you and the ones upstairs, it will be a battery. A very nice experiment."

Delilah wrinkled her nose. "Right. Not nice. So where's your boss? The Slovakian mobster who hired you. We need to talk to him to get my mom free, right?"

The witch's eyes narrowed and Andrew could feel a surge of anger in the charged air. "I do not have boss and am not mobster. I am independent contractor. I am partner. Very good pay in protection and freezing. And in finding. You have found your mother without other clue, yes?"

She nodded. "Just with maps and cards."

He stood up straight and pointed a thumb at his own chest. "I find anyone. I am like dog, but sniffing all over world. Your mother, she hide herself very good, but I find her when contract say find her."

She glanced at Andrew, stymied.

He said, "So your 'partner,'" he did the finger quotes and everything, "does he know it's too late and the FBI has the data?"

"He knows because I tell him. Serena, she said you would have turned it in by now." He sneered at Andrew, but smiled smugly at Delilah. "He say she is useless now, but I keep as many witches and shifters as I want. He want his people out. Before they go, before I go, you arrive. Is good those clumsy idiots did not drive you off the road, no?"

Delilah's grandma had been right and they had to move right away. On the other hand, they could have stopped the moving cars with fleeing mobsters. Who were, apparently responsible for trying to make her crash on the highway after visiting RFB Inc. with Lac. The puzzle pieces were falling into place in Andrew's mind.

Even so, maybe they should have been just a bit slower, because right now they were caught in a trap instead of chasing cars through the streets of South Wheeling.

There was a crash from the stairwell in the corner and something thumped against the door, then gunshots blasted.

Delilah just wished her mom had told her about this whole Slovak mob and going into hiding and whatever. If she had known, maybe they could have rescued her sooner without being here in freaking West Virginia, in a condemned building with mobsters with guns and a freaking evil magic user.

Delilah reached out with her mind, glanced off of Crazy Warlock-ovitch's shell, touched her mother's aura to be sure she was still alive, then scanned out further. Lac, Buho, Trent, five unknown minds. She nudged Andrew and whispered, "I can't sense Ferguson."

He blinked at her twice. "You can sense everyone else?"

"In the building, yes. It's the maximum of my radius. Do you think he's dead? Or in a corner where I don't see him?" She turned to the evil bastard, who was listening with his head tipped to one side. "I guess your partners have killed one of our people."

The warlock blinked his pale eyes and shrugged. "There is one person who leaved a few minutes ago. You all should have leaved. Except you, my Delilahshka. I was tasting your magic as it looked all around the building. Is very good magic, maybe not as watery as I thought. I teach you and you might be adequate."

"Are you negging me?" she asked in astonishment. She'd had guys try to tear her down in order to get in her pants, but apparently this ass was doing it to get her magic on his side. And maybe to get in her pants. Ew.

Andrew and Alex made small, matching snorts of laughter.

The asshole raised his pale eyebrows. Everything about this guy was pale, except his magic which was dark, of course. "I do not know this … are you saying nagging? I know nagging, yes. I am not nagging, I am telling."

She didn't think it was worth her time to explain negging to this guy, since they had much bigger problems. The idea that he would try to breed magic to magic made her want to puke.

"I speak many languages, but English is not of my favorites. Pronunciation is too…" he waved one hand to demonstrate whatever he wanted to say.

She had to agree English pronunciation was kind of a mess, but it generally worked for her purposes.

Another crash and thump in the stairwell and someone ran overhead. The witch sighed in the most put-upon manner she had seen since high school drama class. "I must make sure my partners are safe. My contract says to protect them. We do not have time to talk now, my little one."

And suddenly she was locked in place. And then a voice, the asshole's voice, told her to get up and walk to her mother. She couldn't stop herself as she stood and walked and sat on the floor. Then everything went dark.

Andrew could only watch as Delilah stood and walked past him like a marionette, shuddered as she stepped over a spot on the floor, then collapsed into a heap beside her mother's chair. He could see her breathing. It felt like the silence had earlier, this freezing, only he could hear more crashing from upstairs and his own heartbeat and breathing, he just couldn't do anything. And this powerful magic user was going to make Delilah his student whether she wanted it or not. And, if he understood correctly, make her the mother of his children.

Alex grunted beside him, but Andrew couldn't turn his head and had to assume he was just as frozen.

Fucking hell.

A door, probably the stairwell one, but he couldn't see it from where they sat behind the counter, banged against the wall and there was a sound of scuffling and fists punching. He hoped his team was winning, but they wouldn't be for long if they came into this room with this psychopath who could freeze them with a thought and drain their life out. Andrew tried to shout out, to tell them to run away, but the wizard yelled one word, probably whatever his language for "Stop!" and two bodies thumped to the floor.

There was another crash upstairs and two more shots were fired.

Maybe it was because this fucker was trying to freeze too many people at once without having them in his magic circles, but Andrew found he could turn his head now. Alex was twitching his hand, which had a red mark across the palm. As Andrew watched, the hand grew claws and fur and then faded back to human, his burn mark vaguely pink. He focused all his energy on his own hand and did the same, shifting it to a wolf's paw and back, healing the burn. He usually just lived with it until he could shift again.

"What is this magic you are doing?" asked the evil bastard, appearing above the counter again. "I feel magic happening, but you are not shifted. Maybe you try to escape?"

It wasn't like they could answer, so the man shrugged and walked in a circle around them, squeezing between them and the checkout counter, pouring from a little bucket, salt crystals mixed with something shiny as he sang a little song to himself in a language Andrew didn't recognize. The man stepped out of the ring and crouched down to touch it with one finger and the air snapped shut around them.

Beth would take care of Troy, Andrew thought as the pressure increased on his mind to the point of pain. He'd changed his will to make Alex and Beth the boy's guardians, hoping his son would never have to see his bitch grandma again. She'd sent papers about a hearing the week before and Andrew was afraid she would gain custody if anything happened to him.

Poor Troy had lost his mother already and was about to lose his dad. And Delilah. And his Uncle Alex.

And Delilah would mourn him, if she survived. He wondered if this witch could brainwash her and bend her to his will. Maybe if she survived, she could raise Troy.

Troy!

And he passed out.

Chapter Twenty-Five

"Awake!" boomed a voice inside her head and Delilah gasped to alertness. Her head was pounding like the worst hangover ever and she'd had some doozies back in her teens and early twenties. She was lying on a cold, hard tiled floor. She pushed herself up and saw it was filthy, so she was too, now. Something in her bra was digging into her cleavage and she wanted it to stop. Maybe she'd broken the underwire. But she had on a thick vest thing. What the hell?

She brought her legs up under her, feeling the ache in every muscle as she bumped into someone.

She startled, but turned to see her mom, still tied to the chair and flopped sideways, but just opening her glassy eyes. "Del," she groaned. "Delilah."

Del shook her head to try to clear the cobwebs.

She was in an abandoned shop in West Virginia. Her mom was being held captive and now, so was she. She set a hand on her mom's knee. "I'm here, Mom."

"Thank you," her mom rasped out. "I tried to warn you to go away, but he was blocking me."

"He has your magic tied into your cage here. He's using your magic to work his own."

Her mom nodded and made an effort to sit up straighter. It was a wobbly effort, but she basically succeeded, slouching back in her seat instead of sideways and catching her breath at the effort.

"I mean, Eloisa and Mike have been figuring out the shared magic thing for a while and we've done it a little bit, but this is a lot."

Her mom breathed slowly through her nose. "A lot. Yes."

Del checked her mother's bonds and found handcuffs on her wrists and ankles. She repositioned her mom as best she could so the cuffs wouldn't dig into her flesh and slid a finger in to rub the red marks they'd left.

"Your shifter is waking up," her mom whispered.

"Andrew!" Del spun around and bumped her knee against the jolting electric shock of the magic cage. Her mom gasped, too and she pulled back, rubbing her knee.

Andrew and Alex were both pushing themselves up to a sitting position. Alex rubbed his face with both hands and said, almost conversationally, "Holy Fuck."

Andrew picked up his gun and put it in his holster, so Alex searched around for his and spotted it outside the circle. He reached out one hand and used even worse words as he jerked back and shook his hand. "You ever grab an electric fence?" he asked Andrew, still conversationally.

"Brushed up against them a couple times," Andrew replied and he took Alex's hand and turned it over to check it out.

"Andrew," Delilah whisper-shouted. "The witch is out of the room. What a fucking drama queen."

"Language," her mom said, voice stronger than before.

Del rolled her eyes. "Are you OK?"

Alex see-sawed his hand and made a prissy face in imitation of the asshole.

She smiled. "This is a bitch of hangover."

Andrew nodded. "What's the status of the others?"

She looked up at the ceiling, but didn't hear anything, then she scanned the room. While she'd been knocked out, two more people had joined the fun in the deserted store and they were also sitting up and rubbing their heads.

"Lac?" she called out.

Lac waved at her grimly. From twenty feet away in the half light, she could see bruises and cuts on his face and his jacket had been torn off, his bulletproof vest askew.

"Who is with you?"

He shook his head. "One of the mobsters. I don't know why he's locked in here with me."

"Crazy Warlock-ovitch has no loyalty and no morals, so he'll probably murder your new friend without a second thought."

The new friend, a thin man with long, blond hair in a ponytail, stood and tried to walk out, only to jolt with the electric fence of the invisible cage and cuss in whatever languages he had available. He yelled at Lac, then sat down across from him, pointed his face toward the ceiling and started shouting for help, slipping in and out of English.

"Where's Ferguson?" she shouted over the top of the gangster, who piped down, glaring and pouting.

Lac flipped off the mobster and said, "Ferguson decided he didn't want to die here. He lasted about three minutes total before he noped out a window on the second floor. Sadly, he did not break a leg on the way down. He's probably driving around, giving himself some time before coming back with the cops and saying he couldn't do anything and now he's so sad all these shifters and witches are dead."

The mobster started shouting for help again.

Alex shouted something in a language she couldn't place at all. "As long as we're swearing in all the languages of the world," he said and leaned back on his hands. "That was Cherokee."

Lac let loose a stream of what was surely invective as he shook his fist at the sky. "Vietnamese," he said drolly.

"All I have is high school French and a couple years of Spanish in college," she said.

She startled as her mom shouted something in…German? "Danish," she said simply. "Except I only remember how to talk about the weather. I just yelled at the clouds."

Del laughed and squeezed her mom's knee.

"I feel like we're not taking this seriously enough," Lac announced.

"Oh, believe me, Little Three Feathers," said Alex. "We're taking it plenty seriously. My brother over here is about to explode."

Andrew did indeed look like he was about to have a stroke. Delilah felt guilty for even the moments of laughter.

"I have to get home to Troy," he said. "And I have to take all of you with me." He stared at Del from his circle and she felt the ghost of his kiss. "Now who has a plan? Does this asshole have any weaknesses?"

Silence as they all thought.

"He cannot touch metal," said the mobster who was locked in with Lac, his accent noticeable, but less thick than the witch's.

Del looked at him and could see his aura was dark from the things he had done and seen, but he was devoted to his family. Now, if his family was the crime boss in charge of this whole thing, then he was less wholesome. "How do you know this?"

"He made me put the cuffs on the accountant witch," he said with a shrug. "He would not touch them."

"I wonder if he cannot touch metal or if he was holding onto a spell so hard he would have lost control. Does he have trouble with doorknobs and things like that?"

"He usually pulls his shirtsleeve down, but I have seen him use his bare hand." The man sighed and slouched. "It is the only thing I can think of."

"Well, his absolute arrogance is certainly a weakness," Del's mom said. "Trouble is, he so far has been able to back it up. Monologuing like a Bond villain, though."

"Yeah," Del said, her mind whirring so fast, she closed her eyes to seek the vision teasing at the edge of her consciousness. "Keep him talking." She moved to her mom's back, carefully not getting too close to the electricity around them. "Mom, I'm going to need to read your palm. I can't get the vision to come."

"Do you think you can Read me? You can't usually."

Her mom was always blunt, but Del felt it like a slap.

Her mom took a deep breath. "I'm sorry. And I know. I'm even less useful, because this situation is sadly lacking in spreadsheets." Her mom's quick, tight smile was a balm to Del's soul. "It might be the effect of the circle creating an attachment with Crazy Warlock-ovitch, as you call him, but I've felt like there was something I should know ever since he trapped me last night."

Del nodded. "We're going to have a conversation about why you were hiding from me before, but we'll wait until we get out of here."

Her mom turned her wrist so Del could see her palm and Del took it gently, bending down as she hummed. She ran a thumb over it, noted her mom's nice, long lifeline and was reassured, then closed her eyes, feeling her mom's strength and power and straight-forward nature combined with her secrecy and paranoia. She had the vague thought that she and her mom almost never touched and they should spend more time hugging.

The vision hit her hard as she saw the answer. This connection with her mom was more intimate than they'd had in a long time. She felt her mother's justified paranoia of the last months as she gathered evidence against the Slovak gang and against other dangerous people who were embezzling.

Then she felt Warlock-ovitch notice she was using magic and she shut it down hard before he could grab it. She fell back gasping, bounced painfully with a full-body shock off the magic cage, and flopped on the floor. "Ow. Goddess damn it," she moaned.

"Delilah!" Andrew shouted and she rolled over to see him on his feet, trying to get to her and pulling back his hand with a shake and a snarl.

"I'm fine. I mean, I guess we know now what happens when I try to go through an electric fence. Shit." She pushed herself up to sitting again. "OK, so before the asshole gets back down here, we're going to try something."

In the end, it was both harder and easier than she expected. She sat in front of her mom with her hands on her mom's knees and opened her magic up. She felt the warlock grab at her power, greedy and spiky and doing something to the people upstairs that she wasn't sure she wanted to know about.

But when she and her mom focused on each other and shared their magic only with each other, opening themselves as they hadn't since Del was little and she could climb into her mother's lap and feel warm, it shoved him out, the connection with him dimming and winking off. Her mom gasped and flopped back against her hard chair.

Without her magic holding it together, the circle faded. Del kicked out and scattered a wide arc of the salt from the circle and it popped out of existence. She shivered hard and took a deep breath. She felt Warlock-ovitch scrabbling at her mind, but shoved him out and got up on shaky feet and ran to Andrew's circle.

"OK, focus on me. It helps if the two of you hold hands. Alex, focus on sharing all your magic with Andrew so the witch can't touch it."

She stared into Andrew's eyes and saw them turn to wolf and his teeth lengthen. His ears grew longer and his skull changed shape. Alex whined deep in his throat, his eyes shifting with each blink from human to wolf to cat and back again.

"OK, now connect with my magic," she whispered through gritted teeth as she shoved her visions and cards and everything toward him. And her love. Her respect for him as a man, as a protector, as a father, even as a cop in a questionable system doing his best to make the system equitable. And her hopes for Troy as an autistic person, learning to live in the world, and maybe, just maybe she could be there for him, too.

The card against her breastbone shuddered and the cage flared stronger and they all winced and struggled under its weight. Andrew and Alex shifted slowly and painfully, into wolf form, hunching down until they lost contact with each other's paws and dropped to all fours. She and Andrew held each other's eyes and barely blinked as she felt his magic pop through the invisible barrier. A feral power he barely kept under control. His protectiveness for Troy and for his team and for her. Alex's power riding along, his wildness and pain and love for Beth a feral punch.

Her ears popped and the circle lost its hold on them. She hastily obliterated a big section and leaned heavily on the checkout counter as wolf Alex and Andrew panted, still in their clothes and bulletproof vests.

Alex shifted back to human first, tugging at his clothes and undoing Velcro until he could get everything settled in the right places again. He stood up and dusted his hands off. "Well, that was a bit of a ride."

"Go unlock my mom, please," she said, eyes on Andrew as he closed his eyes and shifted to human, taking off his FBI jacket, vest, and shoulder holster before unbuckling his belt and hiking up his pants and putting his things back on.

She dragged her eyes away from Andrew's undressing and redressing and looked over to where Alex crouched behind her mom, trying a couple different handcuff keys before finding the right one.

"Handcuffs don't have keys specific to them. They're not like house keys or car keys," Andrew said as he set a hand on her hip and leaned down, his face in her hair.

"Makes sense," she said, her heart reacting to his nearness. "I mean, otherwise the same person that locked them would have to be there to unlock them and it would get tricky."

Andrew straightened up and turned toward the rest of the room. "Oh shit. Lac!"

She turned and saw Lac and the gangster both flat on the floor, convulsing.

Andrew grasped Delilah's hand and strode across the room. Or tried to stride, but his legs were weak from the power expended to break free from the witch's circle. They both wobbled and staggered across the room.

"I can feel him trying to regain control," Delilah gasped. "And he's punishing Lac."

This magical cage felt different. Andrew stepped back and squinted his eyes, trying to see with wolf vision, but it didn't help.

"Keep holding my hand," Delilah said, squeezing tightly.

After a few seconds, she said, "He's made the cage collapse on top of them so they're being held down and shocked by it constantly. Give me your gun."

"What? You have no gun training. It would be irresponsible." Good lord, he'd be in so much trouble.

"Then give me some other piece of metal to try to break the circle," she said. "They're fading. He's killing them."

Alex appeared at their side, half-carrying Serena Woods, her chair with its metal legs in the other hand. "Use this," he said, voice tense and pained.

He and Delilah turned it on its side so the metal legs were pointing toward the cage and shoved. The charge ran up the legs and through Delilah into his hand, and he jolted. Serena grabbed his other hand, her grip weak and her aura nearly fried out. She sent a jolt back through him and into Delilah and into the chair and the legs on the floor scraped into the salt. The agony speared through him, flaring for a few seconds before everything went dark and he crumpled, dragging everyone else down with him.

It was only a few seconds later, probably, and whoever he lay on shoved him off roughly. He groaned and opened his eyes, pushing himself free of the blond gangster, who was swearing in Russian. Lac opened bleary eyes, said, "Fucking hell," and passed out.

Serena Woods lay on the floor beside him, her breathing ragged. Delilah knelt on his other side, holding his hand again. Alex industriously kicked bits of salt circle all over the place, swearing heartily.

"He's coming down," whispered Serena. "He's on the stairs."

"We can't stand up to him if he cages us again," said Delilah. "We've used too much of our strength."

Andrew was certainly on his last bit of strength. "Maybe he's used too much of his power, too?" He was trying to be optimistic, but as a pessimist at heart who looked for holes in every scenario so he could plug them up, he figured it was their only chance.

"He was throwing a lot of magic around to trap us and when he was upstairs, I could feel the flares. God, I hope Buho and Trent are OK," Delilah said. "We all need to stick together. We need to hold hands. Yes, even you, random gangster man."

The mobster scowled at her.

"Unless you're thinking of remaining loyal to the guy who just electrocuted you? Or you could run away, but make it snappy," she snarked.

"What is this snappy?" the mobster asked, suspiciously.

Delilah was done with waiting. "Come on, take Lac's hand, I'll be on his other side. Mom, hold Mr. Criminal-ovitch's hand. Let's have Andrew and Alex on the ends so they can use their guns. One of you keep the chair to throw at him, in case he tries to melt your guns again."

They gathered around Lac. She took his limp hand and felt his aura still alive, but flickering. What a horror show this was. She bent over him and kissed his cheek. "We'll protect you, Little Three Feathers."

He made a weird noise like a muffled cat's meow and she figured he'd be all right. If they survived. She sighed. "Magic is supposed to help people."

Andrew squeezed her hand from where he stood next to her. "I bet this guy thinks he's helping himself and the partners he contracts his labors to."

She shook her head. "Yeah, no. What's Slovakian for karma? Because it should be coming to get him."

"Karma," said the gangster, rolling the R slightly.

"What?" she asked, looking at him.

"Karma is Slovak for karma." He shrugged.

"And if we're protecting you, what's your name?" she asked.

He blinked in surprise. "Peter." He pronounced it more like pay-ter.

She felt the jolt of truth run through Lac and into her. "Names have power."

Someone shouted behind the door to the back rooms, probably behind the stairwell door.

"Last chance, Peter, if you will cave in to the evil warlock, it would be best if you ran away now," Andrew growled over her head.

Peter shook his head, his now-lopsided ponytail flopping. "He was willing to kill me to hurt you. He is always hurting us to make us do what he wants. And the others are my friends. Most of them."

Delilah glanced up at Andrew, who looked and felt like he was ready to just shoot this guy and make everything easier. She squeezed his hand and shook her head as the stairwell door banged open accompanied by a woman's raised voice, talking fast in a language she didn't know.

"Brace yourselves," Del's mom said.

The silhouette of a man appeared in the doorway to the back rooms. He flung his arms up and shouted something, and they all froze in the grip of his spell.

Chapter Twenty-Six

Once they were out of here, Andrew was going to spend the rest of his damn life moving and listening to things, because he was tired of this bullshit.

They watched without moving as three mobsters strode in, pushing Buho and Agent Trent ahead of them. In the semi-darkness, which was getting darker all the time as the gray winter day faded to night, it looked like the mobsters hadn't come out unscathed. Buho and Trent, though, looked like they'd taken a beating.

Buho's head came up and he quickly took in the six of them holding hands. His eyes flicked down the line and stopped and Andrew figured he was looking at Peter, weighing up their chances of having him stab them all in the back.

The woman mobster, who had Buho's service revolver sticking out of the pocket of her coat, started yelling at Peter in Russian, calling him Piotr. Since Peter was as frozen as the rest of them, he couldn't yell back, which seemed unfair. Andrew's limited knowledge of Russian told him Peter was a traitor and his mother was something that was probably not polite.

Delilah squeezed his hand tighter, which told him she wasn't as frozen as he felt. He concentrated on his hand and squeezed hers back.

"Now that I have controlled you, I will always have the ability to enter into your minds again," announced the warlock, clapping his hands with apparent glee.

Delilah squeezed Andrew's hand again and he squeezed back. At least so far, they were semi-frozen and not being mind-controlled, so either the witch was slipping or he knew this was enough to hold them and wasn't wasting his strength.

The woman mobster turned to the witch and said some unflattering thing about his mother, too, so the witch pointed at her and she crumpled to the floor. The others stepped back, outrage and fear on their faces. Andrew wondered if they were being controlled or if their fear was keeping them from shooting. Just bang, right in the back before he murders them. They were gangsters, they had probably killed people in cold blood before.

In any case, the witch didn't fear them nearly as much as he should and strode forward and walked around their group. He didn't lay down a salt circle this time, which was progress, but he went all the way around before stopping in front of Serena Woods, shoes crunching on salt and whatever else had been mixed with it, plus years of dirt and who knows what that had already been on the floor. "This time, I will drain all your magic until you die," he said calmly. "I will make powerful babies with your daughter, so your magic will live on in them."

Delilah squeezed Andrew's hand hard and he squeezed back just as tightly. Over his dead body, though that was too close to happening. He wondered if the asshole would control Delilah's mind long enough to get her pregnant and give birth and then what? Take the baby and murder her, probably. That was grim.

The asshole was in front of Delilah, just barely visible from the corner of Andrew's eye. He found he could turn his head slightly to get a better view of her and the others down their line. Alex's head turned slightly, too and Andrew wanted to smile at his half-brother. Ready to attack on three, right? But the spell held them too tightly.

"You are not over thirty, I think, but you are a little old. Hard to see your body with your vest on. Not very powerful, either, but it will have to do. There are so few women of power these days and none who are ruthless enough to be my true mate. I have many girlfriends, though."

Holy crap, did this guy plan to have a whole harem? Or more likely: a line of raped witches who died when they defied him. Did he have a bunch of children around somewhere? The thought of children being subjected to this maniac made him shiver. Which, yay, he could shiver.

But the witch saw the movement and the freezing spell went hard again. "That is cheating, Mr. Wolf Agent."

Again the squeeze from Delilah and he knew he could move a little if he needed to. He held still though, as the witch looked him up and down. "Very strong and determined. I will put you down like dog."

"I am wasting my time," the witch said. "Vladimir!" he issued an order to one of the men who scowled deeply, but put his sidearm in his shoulder holster and fetched a broom from the closet in the back hall. He swept the salt from the circles at the back of the room into a pile, then swept it into a dustpan and dumped it all into a bucket while the witch paced around their group.

"If he gets a salt circle around us again, we're screwed," Delilah's voice spoke directly in Andrew's head. That was new.

He inched his hand closer to his gun, but it took the same effort as if he were dragging a truck.

Vladimir toddled over with his bucket of salt, cast one assessing look at his erstwhile comrade and at the rest of them before thumping the bucket down at the witch's feet and walking away in spite of the witch arguing at his back, waving his hands. The man crumpled to the floor and the witch turned back to them.

Behind him, Andrew watched as Buho and Trent exchanged glances. There was now only one mobster guarding both of them and he was holding his automatic weapon loosely with the muzzle pointed at the floor. They had their hands cuffed behind their backs, but Buho's gun was only feet away from him, sticking out of a coat pocket. Of course, if Buho did a semi-shift and got his hands free, he couldn't shoot the witch without risking hitting one of them. At this point, if he could have, Andrew would have told Buho to take the shot anyway, because otherwise, they were all going to die here. Except maybe Delilah.

Of course, there were still one or two more gangsters upstairs, though they might be dead or incapacitated.

And they still had Strickland outside, going mental because their earpieces had been useless for almost an hour.

There was a slight noise, just a little scrape, from the window off to his left and Andrew wouldn't have turned his head even if he had been able to. Buho stretched his neck and casually glanced over and his expression didn't really change, but Andrew knew him so well that he saw the tiny smile of his friend's eyebrows.

Buho's shoulder moved slightly and Andrew knew he'd freed his right hand and was waiting for a good moment.

The witch, meanwhile, lifted the bucket and was drawing a line around them, muttering in his sing-song way.

Buho moved as swiftly and silently as his owl form could ever have, scooping his gun up from the collapsed woman and holding it to the last mobster's head, yanking the larger weapon out of the man's hands.

"Kazimir Kazimirov, put down the bucket and put up your hands!" Buho shouted.

"Kazimir Kazimirov," thought Delilah's voice, "I have your name, I control you now."

And a silent zap of agreement from her mother.

Andrew tried to speak in her mind to tell her that with a name like that, this guy was Russian or maybe Ukrainian, but he was sure he didn't get through. Or maybe it mattered a whole lot at this precise moment.

Kazimirov set his bucket down and turned deliberately. He set his hands on his hips, then waved one hand dismissively and Buho, Trent and the last mobster standing were frozen, too. "These gangsters are nothing to me. I only waste my energy controlling you so you don't distract the magic."

The division of the witch's attention had loosened Andrew's muscles another notch or two and he let his hand creep closer to his gun.

Kazimirov took his bucket and finished his circle, but he'd drawn too close to Alex, who shoved out a foot and broke the circle again just as it was closing in on them. The magic popped out of existence. This time Kazimirov was pissed.

He froze them down hard and strode toward Alex, reaching into his own shoulder holster and coming out with a gleaming, silver knife.

"Fuck! Fuck!" Andrew screamed in his own head.

"Put down the knife, Kazimirov, and back away from the people," bellowed Strickland through the broken pane of glass that had been the source of the cold, cold breeze.

Kazimirov turned, genuinely surprised this time, and Andrew felt the power pull out of him and into Delilah and all the way down the line, because suddenly, Alex grabbed the chair and swung it hard at Kazimirov's head, connecting with a dull thud. Kazimirov reeled away and they were all free. Delilah dove on top of Lac and Peter dragged Serena Woods down.

There was a shot and sounds of fighting from Buho's end of the room.

Kazimirov slashed the air with his knife and Alex screamed and staggered backwards, gun only half out of his holster.

Kazimirov turned toward Andrew, knife raised and hand pointed, then was punched backwards, Andrew only hearing the shot after the witch was falling. Andrew advanced on him, gun steady and ready to take a head shot, but Kazimirov was on his back on the floor, unmoving.

"Everyone OK?" Andrew demanded.

"Lac's waking up," Delilah said after a pause.

"So are the gangsters," Alex said, and hauled the cuffs out of a pocket to slap on them both before they could get their wits about them. "The knife fucking hurt, but it's only a surface wound." Alex could have been spurting blood and told them he was fine, especially with the adrenaline as high as it was.

Andrew barked out, "Get me metal cuffs for the witch, too."

Buho frisked the guards and brought a pair over. He went to put them on Kazimirov, but hesitated when he knelt down. "Miller. I think he's dead."

"Get back," Andrew demanded and Buho eased away, eyeing Andrew warily. "Delilah, is the witch dead?"

He felt her aura brush his as she came up to his side and peered at the witch on the floor. "Almost. Or he's tamping down his aura like when he was invisible in the shadows. I can't tell. Either way, I'm not touching him."

"He's lost a lot of blood," Buho said. "There's a puddle."

"Don't touch the blood!" cried Peter.

Buho scrambled back, checking his hands. "What?"

"His blood, it gets on you. Is worse than circle."

Kazimirov sprang back to life, lunging at Buho with his silver knife. Buho was fast, though and rolled out of the way and Andrew shot and shot and kept shooting until his gun clicked. He lowered it, hands shaking, staring at his tormentor.

The echo of the gunshots faded and the room was silent.

"Dead," whispered Buho. He cleared his throat and called out, "All clear down here, Strickland!"

And the doors banged open all around and cops came in, guns drawn. Andrew set his on the floor and put his hands on his head, knowing the drill of disarming everyone until the good guys and bad guys could be sorted out.

Strickland dodged through the crowd, striding in from the front and directing traffic, pulling the FBI team and Delilah and her mom and Lac over to one side.

Strickland clenched Buho's forearm, obviously not willing to let him go.

Delilah argued with Strickland, standing over Peter, who sat on the floor with his head on his knees and his hands cuffed behind him.

Andrew went over and agreed with Delilah that yes, he had sided with them, but with Strickland that yes, he was part of a gang of kidnappers and he had been trying to subdue Lac up until he'd been betrayed by the witch who was now dead.

Lac and Serena were sitting side by side on an ambulance gurney, having their injuries checked over.

"Andrew," Alex said right next to him, clapping his hand on his shoulder, making him startle. "Shit. Sorry. Well fuck, you're having a meltdown."

"I'm not having a meltdown," Andrew said, but his voice was thready and when he went to rub his face with shaky hands, he felt tears. "We almost died, Alex. Troy was almost an orphan."

His brother got up close to him and spoke to him quietly. "OK, it's OK. We're OK. Troy's OK. Delilah's OK. The only dead people are one of the guys upstairs and the scary witch dude."

"We're OK." Andrew nodded somewhat drunkenly as Alex led him off to the corner, covering him so no one would see him cry. "I killed the scary witch dude and I don't think I could have done anything else."

"You're right. I don't see any other outcome. He was going to murder us, presumably to fuel whatever spell he needed. At the time you shot, he was coming at Buho with a big knife."

"Self-defense still leaves a stain." He'd killed four other people before, all people trying to kill him, but it wasn't something he could forgive himself. And this time, he'd shot and shot and shot, even though the asshole was dead after the first two bullets.

"Yeah," said Alex. He'd been undercover and dealt with some scary things.

"You're a good brother, Alex. I love you." Tears flowed more freely and he hugged Alex tightly.

"Aw shit, you're squeezing the tears out of me, too," Alex said and squeezed him back. "Love you, too." He laughed. "I never thought we'd say it. Now enough mushy stuff, I'll go get Delilah and I'm going to call Beth."

"Yes," Andrew said, leaning against the wall behind him. He fumbled for his own phone and called Beth himself. "Beth?"

"Is everyone all right? Is Alex?"

Shit, he'd scared her. "Yes, we're all OK. Alex will be calling you in a second. Is Troy OK?"

"He's been upset since you left, he's been playing with his tarot deck and rocking. Are these Delilah's cards?"

"She gave them to him." And showed him the cards and told him the meanings. And loved him and was patient with him.

"Tell him I'll be there as soon as I can and we're OK. And Beth?"

"Yes?"

"Thanks for staying with him. If Ferguson shows up there, be wary. He slipped out about three minutes into the op, about an hour ago, according to Lac, so who knows where he is."

Silence from the other end, then he heard her relay the message to someone and then Gaines's deep sigh and slow, weary cussing. Then Gaines came on the phone. "What happened?"

"I don't know, exactly." He told him what Lac had said.

Gaines sighed again. "That asshole. Why's this phone keep beeping?"

"Three Feathers is trying to call his wife. I'll have Lac fill everyone in on Ferguson later. And thanks for protecting my son, Gaines."

"Sweet kid. Worried about you."

Then they hung up and Delilah trotted to his side and put her arms around him and he had to turn his back to the room so he could cry.

Chapter Twenty-Seven

By the time they'd sorted out prisoners and injuries, done an initial debriefing, and Trent, as representative of the local FBI, had confiscated all the guns, both to return to the armory and to run ballistics tests, almost two hours had passed. Delilah had watched as Andrew regained his composure. Or, more precisely, as he built his composure on top of the turmoil inside himself. She was pretty good at reading auras and understanding people, and all the deep, painful emotions he was always tamping down were definitely being tamped.

They'd also found a nutrient drink and some sports drinks with electrolytes for her mom, who had only been given water for the last day. The EMTs wanted to take her to the hospital, but she insisted she was going to be fine and she wanted to stay with her daughter. Delilah looked her mom over and other than being sleep-deprived and having most of her life force drained out of her, she was doing pretty good. She wished Eloisa were there to do a more precise examination, but she was pretty sure her mom would be fine given a little time.

Andrew pointed out he was disarmed and couldn't protect her, but she said she was in no danger.

Once in the car, Delilah retrieved her handbag from under the seat and took out her cards. No, her mom was in no immediate danger that guns could solve, but there was still something lurking. She couldn't get a good read on it, but she told Andrew, who looked pained and got another bulletproof vest for her mom.

She, Andrew, Alex, and her mom entered the Bureau bearing fast food and grim silence and went straight down the hall to the conference room where they'd left Troy and Beth.

Except it was empty.

"I don't like this," her mother said. "What's your read, Del?"

Del would have to think later about her mom deferring to her in anything at all. "Not good."

She took a breath to call out for Troy and Beth, but Andrew held up his hand for silence. "No, it's not good."

Alex was past high alert and onto critical malfunction and reaching for the weapon that was no longer in his shoulder holster. "Fuck," he whispered. He pulled out his phone and dialed Beth's number, but there was no answer. "Double fuck," he whispered.

"Are they still in the building?" Del's mom asked her.

She pulled out her cards again, shuffling them hurriedly and pulling out a couple cards, even as she scanned outward for Troy. An innocent child, the Page of Pentacles, the card she linked in her head to Troy. A sweet child who'd been through too much and needed security. "But where?" she asked as she went to turn the other card over.

She fumbled and dropped the card and it drifted to the floor. Andrew immediately crouched by the table and picked it up and handed it to her. With another card.

"I only dropped this one," she said, holding up the Tower. "Which is a terrible card to pull in the circumstances."

She held onto the other one, another Page of Pentacles, but with a slightly different picture. "Mom, is this from the deck you kept in the kitchen drawer?"

Her mom took it and squinted at it. "I think so. How'd it get here?"

"I gave the deck to Troy." She took the card back and closed her eyes, waiting for something to come to her. "He's still here. I think he left this one behind on purpose. Are there more on the floor?"

Andrew and Alex both crouched down and Alex soon came up with another. "Emperor?"

He handed it to her and Del almost smiled. "It's the archetype of father. It's you, Andrew."

She held one in each hand, but the echo was faint, so she placed them face up on the little table. "Andrew, come and touch the cards."

"We're wasting time," Alex hissed.

Andrew, though, came over and put his hand on top of the cards and she crashed straight into a vision. "It's a back office near a door to the outside. Gaines is standing between them and whoever is responsible for this. I can't see who it is, but it's a man."

"Ferguson?" Andrew asked.

She shook her head. "Maybe. Troy didn't like him from the start, whoever it is."

She opened her eyes and picked up the two cards Troy had left for her, one in each hand. "Follow me."

"Oh no," said Andrew, "you tell us where to go and you stay back."

"I don't know my way around and unless you have a map of this building with you right now, the only clue I have is the cards in my hands," she said.

"OK, so we'll be going into the secure areas, which is a huge no-no. Stay behind me and tell me which direction to turn at each corner. When we find them, you retreat."

Alex, meanwhile, was stripping down. "Going bobcat," he said succinctly before he did just that.

"Better for the sneak and peek," Andrew told her and started to undress, too. "I'll go wolf for the assault. We have no other weapons."

Her mother shot her a sly look before turning her back. He stripped down to boxers and bare feet, though, and didn't shift. She wanted to tell him to put the bulletproof vest back on, but figured it would hinder him as a wolf. He handed her a handful of zip ties and she shoved them in the back pockets of her jeans where they dug into her butt. She picked up pants for both shifter men and rolled them up under her arm.

She allowed herself to be distracted by Andrew's body for only a half a second as she followed him into the hall, her mom crowding up behind her.

They turned left and right and left again in the empty offices. She heard a murmur of voices behind one door and they paused, Alex and Andrew listening intently for a moment before moving on. She had the urge to knock and tell them there was an abduction going on right then, but something told her it would escalate the violence and she wouldn't like the outcome. She knew where to find people once the action was over, though.

She clicked her tongue, the signal they'd agreed on, outside the door to a room labeled Housekeeping, and everyone stopped, her mom bumping into her back.

Del touched Andrew and put a minor cone of silence and a protection spell on him, but when she whispered to ask if he wanted a look-away, he shook his head. Alex, though, she gave all three at his nod. Then she took her mom's hand and put a look-away on both of them.

Andrew could still see her and he bent down and kissed her hard and fast. Then he nudged her and her mom to stand with their backs to the concrete wall, out of sight and out of danger of bullets, then reached over and opened the broom closet door a few inches to let Alex in.

Andrew let his eyes go wolf, more sensitive to light and dark and movement than human vision, but less able to see fine details or color. But he was pretty sure he wouldn't be quizzed on color in the next few minutes. He remembered his ex, Troy's mom, when they were dating and he'd been stationed in Florida, trying to get his opinion on paint chips during the time she'd been hinting they should move in together. He had wanted to tell her he was a wolf shifter and didn't have half the spectrum half the time, but knew it would be a mistake.

He stood back as Alex slipped in, sneaking along the wall. Andrew could barely see him and hoped the assailant's human eyes couldn't find him in the partial darkness.

"Who's there?" the man demanded, an edge of hysteria in his voice.

"The door comes unlatched sometimes, Ferguson," Gaines replied in his despondent, laconic manner. "There's a work order a couple weeks overdue on it."

Well, they knew now where Ferguson had gone and why he'd left so soon after they started their invasion of the old store. Not only was he an asshole, but he was working with the mobsters, or at least with the dead witch. The door banged shut again and promptly bounced open. The asshole didn't even look into the hallway, thank goodness. He closed the door more carefully, though, until it clicked.

Well, shit.

Another man's voice ranted about when would their ride get there and why the fuck were they taking a woman and child with them, because they could have just bailed a couple hours ago.

"Kasimirov wants shifters and if we control the woman, we control the kid. We can ditch the woman later," said Ferguson.

Andrew was surprised Alex didn't tear the man's throat out immediately. He could smell the guns, though and understood the caution of not letting shots be fired in an enclosed space with cinder block walls and metal shelves, especially when one's loved ones might get hit by ricochet.

Troy whined softly, his sweet wolf voice both distressing and a relief. Delilah held her hand over her mouth to hold back a gasp. Andrew nodded at her, hoping to give her reassurance, but she gripped her mother's hand harder, looking like she wanted to cry. Serena Woods had what could be described as a game face. Ready to kick butt. Too bad she was still pale and wobbly from her recent ordeal.

He waved Delilah over and whispered, "I need you to open the door again, but stay back."

She nodded and he told her to wait for his signal. Then he turned his back and dropped his boxers, shifting at nearly the same time. When he shook out his fur and turned back, Serena was looking at the ceiling and smirking while Delilah was hiding her grin.

He listened intently at the door, then when he heard footsteps right behind it, he nodded at Delilah, who turned the handle silently and pushed the door open just an inch.

"Shut the goddamn door, Wilson!" Ferguson growled.

Instead, Andrew flung his body through the door, and slammed into Wilson's legs. He shouted and staggered back as Andrew leaped past the rebounding door. A shape out of the corner of his eye was Alex leaping at Ferguson, claws and teeth out, transforming into a wolf and burning off the look-away spell as he sprang. Beth shrieked and turned her back, protecting Troy with her body. Andrew leaped at Wilson's face, and the man bounced off the metal shelves, toppling bottles of cleaning supplies, but caught his balance far too quickly. He swung a handgun toward Andrew, who crowded in and clamped his jaws on the man's arm, tasting the wool of his overcoat, then as he bit down harder, blood. Wilson screamed and his gun clattered to the floor.

Ferguson got a shot off and Beth shrieked again. Andrew couldn't see her as he was focused on holding down Wilson and keeping track of Ferguson, but he hoped like hell she and Troy hadn't been shot.

Wilson tried to throw him off, but Andrew held on tight, knowing his teeth were tearing a bit more of the man's flesh with each movement, but just not fucking caring. Wilson punched him in the head and he sure as hell cared about that.

"Freeze!" shouted Delilah from the doorway, her voice laden with power.

And, fucking hell, they all froze in their crazy tableau. She darted in and eased his jaws off of Wilson's arm and unfroze him, then disarmed Ferguson and unfroze Alex, Beth, and Troy.

"Sorry, sorry," she said. "I know we're all going to have flashbacks about being unable to move, but I didn't see another way."

Andrew shifted back and she gave him his handcuffs.

Del said, "I'm going to go alert those people we heard talking, OK?"

"Sure," he said. "Take your mom with you. I don't want anyone alone."

She hesitated and her eyes cut to the door. "Um, Mom powered the spell. She's going to have to sleep it off."

"Shit," he said.

He went out and grabbed his boxers and hastily pulled them on, crouching down to check Serena Woods' pulse and to rouse her. She gripped his wrist and said, "It worked?"

"Yeah, it worked. We'll get you someplace more comfortable in a minute, OK?"

She smiled as her eyes drifted closed again.

He tossed Alex's pants to him and Andrew and Delilah backtracked up the hall and started banging on doors until seven people were out in the hall. Just then, the door to the public areas opened and Strickland and Buho marched in.

Strickland led with, "What the fuck is this message, Miller?"

"Attempted abduction of my son and Alex Three Feathers' wife down by the back door."

"How'd they get in?" asked one guy who looked about fifteen, though Andrew knew he had to be at least mid-twenties. Just an infant. He felt ancient.

Buho shook his head. "Fuck a duck, it's Ferguson, isn't it? I thought he'd chickened out or hated us so much he didn't want to risk himself, but he's working for the gang."

"Him and a guy named Wilson," Andrew said.

This brought more consternation than the mention of Ferguson. The rest of them didn't seem surprised that Ferguson had been doing something shady, but Wilson was another story.

"We're going to need an ambulance. Three Feathers is doing first aid on the guy I bit."

Their audience got even more uneasy and the infant whispered a question to the guy next to him.

Andrew stared at him. "I've been repeatedly frozen, shocked half to death, had guns pointed at me, and rendered deaf today, and he threatened people I love and tried to kill me. If he loses his fucking hand, I'm not going to cry."

Delilah set her hand on his back, rubbing it gently, transmitting calm to him, since he'd already cried once and didn't want to do it in front of the entire Wheeling Bureau. Shifting had taken the red out of his eyes, or at least alleviated the burning feeling.

Strickland insisted on seeing what was happening and Buho had everyone else scrambling to make phone calls, wait for the ambulance, and, with a little more info, figure out what ride Ferguson and Wilson had been waiting for and if it wasn't someone they'd already arrested, to take them down, too.

As he and Delilah headed back through the maze of the building, she said, "I know you should probably put your shirt on, but I'm enjoying the view."

He grinned at her and put an arm around her shoulder. She ran one hand across his abs and he flexed for her, because it turned out he was vain.

Once back at the housekeeping closet, a group had gathered, but Andrew pushed through to where Beth stood, still holding Troy close. Andrew wrapped them both in a quick hug and then took Troy in his arms and held him tight. Troy shifted to human and snuggled in closer. Beth handed over his sweatpants and Andrew crouched down to help him put them on. When he stood again, Troy in his arms, the boy whispered, "Dad."

And Andrew found himself crying again.

Chapter Twenty-Eight

ONCE THEY'D REVIVED SERENA again and she'd declared herself ready to go, once they'd again been debriefed, once Troy, in wolf form again, had fallen asleep against Andrew's chest and warmed his heart, it was nearly midnight, so they all spent the night in a hotel, but a much nicer one than the night before. Delilah and Serena shared a room and though it had a communicating door to Andrew's room and he asked them to leave it open just in case, there was no chance of more lovemaking.

Had it only been twenty-four hours since they made love with their pajamas on?

Alex and Beth had a room in the same hotel and based on Beth's rosy cheeks and Alex's grin the next morning, they'd had the sort of post-adrenaline survivor sex that Andrew craved. Strickland and Buho stayed later at the Bureau than the rest of them, so when they crossed paths in the morning, it was only the subtle scent on both of them that said they'd also shared a room.

As for Andrew, he'd shifted to wolf form and curled around his baby son, barely sleeping and on high alert. And also very jealous of his brother, his sister-in-law, and his friends.

He was jittery from lack of sleep in the morning and let Delilah drive. He moved Troy's car seat to the passenger side and though Troy had been hesitant to get in it, he seemed happy once his dad was in the back with him, legs stretched into his foot well.

He'd get Delilah a bigger car, he thought, then realized they hadn't talked about their future. And maybe she liked this car.

And maybe the bullshit Ferguson and Wilson had been spouting would convince everyone it was Miller and the others who were crazy. They said they'd been giving Beth and Troy a tour and Andrew and Alex were crazy shifter sons of bitches.

Andrew could still get fired, arrested, and disgraced. Already, he was going to have to undergo a full investigation because he'd shot the evil witch. What if they pushed him out of the FBI? What if he dropped out? And what the hell he'd do after that, he didn't know.

Then he closed his eyes to doze as they bypassed Youngstown and got on the Ohio Turnpike and dreamed a whole conversation about quitting the FBI right away with a reduced pension and finding something to give him a more relaxed schedule. But what? Maybe being a PI. Maybe helping Serena with investigations. Maybe...he didn't know.

He'd never really learned anything other than to be a cop and he was a damn good one. Maybe he'd go back to school for....what?

And make babies with Delilah, maybe ones with shifter magic and her sort of magic.

He startled awake as they slowed and turned off the Turnpike onto 77 heading north into Cleveland. He rubbed his face and found Troy watching him, his deck of tarot cards in his lap. Troy handed him a card with a naked woman pouring water with a big star and seven smaller stars over her head. It said The Star at the bottom. He wondered what the meaning of it was and pulled out his phone to find out, but instead asked.

Serena half-turned in her seat. "Why do you ask?"

"Troy handed me the card."

"Right side up?" she asked and when he said it was, she smiled slyly, in a way that made her look exactly like Delilah. "It means hope, renewal, and inspiration. And a period of peace and love and growth. Though, as I'm sure Del has mentioned, it has nuances based on the cards around it and on what the Seer can See."

Del sighed. "Troy understands the cards, right Troy?"

He looked at his son and wondered if he'd sorted through the whole deck, which was already starting to look grubby because the kid was five, after all. Or maybe he'd pulled just one card and handed it to Andrew.

"Is there a way to test if he has your sort of psychic powers?" Andrew asked.

"Hmmm," Serena said. "I don't know an exact test. I've only checked out older kids and adults and it's not so much a test as a survey of strengths. Like one of those tests some jobs make you take, but talking about their experiences and trying spells."

He nodded and watched his son, his baby boy, wondering if the kid didn't already have magic inside him other than the shifter magic and intuition and the wolf senses that were stronger than regular humans'. Troy got tired of him staring and turned his head away. Andrew murmured an apology.

"Am I dropping you at your apartment?" Delilah asked. "Did someone get your car repaired?"

"I don't even know what day of the week it is," Andrew said. "If it's Monday, I was supposed to call in. Pretty sure I can say now that I worked all weekend. Buho was going to get my car seen to, but I doubt it would happen before today."

"It is Monday. So...your apartment? Or we could drop Troy at school and take you to work?"

Andrew looked at Troy, who was frowning in a way that meant he was about to start whining. "I already told his school he'd be out this week. I need to go home and spend time with Troy," he said. "I'll call the office so they know for sure I'm not coming."

He proceeded to call and while he talked to Strickland, who must have gone straight to the office, she reminded him he needed to talk to the Organized Crime unit, half of whom had gone to Wheeling during the night. She reminded him he should have stayed there to help wrap things up.

And yeah, they were going to see it as a mark against him that he didn't, but he had his son and two other civilians to take care of.

Aware of those three civilians in the car with him who were able to hear every word, he told her he would talk to her later and hung up to call Quentin, who was even more pissed off than usual and told him to come in after lunch. And his car was probably being towed.

So Andrew called the motor pool guys, who said his car was not going to be towed if they could help it and they'd look at the car and let him know if they could at least drive it to a mechanic. Most of the motor pool guys were shifters, some open, some closeted, and always had his back.

"Home then. And you can get your things, unless…" Did he dare ask her this in front of his son and her mom?

"Unless?" Serena chimed in when he didn't go on.

He cleared his throat. "I mean, you're going to want to take back your valuables. And I was told your house was broken into yesterday."

Serena looked particularly grim. "Yes."

"But Delilah, you're welcome, to, um…" move in? They'd only met a week ago. "Visit? Any time you want?"

"Leave a change of clothes and my shampoo at your apartment?" she asked, a wary look on the little bit of her face he could see in her rear view mirror.

"Yes," he said with relief. "And come over as much as you want."

"And babysit Troy?" she asked.

Oh. That must be why she was wary. "In a pinch, I would appreciate it, but I'm hoping to find an after school program or daycare for him."

She looked slightly less wary, but still on guard. "Well, for now we should pick up our valuables, Mom. Or do you want to look at the house first?"

The two of them discussed what Delilah had brought over and Delilah almost missed the exit. Serena stared assessingly at her daughter, then glanced back at him. "So you didn't find the other safe."

Del huffed. "In your office? I found the one in the waiting room."

"No, in the house," Serena sat back with a smug smile. "Well, I guess I do have a few secrets left."

"Didn't I say we were going to talk about secrets and why you didn't tell me anything? I mean, we were blindsided by your disappearance, Mom."

They bickered for a few minutes, but without heat. Andrew watched behind them carefully in case they were being followed. At this point, they didn't know how many more Slovak and Russian mobsters were around, though Quentin said there were more, or if the evil Kasimirov had a brother or sister witch, or one of his "girlfriend" witches who would come after them.

When they reached his apartment building, Delilah swiped the guest card to get into the parking garage and hung it on her rear view mirror before parking in his usual spot. Andrew had his door open when Delilah said, "Wait."

He clicked his door shut and waited while she reached into the foot well by her mom's feet and took her box of cards out of her purse. "I've got a creepy feeling about your apartment. Or maybe about Mom's house?" She shook her head. "Give me a minute."

While she was laying out cards on her lap and on the console, Andrew got out of the car and called Strickland again, but got bumped to voice mail. Quentin didn't give a rat's ass about him, but Andrew called him anyway, asking for backup to his apartment and people to check out Serena's house.

He had gotten his sidearm back early in the morning due to Strickland's intervention, but didn't want to have to go into his own home - or anyone else's - with gun drawn, especially not after the last few days. He shuddered once, thinking about the helplessness and anguish he'd felt and the rage at the warlock. Then the smell of blood and death he had caused.

"OK, I think someone tried to get into your apartment and we need to be cautious, but the locks and the wards I set held them off. But someone's in your house now, Mom."

"Well, we have to go there and stop them," Serena Woods said.

After a round of Hell No, Andrew called Quentin again, who said he'd sent out the cops and was sending two guys over, but he wanted to know how Andrew knew this and he said surveillance video and got off the phone as fast as he could. Not because he didn't believe Delilah, but because he knew Quentin would not.

"OK, look at it this way, Mom: if there's an intruder, the first thing the cops say is to get out of the house. We are definitely not going over there. It's probably more mobsters, extra pissed because we got their friends arrested and killed their witch."

Serena finally subsided and they all trooped to the elevator.

As they went up in the elevator, Andrew got the feeling in his gut that Delilah was wrong about the safety of their apartment.

"OK," she said as they passed the ground floor, "I'm feeling less confident that your apartment is safe." As she pushed the button for the second floor, he noticed her pink nail polish, so smooth a few days before, was nicked and flaked. "Let's take a moment to think before walking into the hallway right outside your door."

"I'll check it out and you stay here," said Andrew.

"You might need magic," said Serena. "I'll come with you."

"No spreadsheets here, Mom," Delilah said, "and you're still not a hundred percent."

"And you are? We're all tapped out."

The doors opened on the second floor hallway - beige and bland passing for classy, just like the rest of the hallways. He stuck his foot out so the door couldn't close. Andrew took out his phone and called Quentin, asking when backup would get to him. Quentin let it go to voice mail, the asshole. He called Strickland again and she said she'd send Buho and one other, but it would be twenty minutes.

The elevator pinged and murmured, "Please do not block the doors," in a soothing voice.

Then the stairwell door burst open and a man with an automatic rifle lunged out and pointed it at them.

"They weren't in the apartment," Delilah said. "I asked the wrong question. No wonder the answer was fuzzy."

Andrew refrained from saying anything sarcastic and instead pushed the rest of them into the elevator, shoved Troy into Delilah's hands, and told them to hit the emergency stop button between floors, which would sound an alarm. The doors closed on their anxious faces, yelling at him to get in the elevator, too.

"Keep your hands up," said the man. No accent other than East Cleveland on this one. Andrew sized him up. He was as tall as Andrew, but thinner. Sadly, he seemed to know how to work his weapon, displaying a competence either from the military or from years of mobster experience. "I want your weapon on the floor." He hit a button on his waist and announced he had the werewolf, but the women and kid were in the elevator.

"Do you want my hands up or for me to get my weapon out?" Andrew asked, channeling his half-brother, who had become a total smart ass. Or already had been, but had been wound too tight before.

"Take your coat off so I can see your weapons, then hands back up," the guy decided.

He apparently didn't have any sort of cuffs, because a thinking person would have restrained Andrew.

The elevator light started blinking, and the alarm sounded a pleasing ping-ping-ping. It wouldn't do to scare the upper middle class residents who owned condos in the building. There was also a fire alarm in the elevator for serious emergencies, but he hoped the building's super would call up to the elevator before Delilah and Serena decided to pull the alarm. Still, a full-scale fire drill might flush out these bad guys.

"How many of you are there?" Andrew asked as the man marched him toward the stairwell, not getting close enough to disarm or be disarmed, but muzzle pointing at Andrew, who was not getting any ideas. At least not ideas he could use quite yet.

"I'm not stupid," the guy said. "Enough so any floor your girlfriend comes out on, she'll come up against one of us."

"All ten floors? Where are we going?" Andrew asked.

"Up. You're going to let us into your apartment and we're going to go through your things. And we're going to have a talk about how you killed Kasimirov."

"I don't suppose you're going to accept self-defense?"

The man snorted. "Not up to me. I can't be sad because he was a nasty shithead, but he was a *useful* nasty shithead and the boss is fucking livid."

"Here I was hoping one of those arrested yesterday would be the boss." He turned the corner and the guy was just close enough behind him that Andrew couldn't run and hide in the stairwell or swing around and kick him in the face.

"You are never going to see the boss, you mangy freak," the man said, with surprisingly little heat for being deliberately insulting. "We've got a lieutenant here who is going to figure out what information got leaked and who's responsible, other than you and your girlfriend and her mother."

The guy clicked on his mic again. "Yep, almost to the third floor now. The others still in the elevator? ... I don't know ... Probably still second floor or close to it."

Andrew could barely hear the voice at the other end, only enough to pick out a few words. He figured, though, they were trying to get the others out of the elevator. He should have reminded them he loved them and to not get out of the elevator, no matter what happened. Because, yeah, he hoped Troy knew it and he hoped Delilah knew it, but he'd much rather die and have these guys either picked up by the cops or chased out than have a hair on the heads of the others hurt.

"Open the door," this asshole behind him said, so Andrew did. He thought they should have keycard locks installed on each fire door so people could only exit at the lobby, but the fitness people liked to take the stairs and insisted they visited each other all the time. He didn't think he'd ever seen anyone in the stairwell and you had to swipe a card to use the elevator, too, but whatever. Maybe after this, better locks would be installed. Not that taking out a key card or entering a code would have helped him much in this situation.

What would help him was a bigger gun and one less asshole.

The guy was behind him, standing at the top of the stairs and, saints be praised, he was a little too close and looking at the door instead of at Andrew. The strap on the weapon meant Andrew wasn't going to get it from him, but...

He turned and kicked out hard and the guy went flying down the stairs with thumps and a loud clatter and, luckily, not a spray of bullets. Andrew took off upwards, drawing his pistol.

This building was nicely insulated, so apparently no one heard the thumps and clatters. He continued on to the fourth floor and looked through the window in the door before slipping through. Another guy was standing with his back to the stairs, automatic weapon pointed toward the floor, unaware of his surroundings.

Andrew grabbed his gun away and after a brief struggle that ended with him half-choking the guy with the gun strap as he flattened him on the floor, Andrew zip-tied his hands and feet.

"Yippee ki-yay, motherfucker. That's how it goes, right?" Andrew said, panting from the exertion.

The man's eyes went huge, probably because Bruce Willis killed a ton of terrorists in Die Hard. Andrew patted the guy down and took a knife off him plus his comm link, which he wiped on his shirt before putting in his own ear, then knocked on a few doors until a couple answered, eyes huge at his gun, and he flashed his FBI badge and asked them to call 911 and to otherwise stay in their apartment, in case the guy got loose.

The guy, about fifty and fit, said, "But I have a handgun -"

"No," Andrew told him. "This is an active crime scene and I'm waiting for backup and do not need any more firearms waved around. The cops might shoot anyone they see who has a gun. Feel free to stay inside with your door locked and shoot at anyone who breaks in, but do not bring your gun into the hallway. If you have phone numbers for anyone else in the building, tell them to stay inside with doors locked. Or to stay out of the building. Also, call the super and tell him to not unlock the elevator. There are more criminals running around and people are sheltering in the elevator."

And he texted Buho, went back to the stairwell, and down to his own floor in search of mobsters.

Delilah could live with the annoying ping-ping-ping of the polite, upper-class alarm and the robotic voice asking them to unlock the elevator. She could even live with the building's super - were they called that these days? Or did they go with concierge or something? - asking them to explain themselves and not believing them. He didn't unlock the elevator, but agreed to call 911, if only to arrest them for trespassing.

Troy, however, couldn't go much longer without a bathroom and the ping-ping-ping made him cover his sensitive ears and rock where he sat on the floor with her mom.

"Ma'am," the super's tinny voice said again, "I'm going to have to deactivate the elevator completely. It'll settle to the lobby and the doors will open."

"No!" Del and her mom said in chorus.

Del said, "Listen, there are people with guns and they specifically want to catch us and FBI Agent Andrew Miller who lives on the third floor. If you unlock this elevator, we will settle and our doors will open and who knows who will be standing there."

The concierge's voice went up an octave. "Ma'am, I...I'm sorry."

The elevator jerked once, then began to sink.

"They're going to end up in the lobby," the concierge said to someone. "Ma'am, he's got a gun pointed at my head and I don't want to die."

There was a thud and the super grunted. She hoped he wasn't seriously hurt and she would thank him later for telling them as much as he had.

She got Troy to his feet and had him stand against the front wall of the elevator, out of the line of sight of anyone waiting. She set a look-away spell on herself and turned to help her mom, but she was already a mere shadow.

They both stood off to the sides, and waited as the elevator creaked downwards.

Chapter Twenty-Nine

"They're going to end up in the lobby," Blake the concierge said. "Ma'am, he's got a gun pointed at my head and I don't want to die."

This was not happy news for Andrew to be hearing on his stolen earpiece.

Andrew abandoned the idea of going to his own apartment and barreled down the stairs, leaping down multiple steps at a time and swinging around the turns. He paused long enough to check the man he'd knocked down the stairs, as he was still lying there. He was breathing and starting to move, so Andrew zip-tied him and took his gun and two knives, too. He was starting to look like Rambo, but he sure as hell wasn't going to leave a weapon around. Just for the heck of it, he took the guy's comm earpiece.

Strickland had reminded them the day before to secure their own weapons and communications and it could tip the balance away from the mobsters toward him. They just had to survive until the cops and more FBI could get there.

He slowed down and listened, keeping his own footsteps soft and his guns from rattling and paused at the door, checking through the tiny window, remembering the door from this hallway to the lobby was mostly wavy glass and someone could see him moving if they tried hard enough. He slid out and eased the door shut with a quiet thunk, plastering himself against the wall and holding still.

The good thing about the wavy glass was the lights of the lobby made it easy for him to see people moving out there, too. The gangsters had gone silent in his ear and he wondered if they knew he had their comms. Or else they had a prearranged signal of which channel to jump to. Either way, he damn well hoped it didn't mean there was another witch casting silence spells.

He eased toward the doors and knew he was just a touch too late when some guy, this one with an accent, shouted, "Come out with your hands up!"

Delilah sure as hell wasn't going to do that.

Motion and a shadow outside the door, someone staying back, but looking in at an angle, and a guy saying, "I don't see them, but I can't see into the corners."

"Well, unless they went out through the top, they're still in there," said the first shouter, accent heavy. "From what we were told, they're too short and besides there's the little kid. Go in and look in the corners."

"And you say they're witches?" the unaccented man replied. "Yeah. No."

"They are not like Kasimirov. They are nice witches who tell fortunes and shit. One's an old lady accountant. She's not a danger to us."

Del heard her mom barely whisper, *Old lady*, and felt her pulling magic together.

She had only heard those two voices, but it didn't mean there weren't other people out there. She put extra protection on Troy and a silence spell so no one would hear him if he moved. And she thought of Andrew, somewhere alone, maybe already captured, maybe already dead. She hadn't heard any shots fired, but this place with its carpets and thick walls was a lot more sound-proofed than the abandoned shop in Wheeling. "Wait here for us and your dad, OK, sweetheart?"

"Troy," the boy whispered.

She could only hear him because the spells were hers, but she thought he was protesting that she called him sweetheart. She was the one who'd called Andrew out on not using his son's name, after all. They would figure it out later.

The two men bickered for a minute and the accented one came in to check out the elevator.

She stretched her hands in anticipation.

And had a gun muzzle pointed at her face as the man stood outside the elevators at an angle protecting him from her mom. "I can barely see you, but there you are. Come out of there with your hands up."

She put her hands up and let the look-away spell drop. She was going to have to save her energy.

"Where's your mother and the boy?"

"I boosted them on top of the elevator. There's an escape hatch. There's also a ladder in there, so they're climbing to safety."

Fifteen feet away from her, someone scanned their card and entered a code to come in the front door. She shouted, "Get out! They have guns!" and the woman dropped the door shut in surprise, then made a shadow with her hands to peer through the glass. She looked shocked when she spotted the giant guns and Del waved her away, so she took off down the street trotting along in high heels, fumbling in her giant bag, probably for her phone.

"Sorry, what were you saying?" she asked the accented man, being as calm as possible just to keep him on his toes. She wondered if hysterical would distract better.

"They are not climbing a ladder," the man said. "It's ten floors to the roof."

"Well, they might have pulled open some doors by now. I wonder if they can get up on the roof, though."

The man, about her age with white blond hair and a pouty mouth, made the cardinal error of taking his eyes off her. She grabbed his arm and smacked him with a knock out spell and disappeared again, scampering a few feet away as quietly as she could.

He staggered and dropped to his knees before face-planting on the well-padded, patterned carpet.

The other man rushed at where she'd just been and she grabbed at him, too, but he wrenched out of her grasp and backed away.

And finally, finally, she heard sirens and two police cars pulled up out front. She hoped they were covering the garage and the back doors, too.

Another bland sedan pulled up and Buho and three other people piled out of it. Buho waved his hands and they split up, Buho glancing at his phone as he joined the cops, who were standing behind their cars.

As he spoke, they looked alarmed and hunkered down. Yeah, it was actually dangerous, assholes.

The remaining man hit a button and spoke into his mic in what was probably Slovak. Maybe Russian this time. She wondered how many were left in the building. At least one with an earpiece, because the man was listening to someone and not looking happy. Anything which made these assholes unhappy, she was one hundred percent in favor of.

Andrew drew up level with the door to the lobby and peered through, watching as Delilah flattened one asshole and sent the other scurrying. She yelled at the woman from the fifth floor with the red hair and drawn-on eyebrows and sent her tottering away.

When this was over, he was going to have to get to know the neighbors. If the neighbors didn't blame him for this clusterfuck. If he could afford to live here when the FBI fired him. Negative thinking. He shook it out of his head.

The cops pulled up outside and he thought he saw Buho duck behind the cars with them. Buho would save their asses.

Andrew waited as the remaining gunman assessed his choices: give up, take a couple of hostages and hole up in the concierge's office, shoot everyone (Andrew's least favorite option), run down the hallway past Andrew – for which he would need a key card or for Blake to buzz him in, or take the elevator – which also needed a key card. And, yeah, the guy probably had a key card by now.

He didn't like the elevator plan, either, since Andrew had to assume his son and Delilah's mom were still hiding in there, because he'd checked the elevator ceiling back when he moved in and even standing on Delilah's shoulders, they wouldn't have been able to open the hatch without a crowbar. Which was something he'd thought about looking into, but hadn't got around to

The gunman decided the elevator was his best option and yeah, until the FBI and the cops got onto every floor in the building, it probably was. More of the guy's mobster friends were still upstairs. Plenty of places to hide and hostages to take throughout the building.

Andrew eased the door open and was about to burst through and demand the guy put his hands up, probably ending up killing or injuring yet another person, when the man screamed and flailed and then passed out.

Andrew rushed out and knelt on the man's back, aware of Troy's growls and of the deep, wolf cub bite mark on the man's hand, rivulets of blood just starting. Delilah bent down and snatched up Troy, who barked and growled louder as she dropped the invisibility she'd put on him and held onto him as he squirmed, trying to get at the man. Andrew was busy with zip ties and thanked the lord he had his usual twenty or so stuffed in every jacket he owned as he bound both the unconscious men.

Meanwhile, Delilah went to the front door and opened it before he could tell her to wait. Luckily, Buho kept the cops from shooting her or throwing her to the ground.

Delilah's mom popped into existence beside him and patted his shoulder before going to the concierge's office and yelling at the man for not letting them stay between floors in the elevator. He swore at her, but Blake really was a good concierge, so Andrew intervened just as Buho and several cops came in.

Buho gripped Andrew's arm. "We've got people coming in the back and others surrounding the building. How many of these fuckers are there left?"

Andrew shook his head. "I disabled one in the stairwell between the second and third floors and another on the fourth floor outside the elevator. From what the guy in the stairs told me before I kicked him down them, there was a lieutenant here and enough guys to patrol every floor, so I don't know if he meant one per floor or a few guys checking a few floors each. I never went onto the third floor, but it sounded like there were people gathered there waiting for me."

"So probably four or five more," Buho interpreted. "Unless they freed the guys you disabled earlier."

Andrew shrugged, then shivered. The adrenaline was still riding him, but he'd had way too much fucking adrenaline over the last few days.

Buho glanced down at the automatic rifles he had hanging all over him. "Keep the weapons and the lobby secure. Going to evacuate once we've checked the public spaces. Don't worry, Rambo, we'll mop up the rest."

Andrew managed to crack a smile. "I was going for Die Hard."

Buho nodded twice, which meant he was amused. "More urban. Excellent choice." And he was through the hall door.

Delilah eased through the crowd, clutching a growling Troy, who was still in wolf form and swamped in his sweatshirt.

Andrew bent down and nuzzled his son's head. "You did great, Troy. You kept quiet and still until you knew it was time to bite the bad man."

Troy's growl finally died out and a whine built in the back of his throat.

"I can't hold you right now because I need to be sure no more bad men show up." He stood and looked at Delilah, her expression grim. "You did great, too. You got one and your mom got the other. I hope you never, ever get put in this sort of situation again, but you can handle yourself."

She smiled slightly. "Kicking ass is the Woods family way."

"Absolutely." Del's mom popped out of the office, apparently finished with the super. "Defensive spells only, of course. Evade and disable."

"Though some of those spells can be used offensively," Delilah smiled bigger and more smugly.

"We certainly had enough of offensive magic over the last few days," her mom said. "I can hardly wait to get back to my spreadsheets."

And Serena Woods marched off to talk to the cop who was standing just inside the front door.

"Hey, uh, Mr. Miller, and uh, ladies?" Blake the concierge said from the door of his office.

"Yes, Blake?" he asked, trying to look nonchalant and nonthreatening in spite of his arsenal.

The man blinked several times, his square face scrunched up in what looked like pain. "I'm sorry about the, uh, elevator thing."

Delilah turned slowly, still holding Troy close to her chest and stared at him for several seconds, then nodded. "You were frightened, too. Apology accepted since it turned out all right. And thank you for warning us there were guns waiting down here."

Blake only looked marginally appeased and like maybe he'd start swearing again, but she turned away and he glanced around at all of them and slunk back into his office.

Chapter Thirty

"And just where is Shalonda?" Delilah asked her mom.

Her mother's blush and a shift in her aura told Del she'd hit on something.

"In Argentina, as far as I know," her mom said before she turned back to her home office desk. She'd had Del help her carry it into her room when Del moved in and that sucker weighed about a thousand pounds due to the sturdy metal legs and sides. Del and her mom weren't very physically strong, so it had involved a lot of grunting and bickering, but Mom refused to get anyone else to help.

And thinking of that, Del squinted at the desk, trying to think of who else in the family was strong enough to have been of assistance. And why it had to be a secret. Why couldn't they have offered twenty bucks to the teen football player brothers who lived three doors down?

Del looked back at her mom, who was unlocking the top right desk drawer, studiously staring down into it.

She glanced up at Del and shook her head. "That's not a relevant secret, because there's nothing to tell. I mean, once this all finishes and she's back from the wedding she went to, we're going to go out to dinner."

Del grinned and watched her mom blush again.

Then she looked at the desk and reached into the pocket of her jeans, pulling out her key ring. "So this little key from the safe at work goes to this desk?"

Her mom's blush faded and she narrowed her eyes at Del. "You only just figured it out?"

"I left here in a hurry before we found the safe at work. We didn't exactly have time to puzzle it out before we were followed and leaving the state and all." She felt her own cheeks heat as she thought of their intimate night in the horrible motel with bleached sheets. "I almost forgot about it."

He mom nodded. "Since I'm not keeping secrets anymore…" She pulled out her own key ring from the pocket of her baggy, beige cardigan and fitted a second small key into something in the back of the drawer. "See? A little hidden compartment." She pulled out a small stack of hundred dollar bills. "A couple thousand dollars only, but enough to want to lock it up. And it worked. The bad guys didn't find it and the FBI either didn't find it or they left it alone. Not enough to make them suspicious, knowing I'm sort of paranoid and might like to keep cash on hand."

She got up, though and went to the right side of the desk and reached around behind where the desktop stuck out a good six inches behind the metal filing-cabinet type body of the desk. She fiddled with something and pushed and after a screech of metal, came out with her phone.

"Holy shit, Mom. I thought they took your phone and you'd never see it again."

Her mom shrugged with a smug little eyebrow twitch. "That was a burner phone."

She reached back down and pulled out her laptop and set it on the desk. Del shook her head. "And a burner laptop."

"It was my old one. I had a bad feeling about the whole thing and decided to take the backup instead when I went out the side door of RFB and drove off."

Del sat on the end of her mom's bed, shaking her head. "Maybe a little warning next time when you get a bad feeling and go into hiding. I had a creepy feeling about what's his name, Mr. James, but he was a creep and an embezzler."

Her mom brushed one of her unadorned, dry-skinned hands over the top of the laptop. "Yeah."

Del looked down at her own hands with their chipped pink nail polish and thought about the last few days.

"I'm sorry, Delilah," her mom said softly. She sat on the bed next to Del and patted her leg twice before crossing her arms over her chest. "I've been working alone for such a long time I don't think of everyone else's feelings, necessarily."

Del loved her mother, but thinking of other people's feelings had never been high on a list of her mom's admirable qualities. She didn't say so, because she loved her mom. "Well, it's not like I was working with you, more like answering your phones."

"You're really good with clients and feelings and... well, with finding me, first when I blocked you and then when the warlock did. And taking down the asshole. I thought I was dead. Then I thought you would be too, and I couldn't stand the thought."

Del patted her mom's leg, taking and giving comfort.

"I think I should take you along with me to client meetings. You can get a read on the people and I can get a read on the books."

"Really?" Del smiled, thinking of herself sitting unobtrusively behind her mom in meetings, taking notes and shuffling through her cards. "I don't really see how it would work."

Her mom shrugged. "I'm not sure, either, but I have a good feeling about it."

Del patted her mom's leg again. "Thanks." For seeing her, for acknowledging her magical talents had value.

"I offered Andrew a job, too," her mom added after a minute of silent contemplation.

"You what?" Del hadn't seen this coming.

Her mom wobbled her head side to side. "I'm thinking we could branch out into other investigations. He's a hundred percent honest and hardworking, he's spinning his wheels in the FBI, and as a single parent, he needs something more flexible than flying across the country at a moment's notice. I wonder if the FBI would hire him freelance as a consultant. They probably pay well, though not extravagantly."

"They hire psychics as consultants, too. Lac Three Feathers' girlfriend and some others have done work for them. They could hire you, for that matter."

"They're probably too pissed off at me for not contacting them nine months ago, when I first figured out the Slovak gang was embezzling from small businesses."

"RFB isn't small, is it?"

"They're not huge. This is their only office, after all, though there's some programming and customer support work they've outsourced. That's how the money was being moved. And from there into Bitcoin." Her mom wrinkled her nose, her expression every time cryptocurrency came up.

A few more seconds of silence, then Del asked, because she couldn't not ask, "What did Andrew say?"

"He said thank you and he was considering his options."

"Did you ask Alex, too? Or Lac?" They could have a big, kickass psychic-slash-shifter PI agency.

Her mom shook her head. "Alex still loves his work and Lac desperately wants to be in the FBI. I'd want to start small, anyway. It'll be hard enough to let go of some of the control. I'm getting older, though."

Del snorted. "You're fifty-five, not eighty."

Her mom shrugged. "You know, Andrew's closer to my age than to yours."

Del paused. "I hadn't thought about the age difference for quite a while, to be honest, Mom. He's basically right between us in age. I think?" Yep, still hated doing math in her head. "He's an old soul and I guess I am, too." She would have to reflect more on why she didn't feel it mattered. They fit together.

Her mom smiled, a bit sly. "I'm not ready to retire. I don't want to work forever, though. I mean, after I retire, I'll keep doing pro-bono or low-cost work for charities and individuals."

"And spend the rest of the time on vacation with Shalonda," Del said the other woman's name in her sing-song voice.

Her mom blushed again. "We'll see."

Del shook her head behind her mom's back when she stood up.

Del saw already.

His phone vibrated with a call just as Troy was falling asleep after ten times through his favorite book, right when Andrew had been ready to sneak away. He had plans to finish cleaning up from supper and maybe sit on the couch and do nothing at all for a little while to see if this time Troy would give him a few minutes before he woke up and started whining for Andrew to shift and lie down with him. It had been a hell of a weekend, so he expected the whining to start before he was out of the room.

He'd been thinking of texting Delilah, yes, or maybe calling her, but in a few minutes, not right then.

He denied the call with a text saying Troy was just falling asleep, then peeked at him to see if it were true. Thankfully, it was. He quickly turned off the vibration of the phone so it was completely silent and snicked Troy's door shut.

I'm downstairs now, Delilah texted back. *I still have keycard, but didn't want to intrude. May I come up?*

Of course, he replied immediately, then went to brush his teeth.

He heard his front door open and close a few minutes later as he was putting the stew pan to soak in the sink.

He turned when he smelled her wild, green scent with the overlay of spice as she came into the living/dining room. She hesitated in the archway, beautiful and rounded in leggings and a large shirt with her puffy coat open over it. She slipped off the coat and went back out to the hallway to hang it up on a hook, so he took the moment to rinse his hands and dry them and run them through his hair to be sure it wasn't sticking up funny.

Then she was back, her smile faded. He realized he was frowning and tried to smile as he gestured for her to have a seat on the couch. He sat at the other end of it. Despite her smile, he didn't know how this conversation was going to go.

"I meant it when I said -" he started, just as she said, "We need to talk about - "

He nodded. "You go first."

She took a deep breath and smiled. "So, relationships are hard for me. You'd think they'd be easy because I can sense emotions and figure people out quickly, but with some people - some men - I don't really know how to bond and I get high expectations based on the first rush of attraction and hormones and how his interest is focused on me."

Yes, well, his emotions and interest were focused on her.

She picked at her nail polish. "And I feel all of it for you. The good parts. It's actually better for me with you because you are older than me and have a job and a life and Troy and I'll never expect a hundred percent of you."

He scowled. What was she talking about? "You should not expect less than a hundred percent of any relationship."

"I'm explaining this wrong." She blushed and somehow, the mint and green and spice scent got stronger. "I've always dated people who didn't have a whole life yet, so we grew apart as we changed or we didn't know what we wanted. But I think that you, with your well-established personality and a beautiful son and a job...well, Mom said you were thinking about joining her in investigations or whatever and I can see it as a possible path for you and can see you staying in the FBI if you'd rather, and I can't see exactly what your future will be, but – "

She took a deep breath. "I'm getting off track. What I want to say is that I know I'm important to you. And I can sense it won't change and I could be an important part of your life. And I want all of it."

He nodded when she fell silent, still blushing. She looked down and brushed wolf hair off her black leggings.

He cleared his throat and said, "I meant what I said in the car. You can come over whenever you want."

She smiled slightly, looking unsure.

"We were in the car with your mom and my son and I couldn't tell you how much I desire you and how much I want you here with me." He paused, grimacing with regret. "I should have mentioned how much I respect you and your magic. How I think you'll make a great psychologist, or an investigator with your mom, or anything you want to do, especially if it has to do with understanding people and helping them. And I fell in love with you when you read Troy ten books without flinching."

She looked stunned, maybe her eyes were wet. She said, "Now is a better time, because I can say I'm falling in love with you. Or I might have fallen in love with you when you asked me for ketchup packets for Troy. We only met a few days ago, but they've been an intense few days, obviously. And I think you're wonderful. And I'm saying that as someone who can sense your emotions and, without being too intrusive, your personality."

He grinned, delighted by her. "Going back to the start of what you just said: I'm falling in love with you, too."

She smiled back, blushing again and his cheeks got hot as well.

He took a deep breath. "I'm a lot older than you and I'm set in my ways and have a definite routine and way I like doing things. And I don't understand nail polish, but I find it wildly attractive on your hands."

She chuckled and looked at her hands. "My mom pointed out you're closer in age to her than to me. But you're adapting to Troy's schedule and his needs and though I'm kind of a mess sometimes and I haven't figured out my whole life yet, I live up to my promises and obligations. If you can be flexible enough to fit me in, I can be solid enough...rigid enough? Routine-based enough?" She took a deep breath and let it out slowly. "I mean, I won't ever mean to mess you up, but I hope you can make a space for me."

He had to blink a few times before he could speak, because flexible and rigid certainly had given him some ideas. Her eyebrows went up and she blushed redder, so she probably could tell what sort of ideas he was having.

It was his turn to take a breath. He could smell her arousal and her pheromones were going to make him feral. "Yes," he said. "Yes to a space for you, however and however much you want to be in my life. In our lives. If you want to live here or just visit or...whatever part of your time I can have."

She shook her head. "We both sound a bit pathetic when we both know we'll bend over backward to help each other. And risk our lives for each other and for Troy."

Bend over backward, added to flexible and he was getting even more rigid. "It's the day to day life which can be hard," he said. "It's where my past relationships failed."

She nodded, her expression sympathetic. "Mine too. But can we sort out the details later and feel our way forward, because our auras are screaming to have sex and you just said hard and I said feel and I can't stop thinking about it."

He lunged toward her, faster than she expected, because she squeaked, then laughed into his kiss.

He stood after only a moment of the hard kiss and pulled her up by her hands. "My room, door locked."

She shivered and tiptoed down the hall with him, pausing by Troy's room to listen to him breathe in his sleep, then they were in his room, undressing each other as they kissed and groped in a tangle of hands and clothing.

Naked, she pushed him back on the bed and then…didn't join him. Instead, she turned and grabbed her suitcase from the corner and unzipped it. "Condoms," she said breathily. "And a cone of silence."

Delilah rolled a condom onto him, dropping the other three from the strip onto a pillow and climbed over him to sink down on his impressive erection, gasping as he growled. His strong hands gripped her waist, holding her still when she tried to rise up.

"Hold still. Just… give me a second," he grunted.

She leaned forward, breasts smashed against his chest and kissed him, pouring her urgency and desire into him, but already happier now she was filled by him and their auras were mingling along with their breath. He kissed her back, his tongue tangling with hers, the movements becoming more languid and sensual as his hips rolled under her once... twice...

Their rhythm was slow and their movements small as she ground down onto him, circling her hips as he circled his. His hands went to her ass and he held her tightly against him, rolling his pelvis against her clitoris, so much like the dry humping in the hotel, but infinitely better.

The wave of almost-climax rolled through her and she pushed up slightly, gasping, her weight pressing down on his pelvis, which made them both groan. One of his hands slid up her sides and to her nipple, which he rolled and pinched in time with the rolling hips and she whimpered.

"Delilah," he whispered, "I can't..."

He put both hands firmly on her butt and rolled them both over, pulling out completely, panting harshly. She half sat up, reaching for him, but he said, "Wait."

She paused, legs wrapped around his waist, so close to orgasm and so eager for him to get back inside her she wanted to cry.

He searched her face, then let his eyes pass down her body, his attention brushing everywhere she wanted him. He leaned down and paused with his face a centimeter from hers. "I want this to be perfect."

She almost climaxed as he kissed her gently, slowly, his hands drifting slowly down her sides and up to her breasts.

She almost climaxed again when he massaged her nipples with his palms and his pelvis lowered firmly onto her, his hardness pushing between her legs. The pressure was a reminder that dry-humping in a smelly motel room had been the best sex of her life up until right then.

He lifted his head, his wolf-yellow eyes almost glowing in the low light and she felt the magic swirl around them, brushing against their skin. He let out a long, slow breath, then slid down her to lick at her nipples and nibble down, down over her belly until he reached her pussy. He paused there, breathing through his nose. Smelling her?

He tipped his head back to meet her gaze and gave her a big, happy grin. And she knew she was in trouble from this beautiful man who had her heart.

He looked back down and gently, almost experimentally, touched her clitoris with her tongue.

She gasped and shivered.

He grinned up at her again, so she went up on one elbow to caress his face. He closed his eyes and leaned into her hand as she petted the slight rasp of his cheek and ran her fingers into his short hair. He bent down and licked her from her opening to her clit and began to eat her out in earnest. It took about half a second for her to climax the first time, but he continued, unrelenting until she shook and shivered through another, stronger orgasm.

Her own wails and gasps and unladylike grunts were still ringing in her ears as he rose up on his knees and reached for a fresh condom, pulling off the old one and rolling on the new. He lifted her legs deftly to settle into her, making her shiver and gasp again.

A pause as he looked into her eyes, intent and serious and one hundred percent focused on her. Then he began to thrust in earnest.

Several minutes later, when their breath evened out and Andrew had thrown away the condom and Delilah had removed the cone of silence so they could listen for Troy, they lay under the covers on his big bed, legs tangled, holding each other.

"Will you move in?" he asked. "I don't want you to go."

She hesitated for a moment. "I will. Maybe not right away, because though my mom is pretending everything's fine, I don't think I can officially move out until she's more settled. Do you see what I mean?"

He nodded. "You were both scared for each other." A few seconds of silence. "Will you stay tonight? Because I can't let you go."

She burrowed into his chest. "Yes, please," she said around a yawn.

He didn't think he'd be able to sleep without her in his bed. Maybe not ever again. But he was smart enough and tired enough to not say it right then. Perhaps they could buy a big house and share with her mom. Or a duplex. His mind drifted to housing arrangements and landed on extra bedrooms in case they had more children and he smiled.

And Troy started whining from his room and his door thumped open and the whining was coming up the hall.

Andrew scrambled from the bed and pulled on his boxer shorts as Delilah rolled out her side and felt around the floor until she found her leggings and a shirt and pulled both on as the handle jiggled and scratching started on his bedroom door. Andrew unlocked it and eased it open, reaching down and picking up his pup, who jammed his head against Andrew's chest and whined louder.

Andrew looked over Troy's head at Delilah, who smiled and lay down again. "Would you like to sleep in here, Troy? The way all three of us slept in the smelly bed in the motel?"

Troy's hairy head bobbed against Andrew's chest and he carried his baby boy to the bed and set him down next to Delilah, who asked permission before scratching behind his ears.

Andrew shifted to wolf and hopped up on the bed. Delilah helped him with the covers and he curled around his son, his woman scratching behind his ears before smoothing her hand down his side.

Troy yawned with a whine and shoved his face into Andrew's chest more firmly. Andrew yawned too, then Delilah. Then they slept.

Other Books by Philippa Lodge

CONTEMPORARY ROMANCE

SOMETHING DIFFERENT
   Beatrice and the Houseplants (coming soon)

Greatest Hits (New Adult)
Chill
Hot Rocks

PARANORMAL ROMANCE

This Magic Heart
   Train Wreck

The Shifter's Heart
   Memoirs of a Fox
   The Wolf Knight's Tale
   On the Origin of Shifters
   Christmas Spirit (novella)
   The Interpretation of Magic

Of Foxes and Men (FREE novella with signup for my newsletter)

The Joy (and Pete) of Christmas (FREE novella with signup for my newsletter)

The Lion's Heart
Hometown Pride
Secrets of the Pride
Alpha Lioness

About the Author

PHILIPPA LODGE LIVES IN a semi-arid, overly hot part of Northern California with 3 young adult kids, 2 cats, and 1 husband. She does office work by day and writes evenings and weekends. Find her at philippalodge.com or on Facebook or Bluesky.

Sign up for her newsletter by downloading a free paranormal romance novella from Book Funnel at https://BookHip.com/HJNSWPG

Excerpt from Hometown Pride – The Lion's Heart, Book 1

"Wild lion prides keep their females close, but push their males out when they approach maturity. With few exceptions, shifter lion prides, similar to shifter wolf packs, keep all their members forever. Even those who leave the home territory for education, work, or to gain experience, nearly always come back within a few years or even within a few days or weeks."

"Prides and Prejudice: The African and Asian Lion Shifters." The Shifter-Watcher's Handbook: A Guide to North American Herds, Prides, and Packs, by Mary M Renard et. alia, 3rd ed., vol. 1, Random Penguin House, 2025.

Chapter One

As always, his arrival rippled through the tiny Freiburg, California library full of women and children. Angelica Kass, picking up various food-shaped wood blocks that had been scattered across the carpet, glanced out of the corner of her eye at the double glass doors where the big man was silhouetted. Yep. "Freight Train" Tremaine Jones. Contractor and handyman.

He swaggered inside until he wasn't back-lit anymore and she could see the perpetual scowl on a face like he'd hit a few walls in his time, the worn jeans across muscular thighs, the middle a bit soft, and the shoulders and chest broad under a ratty gray t-shirt with brown paint or something icky splashed across it. Like her, he was half-human, half-lion shifter, but he reeked of dominance. He was a few years older than her, maybe three or four, which put him at just over forty, and maybe it was his constant frown or his serious air or the salt and pepper gray of his hair, but he seemed older.

As usual, the babies and toddlers running amok while she and the moms tidied up after story hour were quickly corralled and strollered and baby-carriered and whisked to safety outside.

Tremaine ambled away from the door, staying next to the magazine section as far from the kids' area as he could get, nodding politely at the women who greeted him as they escaped.

Nobody could clear a room of women and children faster than a bad-tempered male lion shifter.

Angelica could feel Tremaine watching her as she rolled the bookshelves back into place, stacked the tiny chairs on their cart, and wheeled them into the small storage closet just off the children's section. She glanced into the office. Her boss' door was closed, but it didn't smell or sound like she was in there with her mate. Where her boss was, Angel didn't know. Maybe they'd gone out to lunch and some afternoon delight. She didn't care, either, as life in the library was a lot easier without Lipstick Lyssa.

She sat in the checkout desk chair and spun it so her knocking knees were hidden. Face to face with the shifter she'd been imagining as she got off every night to ease herself to sleep, Angelica froze and held back a growl. As usual.

"Blues musicians," he grunted as he plunked down the book about Middle East politics he'd checked out two days before. It was his usual demeanor, ever since a few weeks before when he strode into the library, fierce and rugged and covered in dirt, looking for information about Leonardo Da Vinci.

He scowled in response to her scowl. He was one grumpy bastard, Freight Train Jones.

But then, so was she.

She couldn't fault him for his wide-ranging intellectual curiosity, either. He checked out a book or two every few days and always had something to say about them when he came in demanding something completely different.

At night, alone in her bed, it didn't matter. She'd glimpsed him naked one time after he shifted, because clothes didn't shift, they fell into a pile or tore. His shoulders were drool-worthy and his cock looked more than adequate. And then he turned his back and she saw his tight butt. In her imagination, he had stamina. Even in this pride of goddamn over-sharers, she'd never heard if it was true, but then again, he'd been back in the area for less than a year and hadn't dated anyone as far as she knew. Since she would only ever experience him in her imagination, she didn't care.

She told herself she didn't care.

Not that she was bitter or anything.

"Lyssa is out and will be able to help you in a bit. In the meantime, music is 780." Her boss had chewed her out for giving reference help twice that day already. She waved a hand toward the shelving and thumped her knuckles against her monitor. She jerked back her hand and knocked into the stack of picture books she needed to check in, sending them sliding to the floor. The metal cart overflowing with books to be shelved made a pleasant bonging noise when she hit her head on the side of it.

She froze. In the fading echo of the clanging cart, she heard the distant, rhythmic thump of her boss and her ex-boyfriend humping in the big storage closet by the bathrooms. Her goddamn shifter ears heard him moan.

Freight Train – and who the hell had that for a nickname? – stared in disgust as she sat up rubbing the bump on her head. Way to seduce him with your grace, Angel.

Abruptly, she'd had enough.

Made in the USA
Coppell, TX
22 February 2026

72080219R00154